THE
TUTOR

Courtney Psak graduated with a degree in Communications and Journalism from Monmouth University, following with a master's degree in Publishing from Pace University.
She started her career at magazines such as *Cosmopolitan*, *Self* and *Modern Bride*.

In 2015 she wrote her first novel, *Thirty Days to Thirty*, and sold thousands of copies while working as a project manager for Viacom in New York.

Courtney currently lives in Palm Beach, Florida with her husband and two sons. She is a member of the Women's Fiction Writers Association, the National Writers Association, International Thriller Writers and the Mystery Writers of America.

Also by Courtney Psak
Thirty Days to Thirty

THE TUTOR

COURTNEY PSAK

HODDER &
STOUGHTON

First published in Great Britain in 2025 by Hodder & Stoughton Limited
An Hachette UK company

The authorised representative in the EEA is Hachette Ireland, 8 Castlecourt Centre, Dublin 15, D15 XTP3, Ireland (email: info@hbgi.ie)

1

Copyright © Courtney Psak 2025

The right of Courtney Psak to be identified as the Author of the Work has been asserted by her in accordance with the Copyright, Designs and Patents Act 1988.

All rights reserved. No part of this publication may be reproduced, stored in a retrieval system, or transmitted, in any form or by any means without the prior written permission of the publisher, nor be otherwise circulated in any form of binding or cover other than that in which it is published and without a similar condition being imposed on the subsequent purchaser.

All characters in this publication are fictitious and any resemblance to real persons, living or dead, is purely coincidental.

A CIP catalogue record for this title is available from the British Library

Paperback ISBN 978 1 399 748 131
ebook ISBN 978 1 399 748 148

Typeset in Plantin Light by Manipal Technologies Limited

Printed and bound in Great Britain by Clays Ltd, Elcograf S.p.A.

Hodder & Stoughton policy is to use papers that are natural, renewable and recyclable products and made from wood grown in sustainable forests. The logging and manufacturing processes are expected to conform to the environmental regulations of the country of origin.

Hodder & Stoughton Limited
Carmelite House
50 Victoria Embankment
London EC4Y 0DZ

www.hodder.co.uk

Behind every exquisite thing that existed, there was something tragic.

—Oscar Wilde, *The Picture of Dorian Gray*

Isabel

Isabel knows she shouldn't be in here. It is, after all, a private office. But she knew he would be out for lunch, and that it would be empty, and she saw her opportunity. She puts her hand on the door, already slightly ajar, and it makes a slow creaking noise. She gives one last glance back to be sure no one is coming before she steps inside, closing the door behind her with a slight click. She flicks on the light, bringing the dark shadows into focus. A cherry-wood desk as old as the school itself rests in front of a large window that overlooks the campus quad. She can see some eighth-grade students eating their lunches on the benches that line the walkway, while others throw a football, their suit jackets laid flat on the grass, yellow and blue striped ties flung over their shoulders, enjoying the last few days of school before summer begins.

 A prickle of heat dances on the back of Isabel's neck as she lowers her head to avoid detection. Her long, jet-black hair falls forward as she gingerly pulls at one of the desk drawers. Her fingers flip through the files, but she doesn't find what she's looking for. She tries several others but still comes up empty. She shoves the last drawer closed with a huff. The head of the school, Daniel Lopez, is a very clean and organized man. Nothing is askew on his desk. He has a green Tiffany lamp that sits to the right of his brown desk pad, which he balances out with a family picture in a gold frame on the opposite side. She eyes the portrait with a twinge of jealousy at the image of him with an arm wrapped around a man she assumes is his adult son in a stadium at a baseball game. She finds herself imagining she too is at the game and wonders what Dan would be like as a father. He does seem to have a paternal instinct around Isabel, but she figures it's because she's barely out of college, graduating only a year ago. Isabel takes in the familiarity of Dan's features and feels that with her tanned olive skin, broad face, and espresso almond eyes, she too could look like a member of this family. A glint of light reflects off the frame, pulling her from her daydream. Something silver among the gold. She flicks her eyes down at the desk pad and pulls it slightly back. The sound of metal scratching against wood lets her know that there is something underneath it.

Picking up the mat, she spots a key, then turns her head towards the locked cabinet on the bottom of one of the matching bookshelves. Isabel kneels in front of it, inserting the key. With a slight twist of her hand, the lock releases. A stack of manila envelopes sits in a neat pile and she pulls them out, noting the names that are labeled until she sees what she's looking for.

James Clark.

Placing the other files aside, she opens the folder. At the top is the transfer request form that she learned about. She turns the page over to the next form behind it.

Transfer request record for James Clark to be sent to the Pelican Academy, Palm Beach, Florida.

Isabel's heart beats faster. She pulls out her phone, hovering it over the file before hearing the click of her camera.

She wonders why this file was in a locked cabinet, but then flips to the next page. Her eyes widen.

The sound of a thud on the other side of the door causes her to jump.

With hands shaking, she quickly slides the files back into place, locking the cabinet and returning the key to its hiding place.

She is about to open the door when she remembers to turn the light off. Muffled voices stop her from proceeding. She can't tell if they are coming towards her or going away. The lie she has prepared is running on a loop in her head, ready to use at any moment, when the voices stop. She exhales. Cautiously, she peers around before closing the door, although not entirely, just as she had found it.

When Isabel returns to her desk, she looks up the Pelican Academy on her computer. A whitewash of students in uniforms parading with one another carousel across the page below the name of the school and its crest. Not very different from their own private school website.

She scans their social media posts and community chat boards when she sees her in.

A big congratulations to Mrs. Snider on her baby announcement. Rest assured we will find the perfect candidate to fill her shoes until she returns.

Bingo.

Isabel dials the number of the school, chatting with the receptionist about where to send her details, and schedules an interview.

She feels more relaxed now, but there is still a nervous energy boiling inside her. She has a long way to go for her plan to succeed.

"Isabel, working hard through lunch?"

Isabel jumps at the high chirping voice that breaks the silence.

"Jeez, Theresa. Sorry, I was deep in thought. I didn't even hear you come in."

"I just got back," says Theresa, pulling her purse off her shoulder and letting it fall to her desk. She tames her red frizzy hair into a tight ponytail as she peers up at the clock on the wall, smoothing her flyaways. "Should've come to Dan's birthday celebration with us, Isabel. It was the lunch of the century." She gives a slight chuckle.

Isabel smiles. "I bet."

"It really was, actually." Theresa sits down at her desk, putting on her reading glasses, and powers up her computer. "I know you've only been here for less than a year, but Dan pulls out all the stops. We go to the best restaurants and order everything on the menu."

"Uh-huh." Isabel continues typing while she considers the information she just discovered.

"Anyway, the rest of the team should be back any minute now." Theresa types away, then she stops. "What did you have to work on, anyway?"

Isabel blinks in rapid succession. It's not Theresa's business to know that she stayed behind so she could break into Dan's office. "Just running a bit behind on my work. We only have a few more days until the school year ends." She shrugs.

Theresa says something that Isabel doesn't hear, but she nods her along, returning her eyes to the computer at her desk.

A few hours later, Isabel takes the subway through the city. The lull of the locomotive makes her eyelids heavy, and the fast pace makes the vibrant colors of red, orange and gold in the advertisements on the subway wall all blur into one. She has slept little this past year. Not since her grandmother got sick and eventually passed. The only person she had left in the world. A weight of sorrow sits heavy on Isabel's chest as she remembers the light in her eyes. For a grandmother, she was relatively young, in her early sixties, but cancer can come at any age.

The landlord gave Isabel these past few weeks to sort through her grandmother's belongings, to make harrowing decisions about what to keep and what to get rid of, not knowing if she'd be throwing away a piece of the past that meant something to her, or her mother.

That was the other painful part of it. She had come across items of her mother's that her grandmother had held on to. Pieces of clothing she hadn't been able to part with, possibly because at the time it had still had her daughter's scent. Isabel found herself doing the same with her grandmother's clothes. She had little room in her own tiny apartment to store everything, and she debated if it would make sense to get a storage unit. But she realized that it was an expensive way to delay the inevitable.

Isabel, lost in her own head, hears the ping of the subway doors open and sees everyone around her standing up. She follows suit, the white noise of the bustling New York commuters imbuing her and all of 86th Street with a sense of eagerness even though she isn't in a hurry. She allows the flood of people in a rush to funnel out first before following behind. Several bump her on their way to enter the train, but Isabel keeps her head down. She effortlessly bleeds into the background, like a ghost.

The smell of something sour enters her nostrils, quickening her climb to the street. It's times like this that she realizes she wouldn't miss this place much.

She walks the next few blocks until the magnificent white structure of the Met comes into view around the corner, like a beacon. Its uplighting emphasizes the fluttering oversized banners advertising the newest exhibit, beckoning people to come and see.

She lines up at the hot dog stand, smiling at the vendor, but he doesn't acknowledge her. There is no sense of recognition that she's been here several times a week for a while now. She's just another customer to him, which is good. That's what she wants, to be invisible.

After her first bite, she checks her watch and looks at the corner of the building across the street. Most of the faces blend together, the same drawn-looking expressions as people push past one another in a hurry.

It's then that she sees him standing at the window, and she stiffens. His arms are crossed as he looks down at the sea of commuters, clearly waiting for her.

Goosebumps form on Isabel's otherwise smooth skin.

Then she spots the woman, tearing frantically around the corner, weaving in and out of the crowd. The woman looks up at him in the window and gives an apologetic wave, as if she's running late for something.

Shortly after, she disappears into the building. Isabel waits a few moments until she sees her appear in the window, a dark figure against the light. He kisses his wife on the lips, appearing to want her to linger longer, but she pulls away from him.

Isabel releases the breath she didn't realize she was holding.

She stands up, wiping the crumbs of the hot dog bun off her hands. As she looks up again, she freezes. He is still in the window and it looks as if he's staring directly at her. *He couldn't be, could he?* Still, Isabel stands tall as if a dart has struck her.

She takes a deep breath, then smiles and waves, curious to see if she was right or if she was being paranoid.

He doesn't wave back. He just stands with his arms crossed for a long pause before tilting his head back around, as if he is being called by someone, before disappearing into the apartment.

Isabel picks up her purse and slings it over her shoulder, giving one last glance towards the window. "See you in Palm Beach," she says softly.

Rose

Rose is sitting in the back of the town car watching as the palm trees sway in the wind as they drive past. She can't help but see her own reflection shining back at her in the window, dark hair swept up in a bun on top of her head, soft curtain bangs framing her eyebrows. Her white button-down is tied at the ends above her torn jeans. She looks pale compared to the people she sees riding bikes and strolling along the sidewalk. The ocean is a serene mix of aqua and turquoise, lapping against a white sand beach. They stop as an extended golf cart cuts them off, crossing the street. It's full of beautiful, tanned women with designer sunglasses and beach cover-ups sitting on palm-printed seats. The roof of the cart displays a lacquered surfboard and decorative scalloped fabric. The cart parks up at the side of the road and the driver, dressed in white shorts, signals to someone on the beach, indicating the number of guests, while the person on the passenger side retrieves pink umbrellas with white tassels and teak beach chairs with baby pink and white fabric. While the guests in gold-studded sandals pose for a picture in front of the iconic Spanish-style bell tower, the driver pulls out a white cooler from the back and hands it over the retaining wall.

Rose envies these women here to celebrate Labor Day weekend together before returning to their homes, somewhere far away. Whereas she and her family are coming to live here, including her mother-in-law, Evelyn. The thought of it is as stifling as the Florida heat. She cranes her neck to look at the driver's dashboard and notices that it's 98 degrees. She rolls her eyes.

Across from her, her son James is looking out the window, no doubt eyeing the beautiful women that have spilled out onto the sidewalk. His mop of gold hair shines through the sun-streaked window. She can't believe she's old enough to have a high schooler now. One minute he was this skinny, frail kid, but now his shoulders have broadened, his arms are more toned than lanky and he has a protruding Adam's apple underneath his collared shirt which contributes to his deepened voice. It makes her tear up just looking at him. He doesn't need her anymore and before she knows it, he'll be off to college, living on his own. It all seems to go by in the blink of an eye.

"We're almost there," Grant says from the front passenger seat. His voice is calm, but there is a hint of a strain, as if telling Rose to brace herself.

When they got married this past Christmas, she had not anticipated that she and James would be forced to move in with Grant's ailing mother. But that's just how it goes, she supposes. Unexpected things happen that change the trajectory of your life.

Rose anxiously spins her wedding ring around her thin finger as she thinks about Ian, her late husband. A mixture of guilt and anxiety swirl around in her thoughts. While her and Ian's relationship had deteriorated years ago, she stayed for James. But his sudden death still hit her like a bombshell. Suddenly, she was left with nothing. She found that Ian had depleted their life savings, leaving her with barely enough money to support herself and James as she struggled to sell her art.

Meeting Grant when she had seemed almost like fate. In some weird way, it was as if the universe had planned it. She had been drowning, not only financially but in life.

She'd first met Ian at a trade show that she had gone to with a friend. He was eight years older and a furniture designer, but he was doing well for himself, and Rose was attracted to that stability. When she became pregnant, she was scared, but Ian was excited and promised to marry and support her. Being faithful to her, though, was apparently something entirely different. Eventually, she felt like an obligation. A mistake he'd made that he had to deal with.

But then he was gone and as if on cue, Grant stepped into her life, showing her what real love and happiness could look like.

But Rose hadn't anticipated the effect that Evelyn would have on their lives, even when she wasn't present.

When she and James moved into Grant's penthouse apartment overlooking Central Park, it wasn't a surprise to her it was his family's home, where he had grown up. It was a prime piece of real estate, and she could see that you would want to keep it in the family. She had first seen it after an event at the Met, when Grant had persuaded her to come for a nightcap at his place across the street. Rose was taken back by the blue silk wallpaper, cut-marble staircase and Gilded Age furniture. She just assumed as a bachelor he hadn't cared enough to change it.

What she hadn't expected was that when she moved in, he'd still want to leave everything as it was. Like a shrine to Evelyn, right down to the oil painting of her, Grant, and his late father in a gold-leaf frame that looked down upon them in their living room. It was as if every object in that apartment represented their status, something that was off-putting to Rose. But she quickly forgave him when she met Evelyn, realizing it was she who wanted everything as it was.

The first encounter with Evelyn had been for tea at the Palm Court in the Plaza Hotel. Rose marveled at the marble Corinthian columns and large atrium. Crystal chandeliers dangled like enormous earrings from the gold ceiling. If you asked Rose to describe Evelyn, she would simply answer that she was the essence of the Palm Court, an old-world version of New York.

It was like nothing Rose had ever experienced before. Just standing in the space, she felt out of place and insignificant in this world of grandeur. Surely people like Evelyn could see right through her, and she had been right.

"Mother, I'd like you to meet Rose," said Grant, stepping aside like a rising curtain on a stage theater to reveal Rose behind him.

Evelyn stared at her, her dark eyes beady as a hawk's, her taut face framed by a voluminous layered silver bob, à la Jane Fonda. Her thin lips tightened into a frown, and she turned her attention to Grant. "Whatever happened to that other girl you were seeing, Sarah Preston?"

Grant cleared his throat awkwardly.

To Rose's relief, they weren't staying. This was merely a quick introduction before Grant surprised them both with a matinee show where conversation would be minimal. But Rose could feel Evelyn's eyes on her throughout the play, like a laser burning the back of her neck. She had not been invited to join them for dinner.

"I was wondering if you'd be okay with James using the furniture from his old room," Rose had asked Evelyn shortly before they'd moved into the penthouse. Grant had flown Evelyn in from Palm Beach for Thanksgiving—and perhaps also to get her blessing, Rose couldn't help but wonder.

"It's just, this move is a lot for him, and I want to give him a sense of home in his new surroundings."

It had been a frosty New York afternoon, the air as crisp as the vibrantly colored dry leaves that were falling from the trees. But the chill in the air seemed to come more from Evelyn.

"Do you have any idea how much that furniture cost? It was custom-made for that very room." Evelyn's bony finger pointed up towards the staircase.

Rose bit her tongue then. She hadn't wanted to start off on the wrong foot with Evelyn, but suggesting any sort of change appeared to be doing just that.

What Rose had come to learn was that whatever Evelyn wanted, Evelyn got.

"We're here," Grant announces.

James sits up in his seat while Rose turns her attention to the wrought-iron gates opening with a loud, decrepit creak. Amidst a thicket of jungle-like trees, the car moves at a slow crawl, as if it could be engulfed entirely. Then the tires crunch on the gravel as they come to a stop, in front of a cream-colored French baroque mansion.

James is the first to jump out of the car, his hair blowing in all different directions. Rose had noted the sudden change in weather at the north end of the island with interest. She couldn't help but wonder if it was the same everywhere, or whether a permanent storm cloud just circled above her mother-in-law's house like a villainous cartoon. Now, Rose's curiosity is piqued as she contemplates whether the blonde babes heading to the beach are currently struggling to keep their oversized hats from blowing away, or if this storm is even touching them at all.

Grant is second out, the door slamming hard as the wind pulls it from his grip. With his head down, he makes his way to the trunk of the car to assist the driver with the bags.

Rose picks up the wrapper from James's granola bar that fell unnoticed to the floor of the car. She does a quick sweep for any other items that might have been left behind. Grant's AirPods from the plane are sitting in the cupholder. She scoops them up, putting them in her purse.

When she steps out, both James and Grant are about to approach the terracotta steps, lugging the last of the bags towards the front door. She drops the duffle at their feet.

Her eyes settle on the pecky cypress door and a bolt of dread jolts through her body like an electric shock as she worries about what is to come once she steps over the threshold.

Rose flashes back to Grant and her wedding day. She was sitting in their living room dressed in a simple ivory gown, watching as Grant massaged his mother's shoulders, made sure her glass was never empty, tending to her every need, and Rose had admired it. She saw it as a good sign, that a son who took care of his mother would take care of his wife. But as she'd stared down at her empty glass of rosé, she'd also wondered if that really would translate, or if she'd always be second fiddle.

But she had to admit that he treated her better than any man ever had before.

"The caterer is here," Grant had announced.

Rose thought a caterer was excessive when it was merely her, James, Grant, and Evelyn after their small courthouse wedding.

"James!" Grant called out. "Help me with the food, will you?"

"Sure," James called back from upstairs where he had retreated with his video game.

"So, Rose"—Evelyn took a generous sip of her martini, a gold Christmas wreath charm wrapped around the stem—"do you love my son or did you simply marry him for his money?"

Rose was thankful her glass was empty because she dropped it on the robin's-egg blue carpet between her feet.

"Excuse me?" Rose laughed, stunned, as she picked up her glass, thankful that it hadn't broken.

Evelyn shrugged her shoulders and took another sip. "You needn't try to fool me, dear. I know all about your past."

A vice seemed to tighten around Rose's chest as she wondered if Grant knew as well.

Rose hadn't had the best childhood; that was putting it mildly. She'd struggled as an orphan—when she'd been only a child, she had watched both her parents die in front of her. But Evelyn couldn't know everything, right? What she had done . . . No one could know the truth.

Before she could respond, a flutter of waiters in crisp white shirts and black cummerbunds swarmed through the front door, Grant nipping at their heels, pointing to his watch at their delayed arrival.

At the memory, Rose can taste the coppery blood in her mouth as a chilling breeze comes off the ocean. She sucks in a breath, trying to calm her nerves.

Grant turns and reaches for her hand. "Thank you for doing this." He smiles at her. "How did I deserve such an understanding and kind person?"

"Don't call me a saint just yet." Rose clears her throat. "But I'll certainly try."

She squeezes his hand and nods. Grant rings the doorbell at the same time as James reaches up towards the large brass knocker and raps on the door. The wind forces the heavy ring to slam, a harsh bang that sounds as loud as the thudding in Rose's chest. She braces herself as the door slowly creaks open.

Evelyn

Evelyn's Rolls-Royce pulls into her driveway on its return from the Coconut Palm Country Club. Her game of mahjong ran late and as she checks her Cartier watch, she sees that Grant and the others will arrive any minute now. The thought of it makes her stomach tighten. She has been a widow for the last twenty years and has grown accustomed to her solitude. Although maybe you can't exactly call a house full of staff members solitude.

Evelyn has kept busy with her social clubs, tennis matches and golf games, and enjoyed coming home to whatever room she wants to, doing things at her leisure. Although lately, the only thing she has much energy for is her mahjong games.

She doesn't mind when it's just Grant and her. She's comforted when he's here with her. She's able to keep a close eye on him and prevent him from making any more foolish mistakes, like the one he made when he married Rose.

She may have been too demanding lately with him, and Evelyn has to admit to herself that she knew eventually it would come to this. If she was going to constantly call on him to care for her, then of course he'd have to make a choice. His wife or her.

She had been betting, though, that it would've been her. It didn't occur to Evelyn that shortly after moving Rose and her son into the penthouse and James into a new school, Grant would make them up and leave again, suggesting they all move in with her.

But maybe it's better this way. After all, keep your friends close and your enemies closer.

Evelyn knows women like Rose, and it won't take long for Rose to realize that her place isn't here. Evelyn's mansion is not just a place to live, it's a status symbol. An estate that sits on one of the largest plots on the north end of the island, and backs right up to the ocean. Where she is, all she hears is the squawk of the seagulls and the soothing sound of the ocean waves.

She remembers Harrison telling stories of when JFK himself opted to build a bunker on Peanut Island, a stone's throw away from them in the Intracoastal during the whole Bay of Pigs fiasco. At the time, Evelyn loved that this neighborhood in its prime was the crème de la crème for some of the most important people in history: the Vanderbilts, the Lauders, the Pulitzers. She beams with pride over the social circles she has found herself in, and Rose won't stand a chance.

Evelyn steps out of the backseat, a gust of wind threatening to pull at her top wig. She scurries across the stone driveway, leaving Renaldo, her middle-aged driver, to pull her car into the garage. Her heels shuffle as she pulls open the heavy wooden door. It shuts behind her with a deafening thud, causing her to jump.

She checks her reflection in the mirror by the front door, putting her classic white Chanel purse down on the table. She arranges her hair back into its rightful place and runs a pink manicured finger beneath her eyelids, fingertips quivering. She shakes her hands, then smooths out her pink Oscar de la Renta poppy flare dress and straightens her belt.

All set, she thinks, until she sees her gold opera tulle button earring hanging slackly from her ear.

"Martha?" she calls as she tightens it, her hands still shaking.

"Yes, Ms. Caldwell?"

Martha appears in the mirror's reflection, coming out of the kitchen. She is a plump woman in her mid-fifties with white-blonde hair always tightly fashioned on the top of her head.

"They'll be here any minute. Will lunch be ready soon?"

Martha's head bobs. She plays with her gray uniform skirt, something she seems to do anytime Evelyn addresses her.

Evelyn smiles at her via the mirror and Martha nods, turning and heading back into the kitchen.

Evelyn stares up at the vaulted wooden ceiling and puts her hand on the switch to turn on the Grecian gold-leaf chandelier, smiling as she watches it highlight the large vase of white roses that sits on a round wooden table in the center of the wood floor. She wants everything to be perfect. To show that she's attempting to make them comfortable, for now.

The doorbell chime echoes loudly in the hall, followed by the loud thud of the knocker. Her heart practically beats out of her chest. She reaches for the door and opens it with a broad smile.

"Hello!" Her voice is an octave higher than normal.

She sees James, Grant, and Rose all standing awkwardly on the front steps, hair blowing in all directions from the wind, their luggage piled on the front step.

"Come in, come in." She steps aside, allowing them to enter. "I think there must be a . . . storm coming. It was beautiful just a short while ago. I hope we don't have a hurricane."

"There's no hurricane forecast," Grant says reassuringly as he pecks her on the cheek.

"Of course not, and if there were, the residents of Palm Beach would simply pay God himself to move it elsewhere." Rose laughs awkwardly.

Evelyn's face drops in a frown. It's tacky to talk about money, but of course Rose wouldn't understand that.

She rolls her tongue across her teeth. "How is the house in the Hamptons coming along?" she asks Grant.

Grant clears his throat. "They're thinking sometime next year."

"The hurricane last year did a number on it along with many of my friends' houses. I guess you can't . . . pay off a storm after all."

Evelyn's gaze slides over to Rose, who is gaping in mortification. "I'm sorry, I didn't know."

Grant rubs her arm reassuringly.

"I have surprises for all of you." Evelyn's voice spasms. "Come, follow me." She turns on her heels, clacking up the wooden staircase that sweeps up to the next floor with such grandeur that it looks like something out of a royal castle.

They pass a couple of closed bedrooms down the long hallway before Evelyn stops at one door.

"This will be your . . . new room, James." Evelyn smiles. The room has silk fabric wallpaper, and the covers of the fourposter bed match the heavy velvet curtains in a crimson red. It is the least feminine room in the house, formerly Grant's, so Evelyn thought it would be suitable.

She remembers how Grant loved this room. Evelyn had offered to make changes, but Grant hadn't wanted to. Like Harrison, Grant liked to preserve things. "The wonderful thing about homes built in the Gilded Age is they never seem to go out of style. They're time capsules of the wealthy and privileged that stand the test of time," he told her once. But really, Evelyn would bet it was more about ego. By keeping the house in its Victorian era, it showed the generational wealth that flowed through it like the oil fortune it was founded on.

"Woah, a new laptop!" James makes his way over to a dark wooden desk. A laptop in this room stands out like a Starbucks coffee shop would in the late sixteenth century.

"You have to start...school right with the proper resources." Evelyn puts her hands out, palms up towards him, slightly shaking.

"Thanks, Mrs. Caldwell."

"P-please," she stutters, "call me Evelyn."

"Thank you so much, Evelyn, it's too much," Rose says. "You're already being generous enough letting us stay here with you."

It's well masked, but Evelyn detects her remark is disingenuous.

"I'm not done yet. Each of you got a special little something." Evelyn smiles mischievously and steps out into the hall again, then pauses a moment to look out at the stained-glass windows, watching the whitecaps of the waves and the dark clouds rolling in off the ocean. "Looks like we are going to be having...lunch inside." She rolls her head, annoyed. "If you had only arrived earlier, the weather was perfect."

She leads Rose and Grant to their bedroom. The walls are green wood panels lined with gold trimmings. An olive silk duvet rests on a king-sized bed with a matching baldachin canopy above it. She remembers when this was her and Harrison's room, when they would visit Harrison's parents.

Evelyn walks towards the windows and pulls a gold rope cord to open the velvet curtains, letting the light in. She looks out at the ocean, the storm now closer than it was before, about to make landfall. A thunderous rumble echoes through the house like a groan.

She turns to see Grant and Rose standing on the oriental rug that covers the dark wood floor, patiently waiting.

Evelyn points at the closet. "Right this way." She heads towards the double doors to the left and opens them. "Ta-da!"

Grant and Evelyn peer inside.

"What's the surprise?" Rose looks confused.

"Grant, I bought you a new w-wardrobe."

"Thanks," Grant says, looking awkwardly at the floor, scratching his eyebrow for a moment before giving her a hug. He pulls at the performance fabric of one of the polo shirts.

"I was hoping maybe you'd want to get a hobby here, like golf or tennis."

Grant laughs. "Sure, Mom. You've been trying for the last twenty years, but I'll give it a shot, again."

Evelyn turns on her heels to face Rose. "Now for you, Rose. I saved the biggest surprise for last."

Evelyn sees Rose exchange a worried look with Grant, which Evelyn pretends not to see.

"Follow me," she says, cocking her head towards the far end of the hall. The wooden panels, freshly polished, gleam against the brass candle sconces.

Evelyn's heart starts to speed up when she reaches the door at the end of the hall, watching as Rose seems to follow her with a sense of trepidation.

"Am I getting my own room?"

"In a way." Evelyn nods. Then she pushes the door open, and they climb a set of back stairs, usually reserved for staff quarters in places such as this, though nobody has used them for that purpose in years. Evelyn climbs the steps, stiffly, while Grant and Rose wait patiently.

"It's the second set of s-steps that gets me." Evelyn wheezes before opening a final door at the top of the steps, revealing a newly renovated art studio.

The room is small and painted white, stark against the dark wooden floorboards that are scratched and slightly raised in some areas. A painter's tarp is spread out like an area rug and an empty wooden easel sits in the middle of it, a metal folding chair and a folding table alongside it. The room is darkened by shadows with the exception of a stream of light through a small circular window overlooking the ocean. Evelyn flicks a light switch, igniting a harsh white light from the rustic wooden chandelier.

Rose's jaw drops and she looks at Evelyn in surprise.

Evelyn smiles triumphantly. "It was my old sewing room, but I haven't had much use for it since my . . ." She trails off, looking down at her trembling fingers. "Diagnosis." She swallows the word down like a horse pill. "I figured it would best suit you if I turned it into an art studio."

"Evelyn . . ." Rose seemed, for the first time, to be at a loss for words.

"Great, *just* what she needs. Now we'll never see her at all."

Evelyn tries to keep her smile even. She knows from Grant that Rose's art is a point of contention between them.

"Now, who's hungry? I'm sure we could all do with some lunch . . . before you get yourselves unpacked and settled," Evelyn says.

Grant makes his way down the steps, but Evelyn stops and turns back towards Rose. "I'd like you to take note of this gesture," Evelyn whispers to her. "I might be asking for something in return."

Evelyn eyes Rose until she is certain she understands.

Rose, taken aback, merely nods.

Evelyn smiles. "Good."

"You two coming?"

"Be right there," Evelyn calls as they retreat down the set of steps, her smile returning.

"Mom, we'll be right behind you, just a minute," Grant tells Evelyn as he takes Rose by the hand and leads her to their bedroom.

Evelyn smiles tersely and continues on her way but stops in front of James's room when she hears them talking.

"So," Evelyn addresses James, who startles and turns around. "Is that the right model?"

James smiles. "It's great. I can download all my video games on here. The quality will be so much better."

Evelyn sighs, thinking how she wished Grant had gotten into video games as a child. She knows most parents would disagree, but Grant never had many hobbies. He played soccer and lacrosse in high school, and he was mediocre at best. He never seemed to have a focus or a passion for anything. He has always been easily distracted, never settling for too long on one thing, which was why his sudden marriage to Rose was so alarming.

"This isn't going to be a repeat of New York, is it?" Evelyn hears Grant's voice through the door. She glances over at James, who has put his headphones back on.

"What are you talking about? This is my job, Grant. I have to work. Do you understand that this is my last real chance of saving my career?"

"Your life is different now. You don't have to work."

"But I want to."

"So you're just going to go back to neglecting your son and me?"

An audible gasp comes from Rose. "How dare you."

Evelyn knocks on the door. "I'm sorry to interrupt, but I was with James in his room, and these walls are not exactly the thickest."

Grant puts his hands up, exasperated. Evelyn steps aside as he walks out of the room, but she lingers in the doorway.

"I know it's not my place, but it has to be said. It's not very healthy to fight in front of your child all the time. It doesn't set a good example."

Rose looks agitated but then sucks in her cheeks and nods, putting her hands on her hips. "Sorry."

Evelyn taps her fingers lightly on the door, then disappears down the hall.

She doesn't like that Rose is so different from Grant. Grant dresses like a man of privilege, his clothes always well kept. His looks are those of someone who takes care of themselves. Grant is fit, keeping up with his trainer at the gym, while Rose is just skinny. Sure, she has that Keira Knightley appeal, but that was never Grant's type before. He preferred women of leisure, who came from trust funds like him and could spend their weekends island-hopping on chartered yachts or jet-setting around Europe on a whim.

Rose, she imagines, could never even dream of such an idea.

While Grant gets his brown hair trimmed into a side part once a month, keeping his natural curls he had as a baby at bay, Rose has never put a hairdryer to her hair before. Evelyn supposes she doesn't need to; her hair seems to dry naturally into soft waves around her face. It's just that they are so opposite to one another. Grant cares so much about what people think about him and it's so obvious that Rose doesn't. They're like two puzzle pieces from different jigsaws and Evelyn doesn't know how they fit together.

She is hoping that after living here for a while, Rose will realize just how much she doesn't belong in this world. And Evelyn is more than happy to show her that the woman with the purse pulls the strings, and she can't wait to get rid of her.

Rose

Rose lets out an audible sigh as she sits on the edge of the bed, her elbows on her knees and her hands in a prayer over her face. Another groan of thunder rattles the windowpanes.

Her phone vibrates and she sees it's a text from Grant. She finds herself annoyed that he didn't just come back upstairs to talk to her.

I'm sorry, it was rude of me to get upset over your work. It took so long to meet you that I just want to make up for it by spending every day we have on this earth with each other. I'm very proud of you and your work.

Rose, despite being annoyed, can't help but smile. He's at least trying. She knows not everyone is perfect, least of all her. She can't slight someone when even they can admit they made a mistake.

He just needs to understand that her art is important to her. She doesn't know who she is without it. Her work has been what has gotten her through the toughest times in her life; her own form of therapy. She thought Grant had understood that, but the past couple of months he's been more frustrated by it. It was as if he expected once they were married that she would drop everything to be at his beck and call, but she had never once alluded to that. Rose was always going to work because she wants to work. She needs something that is hers. It's what defines her.

She also knows how quickly the rug can be pulled out from under her. First her parents, then the death of her first husband. Though it may seem like Rose has finally gotten her happy ending, she doesn't trust it for a second. The prenup she signed was iron-clad and she knows Evelyn wouldn't hesitate to toss her out on the street should something happen to Grant.

No, she needed her art. It was her safety net; though the rope was slowly fraying, she feared. Lately she had been struggling to sell her art. She needed a big comeback or that would be it for her.

Her phone rings this time and she rolls her eyes, assuming it's Grant. Only just before she picks it up, she sees the caller's name. Lina Prose.

It's as if Lina's ears were burning.

Rose and Lina have been friends for almost twenty years now, since Lina took a chance on Rose when she was barely out of art school. She came to a show that the school was putting on, and Rose can still remember the whispers of excitement as she walked around: "That's Lina Prose, they say she's the best."

"Hi, Lina."

"Darling, how are you?"

"Just getting settled in. We just arrived."

"How is the new M-I-L?" Linda abbreviates mother-in-law.

"Let's just say it's going to take some getting used to."

"Well, use that discomfort and angst and channel it into your next amazing art piece."

"I will certainly try." Rose looks around the room. She feels as if she is in a museum rather than her new bedroom.

"Not to put any more pressure on you, but Art Basel is coming up in a few months and your showcase really has to stand out."

"I know, Lina—" Rose starts, but Lina cuts her off.

"The thing is," she begins, "if you can't make it big with this art show, I'm terribly sorry, but I'm not sure if I'll be able to hold space for you anymore in my gallery."

Rose's stomach tightens into a knot. She has feared this outcome, though she knew it was a possibility. Lina has been delaying this conversation as much as possible, but she has to make a living, too. Still, it doesn't stop the tears welling in Rose's eyes as she thinks about when they first met.

Rose had watched anxiously from afar as Lina had stopped in front of her painting at her first art show. Rose held her breath. While Lina had taken the opportunity to see every piece in the gallery, she seemed to have a routine. At least, that was what the other artists had picked up on. One minute thirty seconds, then she moved on, as if she was counting in her head. The rest of them certainly were. But Rose remembers Lina took her time in front of her painting.

Devastation, as she had decided to call her painting, exhibited a mixture of sharp angles in deep crimsons and bruised purples, a bullet fired through the canvas.

Lina passed the standard one minute and thirty seconds, two minutes, then three minutes. In total, she spent about eight minutes staring quizzically at the painting, her eyes magnified behind her thick square-shaped glasses, her lips pursed, and her arms crossed, one bright red fingernail pressed against her cheek. Then she marched straight over to their professor, who then signaled for Rose to come over. Lina whipped her head back immediately, taking Rose by surprise as she looked her up and down, assessing her. Rose remembers she felt instantly flushed with heat.

Then just as Rose reached them, a smile formed across Lina's face.

"Darling, there is a career here for you."

Rose felt as if she would leap out of her skin just then. A wide smile spread across her own face as she gratefully accepted the compliment, but Lina's unexpected offer left her overjoyed. Her art has been on display in the Lina Prose Art Gallery ever since. Except now, there are fewer and fewer pieces.

"Art Basel is going to be your salvation," Lina says now. "If you can do well there, you'll be back on the map. But you need to find whatever it is you lost. I want to see that fire back. I know things were hard, especially after Ian's death, but take this change of scenery and use it to your advantage."

"I won't let you down," Rose says confidently to Lina, her hands trembling.

"I'm glad to hear it. I'll be in Miami in a couple of weeks, and I'll call you. We'll have lunch."

"Sounds good. Thanks, Lina."

"Ciao."

Rose hangs up the phone and walks over to the window, where the rain is coming down so hard it's pelting the glass like someone has taken a hose to the pane.

"Mom, are you coming down for lunch?" James appears in the doorway, holding his new laptop at his side.

"Yes," she says, turning back to the window.

"Summer storms, they call it." James walks towards her. "The mornings are beautiful and then in the afternoon there are sudden storm clouds that will roll in for an hour, then go away. But when they arrive, they arrive with force, so always be prepared for them."

Rose clearly has to prepare for more than just storm clouds. "Where did you hear that?"

"I just looked it up now." He looks down at the laptop. "I thought it was weird that it was sunny when we got here and then it changed so quickly."

"That's why I love you. You're always curious." She wraps her arms around him and kisses the top of his head, though she knows it might only be a matter of months before he sprouts up and gets taller than her. "Never lose that quality."

"Let's eat, I'm starving." James pulls away from her, her hand slowly sliding from his shoulders. Rose knows that it's partly to do with his age, but she can't help but feel James has been pulling away from her more and more both physically and emotionally since his father's death. Rose has been trying so hard to break through to him, but much like her, he shuts down, locking his emotions inside. She knows she doesn't set the best example when she's been doing the same thing all her life. It's a form of survival. Some memories are just too painful to be extracted. Knowing they can never really go away, sometimes you just have to bury them. But now, Rose wonders if she was wrong in allowing James to do that. Maybe she should've talked with him more about the whole thing. But she was afraid that like a volcano, it would cause all the other tragedies lying dormant within her to erupt. What's left now is the igneous rock that has hardened around them.

"Okay," she says, even though the stress of her call with Lina has made her lose her appetite.

There is a lot of pressure on her right now. She wants to make a big comeback with her art, but at the same time, she needs to make nice in the house. She knows Evelyn doesn't really like her. She clearly believes Rose is not worthy of her son.

But Rose loves Grant, and with him she can give James the life she never thought she could. Opportunities that will change the trajectory of his life if he so chooses. She just wants him to be happy.

Grant has been a bit tough to deal with lately, but the stress of his mother's Parkinson's diagnosis has been very trying for him. Since her diagnosis, he has been flying back and forth between New York and Palm Beach constantly. Evelyn has been particularly needy, almost as if this is the excuse she needed to pull Grant away from Rose as much as possible.

It was then that Grant, who had been burning the candle at both ends, suggested they all move in with Evelyn. Not Rose's ideal choice, but she had to do it for Grant's sake.

Rose has been selfishly looking at the situation as though it's Grant's problem to deal with. But that's not being a supportive wife, is it? He probably feels lost and alone right now. No other siblings to turn to. He needs her. That's why he's so upset about her art—he wants Rose to be there for him. And she should be, she knows that. The truth is, Rose isn't used to ever having support before. She's always had to look out for herself, never needing anyone. But this isn't about her. It's about Grant. Grant who has grown up with a mother who has cared for him his whole life.

A sinking feeling of guilt for both Grant and James takes root in her chest. Rose vows she'll make more of an effort, even with Evelyn, though she knows Evelyn will not make it easy for her.

Rose will kill her with kindness if it doesn't kill her first.

Rose steps out into the hall and takes a few moments to wander the empty second floor. Without Evelyn leading the way, she has a chance to take her time, scoping out each room. While Evelyn's apartment in New York has the same aesthetic, seeing it on a grander scale seems borderline ridiculous, like she is on a movie set for a period piece. She comes to the top of the steps where Evelyn's room sits off to the right. A blinding sheet of gold makes Rose almost have to squint. She feels as if she's just walked into a room in Versailles. The walls are gold-paneled with floral wallpaper that matches the king-sized bed and the layered fabrics of the balustrade hanging above it.

A gray life-size painting of likely some famous ancestor, sits above a wooden fireplace, and a gold and crystal chandelier hangs elaborately in the center of the room.

Rose has to stifle a laugh at how over the top it all looks.

In the corner of the room stands another antique-style desk with a laptop sitting lazily on it.

It looks just like the one James has, but she'd be surprised if Evelyn had a laptop in her room. She'd likely have an office somewhere where she would put that. It also bothers Rose the way it rests skewed on the desk with no wires to show this is its regular spot in the house. So far, everything she has seen looks to be set just so. She worries now it must be James's. Maybe he was snooping like she is and had placed it down on the desk while he wandered, forgetting it was there. She certainly didn't want him to get in trouble for being where he shouldn't on his first day.

Rose feels her throat swell at this familiar feeling. Being somewhere she wasn't supposed to be. That time her father had come home angry and told her mom to go to the liquor store, not giving her the chance to let Rose tag along. Rose didn't want to be around him when he was like that, so she ran back towards the shed, hoping to hide in there. Just as she was about to open the door, a large hand gripped her wrists, pulling her back so hard that she had gotten a bruise.

"I told you to stay out of the shed." He struck her across the face so hard she saw stars. Even though that wouldn't happen now, she still can't shake the memory and without thinking, raises a hand to her cheek.

Rose shakes the thought and grabs the laptop and brings it back into James's room.

She finds the cord behind his desk and plugs it in, lifting the screen to check that it's charging.

Then a second thought occurs to her. While she's remembering it, she should look into putting some parental locks on this. She trusts James, but he is still a fourteen-year-old boy.

She runs her finger along the pad below the keyboard, clicking around as she tries to see what she needs to do. Her attention lands on a file that reads 'NY'.

James can't have already made a file on here, she thinks. He wouldn't have had time. She clicks on it to see what it is.

Rose studies the images for a moment. They appear to be of different rooms from the penthouse apartment in New York. Rose squints, studying the images, wondering why James would have pictures of that apartment and how he had managed these high angles. Rose's stomach lurches when she realizes what she is looking at. This is not James's laptop, it's Evelyn's. Rose stands up so fast the chair behind her tips and she almost falls over herself.

Her hands clasp over her mouth. She can't believe what she is seeing. At first, she thought they were just pictures, but then she sees movement. Their maid is walking through the apartment. *Their* apartment. Which means that Evelyn has hidden cameras and has been watching them this whole time.

Isabel

Isabel tries balancing a black travel-sized umbrella over her head as she pulls one of her bags out of the idling Uber. The driver, ducking his bald head slick with rain, grabs another through the open trunk of the black SUV.

"Anything else?" he asks impatiently, staring at her three pathetic suitcases. Her whole life summed up in a nutshell.

"That's it, thanks." She smiles weakly.

He nods and jumps back into his car, horns blaring at him for being double-parked amongst the pink, white and yellow buildings. He drives away, leaving her to struggle with how she's going to drag all three of her bags into her new apartment behind her.

She looks up at the white stucco building with large windows and balconies that jut out in a half-circle looming above her. The dark clouds move with the wind, giving the dizzying effect that the tower itself is swaying.

It wasn't the most glamorous building on the street, but once she had heard she had gotten the job, she needed to hurry. She paid the first month's rent, sight unseen, and subleased her apartment in New York. Isabel could only hope that the pictures matched the actual apartment.

She closes the umbrella, her feeble attempt at trying to stay dry not working anyway, and she maneuvers all three suitcases to the door. In her attempt to open it, she realizes that it is clearly locked and won't budge.

At the sound of a loud buzzing, she jumps and assumes someone is letting her in. As she pulls the door open, she props one of her suitcases against it and drags the other two in.

"May I help you?" A woman with dark skin and braids, plum lipstick and a clean white button-down smiles brightly at her.

"Hi, I'm Isabel Martinez." She wipes her forehead and arms, trying to dry off. "I'm moving in today."

"Welcome." She smiles. "I'm Gina. The manager's office is down the hall." She points to direct Isabel. "They can get you set up."

"Thank you so much." Isabel smooths her hair down, noticing what a mess she must look in her wet T-shirt and jean shorts. Her hair has become frizzy from the rain and she can only hope that her eyeliner hasn't smudged too much.

She looks around, assessing the lobby. There is a large table with a bird of paradise plant in the middle. Above it, a blown-glass chandelier in the shape of coral reflecting pink on the white ceiling.

On the left is a curved wall with a mural of an ocean and backlit sunset sky above an orange velvet built-in bench.

Isabel shuffles her bags out of the way against the wall, then follows the direction of the receptionist to continue down the hallway. On her way she sees the mailroom, then a room with the words *Manager's Office* etched into the glass.

She takes a deep breath. "Here we go." Isabel pulls on the door and finds a tall, lanky middle-aged man with a thinning brown hairline, shuffling papers at a desk. He looks up when he sees her.

"May I help you?"

Isabel pulls her hair behind her ear before extending a hand. "I'm Isabel Martinez, I'm moving in today."

He smiles, showing a line of crooked teeth, standing up to shake her hand. "9B, that's right. Come have a seat."

Isabel sits down, removing her purse from her shoulder and setting it on the floor next to her.

"Really coming down out there," he says, noting that she is soaked head to toe. "I'm Steven." He puts a hand on his chest. "Let me just grab your paperwork." He turns towards the table behind him where neatly stacked manila envelopes are sitting. He grabs the top one and places it in front of her. "Just a couple of signatures needed." He holds his red tie to his chest as he leans over her.

Isabel picks up the papers and scans them briefly. She sees the rental agreement along with the rules of the building, details about the pool and gym as well as the garage and the common areas.

"Any questions so far?" he asks, not looking at her as he fumbles his way through several drawers until he retrieves a ring with a mail key, a key fob for the building and her apartment key.

Isabel shakes her head. "No."

"Do you have a car?"

"Yes, it's being shipped down here from Pennsylvania. It's supposed to be here by this afternoon."

She is using her grandmother's old car that she had kept in a storage garage, knowing it would come in handy. She was going to drive it down, but when she added the expense of the hotels, food and gas over the several days it would take to drive to South Florida, it had been surprisingly cheaper to ship it and fly down.

"Then you will need one of these." He opens another drawer under his desk and drops in front of her a sticker with a barcode on it. "Put this on your back right window and it will give you access to the residents' parking on the second floor of the garage."

"Thank you."

"Are you going to be needing any additional keys? A roommate or boyfriend?"

He looks at her in clearly a matter-of-fact way, but Isabel can't help but feel uneasy having to explain to a manager with keys to every apartment that she lives alone.

Noticing her expression, he looks down shyly. "If you get locked out, there's a fee of ninety dollars to let you in. The master keys are only meant to be used for emergencies, like a burst water pipe or a fire, for example. And at least two people must be in attendance," he clarifies.

This makes Isabel feel a little better, but only slightly.

He sucks in a breath, as if debating something in his head, before he finally returns to the cabinet and hands her another set.

"Just in case." He half smiles. "To keep in your car or something."

Fifteen minutes later, Isabel is sliding the key into her new apartment door. She breathes a sigh of relief when it appears to match the photos. There is a glass dining-room table on the left. A small galley kitchen on the right with a pantry room followed by a large open living room with sliding glass doors that lead to the balcony overlooking another white building. She walks through the living room, assessing the light brown leather couch that doesn't appear too worn or scratched. Next to it, a glass coffee table sits across from a walnut media console with a flatscreen TV mounted on the wall above it. In the corner is a bookshelf, alternating plants, books and art in each cubby-hole. She opens the sliding glass door and steps out momentarily. The humidity hits her like a wall after being cold and wet in the air conditioning, making the simple act of breathing feel thick. There is a small white wrought-iron table and two matching chairs, otherwise the deck is sparse and could use a plant or two. Isabel identifies the building across from her as an office building, and she appreciates it means she'll have some privacy at night.

Like a blast of wind, she feels herself knocked off balance, her vision blurring as the buildings seem to swirl around her.

Is she really doing this? What would her grandmother think?

An overwhelming grief hits her, and she stumbles, coming back inside to sit on the couch. Her head falls into her hands as she cries.

All Isabel wants is for her grandmother to hold her tightly and reassure her that everything will be fine.

Although she might not say that her grandmother was stronger or braver than her, they did have each other for support at the very least.

Grandma had been beautiful, with light brown hair, olive skin, round eyes and lashes that fanned out so perfectly you would've thought she'd paid for them. But it was rare for her to smile. Her lips always rested in a frown, her eyes had permanent dark circles, and her skin had deeper wrinkles than it should've given her age. Isabel knew her grandmother had had a hard life, but it was the one thing she could never get her to open up about. The loss of her daughter, Isabel's mom, had hit her with a trauma so fierce that she'd folded into herself, hiding from the rest of the world.

Isabel tried to be respectful, the way you wouldn't expect someone who's come back from war to tell you all the horrible things they'd seen. But her grandmother's reluctance to open up made Isabel's life a mystery.

You think you can prepare yourself for someone's death, but still it feels like it came out of nowhere. Her grandmother was getting better, the treatments working. But then she got an infection while she was in the hospital and that was it. Not even really a chance to get her affairs in order. It wasn't supposed to be like this. She was supposed to beat it and live another twenty to thirty years.

When she got the call, Isabel had been blindsided by how rapidly her grandmother's situation had worsened. The dread and fear of being stuck on the subway haunted her, as she remembered coming from work and worrying that she would never get the chance to say goodbye. Goodbye to the woman that had raised her, loved her, and was everything to her.

She'd had a bad feeling in the pit of her stomach, like her grandmother had chosen to go downhill. She'd had a purpose in life, raising Isabel after her mom died. But now that Isabel was in her early twenties, had just graduated college and was already living on her own, she couldn't help but think her grandmother had decided she would no longer fight.

Isabel wanted to get there in time to remind her she still needed her. She had to live for her. Without her grandma, she had no one.

"It's time for me to be with your mother again," she had said, her last few words between shallow breaths. "You'll be alright."

Isabel had gripped her hand tighter then.

There'd always been this underlying sadness that Isabel could never seem to pull her from. It was like she'd finally surrendered to it.

The only part of her grandmother's death that wasn't completely devastating for her was the hope that maybe she'd find a safe deposit box that would unlock all the answers to her questions. Questions she had asked her grandmother, but she had always sidestepped the answers. Isabel wanted to know what her mom had really been like. What had happened to her grandmother that broke her. Something that could help Isabel understand and sympathize with her.

Her grandma said that her mother died giving birth to Isabel, but Isabel always knew there was more to the story than what her grandmother was willing to tell her. She had tried looking her mother up, but her name was so common, the internet was flooded with random professional and social profiles. Nothing in regard to her mother. It was almost as if she never existed.

In the end, there was nothing. It was just Isabel and a lifetime of questions that would never get answered. It felt like experiencing her grandmother's death all over again. The grief of never knowing anything about her past.

That was until she started to pore through her grandmother's things, carefully analyzing every item in her apartment, wondering if there was a particular meaning to it. She catalogued everything with as much detail as possible in case she had to refer back to it. Only, the answers hadn't come from her grandmother's house. They came from her job at the Whitmore Academy. A job that her grandmother insisted she apply for. She wonders now if that was her grandmother's intention, to help Isabel find out the truth on her own.

Isabel had been doing administrative work when she'd stumbled across something by accident. It was the first clue that brought her to the Caldwell family, along with her obsession. When she had finally put the pieces together, she realized she had missed her window when she discovered that James Clark, the stepson of Grant Caldwell, would be transferring to Palm Beach. But she couldn't let this lead slip through her fingers. She knows that this family holds the answers to a secret that will likely change all of their lives forever, and with nothing to lose she will stop at nothing to get what she wants.

Evelyn

As Evelyn sits on the kitchen banquette waiting for the others, her eye catches on a garter snake, slithering across the hedges outside her window. Its yellow underbelly is a stark contrast to its tar-colored top half with a yellow stripe across the middle. Evelyn smiles at it as it picks its head up. Its long, skinny tongue sticks out before retreating into its mouth. Evelyn isn't scared of snakes, especially garter snakes. While they can appear menacing as they slither through your property, they are, in fact, a landscaper's best friend. They eat all the pests like slugs and rodents. Evelyn might even dare compare herself to a garter snake. She may look threatening but really, she's doing everyone a favor. Evelyn knows what's best for Grant, better than he knows for himself, and she will stop any intruders that threaten everything she has worked so hard to protect.

The kitchen door swings, and Grant turns his head around the kitchen before spotting her. He nods at Martha before directing his attention to her.

"How are you feeling, Mom?"

Evelyn makes a show of struggling to open up a pill box, extracting a cream-colored gel capsule that she pops in her mouth and washes down with water. "I'm doing just fine," she says in a sarcastic tone.

A clang of dishes startles Evelyn, who glares at Martha for fussing about.

"There's quite a spread for everyone to enjoy, if they actually make it down here." Evelyn points at the various types of sandwiches, roasted vegetables and an antipasto salad, displayed across the white marble countertop.

"They'll be down in a minute. Can I bring you something?"

"Just a salad . . . please."

Grant pulls a bowl from the glass cabinet and scoops a handful of leafy greens into it.

"Are you sure you still think this is a good idea?" Evelyn cocks an eyebrow at Grant.

"We've discussed this, Mom." Grant puts the bowl in front of her.

"I just don't understand the urgency you had for this m-marriage. If anything, intense emotions like that need to simmer. A break from one another would've been a healthier option instead of moving everyone here."

"She's more like me than anyone I've ever met." Grant narrows his eyes at Evelyn.

"Two wounded birds don't make the nest stronger. In fact, they do just the opposite."

"I am stronger, Mother." He tilts his head and smiles. "Thanks to you."

Evelyn sucks in a breath and averts her eyes around the room. With all the necessities needed for a modern-day kitchen, it was the one part of the estate that they'd needed to renovate. The wooden beams on the ceiling got to stay, but otherwise, they had a state-of-the-art full-size fridge and matching freezer. Despite putting dark wood paneling over it to match the rest of the cabinets, it didn't feel as glamorous.

Evelyn would have thought that Grant would want to eat in the dining room with its carved wood ceiling and two cut-marble fireplaces. They had originated from other European castles and palaces. She knew it was Grant's favorite fact to tell guests. The Vanderbilts had done something similar in Rhode Island.

There is a long rectangular wooden dining table that seats ten. It rests on a blue and yellow area rug with matching wooden chairs. Evelyn wanted to see James and Rose's faces as they dined in front of the oversized windows, rounded at the top, providing spectacular views of the outstretched ocean and beach below. When standing close to the windows, one can see the Olympic-sized swimming pool tiered above the lawn on a stone patio. The pool has sun loungers dotting the edges, while the other seated area is tucked under a loggia. The wrought-iron furniture has cushions in orange and white stripes, with an outdoor fireplace. Catty-cornered to that is a cut-marble bar with metal stools off to the left, looking over the tops of palm trees and hedges that edge the lawn below before spilling onto the beach. Once the weather clears, she hopes they can sit outside for a drink.

"Sweetie, are you sure you don't want to go to the dining room?" Evelyn places her hand on his.

"This is fine, Mom," Grant says.

She can sense then that he's doing this for Rose's sake. He's trying to show her that he too can be casual and laid-back. But Evelyn knows that's not who he really is.

He clears his throat and Evelyn watches as his irritation grows, waiting for everyone else. He grips his knife a little too tight and begins to cut his vegetables, his utensils scraping loudly against the china plate.

Evelyn tries not to wince.

"I'm glad you're here, Grant."

"After everything you've done for me, how could I not be?"

Evelyn smiles. Yes, being here is a much more suitable place for him. She only wishes it was just the two of them.

The door swings forcefully as James walks in, his laptop in his hand. He places it on the table before slinking down into one of the wooden chairs, its legs scratching against the tiled floor. "Mom will be down in a minute," he announces.

Evelyn resists the urge to tell him to sit up straight and explain how much more respectable he would look, but she realizes she'd rather save that comment for when Rose is present to hear it.

"Please, James, help yourself." Evelyn gestures to the spread at the same time that James takes note of the food on the counter and stands back up to do so.

"Thank you, Evelyn."

Evelyn is pleased to see he has manners. "So, are you excited to . . . start school tomorrow?"

He nods. "I'm a little nervous, but I think it will be okay. More nervous about soccer tryouts."

"Yes, I hear you are quite the athlete."

"I was more of a lacrosse player myself," Grant says before putting a roasted pepper in his mouth.

"You were very t-talented." Evelyn pats Grant's hand reassuringly. At least he would've been if he had put any effort into it.

It's all about keeping up appearances, she hears her husband Harrison's voice say in her head.

"Sorry, everyone." Rose comes in, looking flustered and unnerved. "This is wonderful, thank you," she says to both Martha and Evelyn as she notices the spread.

"Getting settled in okay?" Evelyn asks, wondering just what Rose has been up to that has her looking jittery.

"Everything's great," Rose says too quickly. "Thank you so much." She selects a sandwich and puts some salad on a plate.

"Oh, by the way," James says, shoving his fist into his pocket. "I found this in my room in one of the desk drawers. I wondered if someone might be looking for it." He pulls the object out and drops it. It clinks against the wood of the table.

Grant and Evelyn peer at the round piece of copper-colored metal, looking at it curiously.

Evelyn scrunches her brows. "Goodness." She picks it up to examine it, the weight feeling heavier than she remembers. "This is Harrison's wedding ring."

"Who's Harrison?" James asks.

"Grant's f-father," Evelyn says, peering at Grant. "I thought he was buried with this." Evelyn holds it up for Grant to see.

Grant averts his eyes and wipes his mouth with a napkin. "Where did you say you found this?"

James looks around as if he might get into trouble somehow. "In the desk drawer in my room?" he says now, like it's a question.

Evelyn looks back at Grant. "Your old room."

Grant scratches his jawline. "Not sure how it got there, Mom." He stands up with his plate.

She feels a shudder run through her.

Grant puts his dish by the sink. "I have to make a call for work," he announces before leaving the room.

The temperature feels like it has dropped ten degrees. A chill runs up Evelyn's spine.

Rose wipes her mouth with a napkin, then settles it on her lap.

"How did he die?" James asks before taking another bite of his sandwich.

"James!" Rose's eyes widen, mortified.

Evelyn picks at her salad, hands shaking as she considers how to answer the question while at the same time trying to wrap her head around how Harrison's wedding ring was in that drawer. She reflects on the funeral. Harrison looked gaunt and paler than he normally was, his dark hair appearing stiff and stringy compared to his normal soft side part, very similar to Grant's. It was odd seeing him lying in a shiny brown mahogany coffin, lined with white silk.

Evelyn felt so many emotions the day of the funeral, but every fiber of her being screamed with fear, preventing her from finding the courage to move forward. The reality is that even after twenty years, she's still as fearful as she was the day she buried him.

After all, it's because of her that he is dead.

Once more, she sees Harrison lying in his coffin, his hands folded across his middle. That ring, she could've sworn, was on him.

Evelyn remembers back when Grant was a child. Maybe six years old. On a trip to Palm Beach, Harrison drove them out to Wellington. It was particularly muggy that day after a rainstorm, and Harrison insisted on having the windows down in his convertible as they drove out from Southern Boulevard. The air held a thick moisture that felt damp on Evelyn's skin, despite the wind from the drive.

Grant sat in the back quietly, not bothering to ask where they were going. Rather, he just looked out the window observantly, as if playing a game against himself, trying to guess on his own.

"What are we doing all the way out here?" Evelyn finally asked him.

"You'll see." Harrison's dark hair was blowing in the wind but sweat was causing some of it to stick to his forehead. He was wearing a white polo shirt and khaki pants from just getting off the golf course.

Evelyn, already in a bad mood, crossed her arms when they pulled onto a long dirt path leading down towards a horse farm.

"Woah," Grant said in awe from the backseat.

Evelyn glared at Harrison, but he ignored her.

A short man in a pair of riding pants and a polo met them by the stables.

"Mr. and Mrs. Caldwell, welcome." His voice was thick with a British accent. "If you will follow me."

Evelyn trailed behind reluctantly, her heels sinking into the dirt, still moist from the early rainstorm.

Grant followed along behind Harrison like a puppy dog, pawing at his leg for attention. Harrison, in turn, swooped him up onto his hip, leaning over at one of the stables, where a brown chestnut horse with a sleek coat huffed at them.

"What do you think of him?" Harrison asked.

"Woah. Can we keep him?"

"I just bought him for you. What do you want to name him?"

Evelyn's face hardened, but Harrison and Grant ignored her once more as they decided on a name.

"Jordan."

"As in Michael Jordan?" Harrison laughed as Grant nodded his head.

"Okay. Well, Jordan it is. Do you want to take him for a ride?"

"Yeah!" Grant smiled.

"Charles, can you get him all set up?" Harrison turned his attention to the polo player who had brought them in.

"Right away, Mr. Caldwell."

Finally, Harrison turned to Evelyn. "So?"

"A horse, really?"

"Yes, really."

"What is he going to do with a horse?"

"Ride it?" He looked at her dumbly.

"We live in New York City, and we most certainly will not drive all the way out here when we are in Palm Beach to ride a horse."

"Why are you on me about this? What's wrong with buying my son a present?"

"Because you bought him a horse. Which is the definition of spoiling."

"I can't spoil my son?"

"Not to make up for your absence."

"Seems to work well for you," he said, more coldly now.

"I do what I have to do," she replied, her voice low.

"Yes, Evelyn, I know. You do what you have to do, because you wouldn't survive without my money."

He walked out of the stable then, leaving Evelyn with the stale smell of hay and manure lodged in her throat.

Evelyn shakes her head thinking about how Harrison always tried to buy their love, as if it would make up for all the terrible things he'd done. She releases her fork and lets it drop onto the plate with a loud clanking noise that makes both Rose and James jump slightly.

"I'm sorry, everyone, but it appears I have lost my appetite."

Rose

Rose awakens to the sound of a gunshot, causing her to let out a gasp as she jumps upright. It takes a few moments to realize that it's not real. It's only from her dream. The same one she gets practically every night. The screaming and crying, followed by a loud pop and then nothing.

Rose forces herself to lie back down in bed, but she is reminded of the hidden cameras she discovered in the New York apartment.

The question is, why did Evelyn have them? Does Grant know about them? She doubts it, so they must have been there back when Evelyn was living in the apartment. Maybe as a safety precaution after Harrison died and she was living alone? But then why still have them active? Why would you want to spy on your son and his wife? Rose shuddered then, realizing they were for her.

I know all about your past.

Rose's gaze falls on an oil painting of likely a relative from the early 1800s. The man, in his mid-forties, is dressed in equestrian attire with a jutting chin and barrel chest puffed out as he sits on a chestnut-colored horse. He holds a rifle at his side and there is an obedient foxhound at the horse's feet. Rose squints, studying the painting, noticing a hint of red. Are the eyes in fact cameras, watching their every move? She thinks of the oil painting at the penthouse that Evelyn wouldn't let go of. Was it all some sort of façade? Rose lifts her head to examine the painting further, but she soon realizes the moonlight is catching the paint, causing the shine she's seeing.

Rose wants to ask Grant about the cameras, but it's a weird thing to bring up. She only knows about them because she was snooping around his mother's room. That's not putting her at a good starting point.

She tosses and turns until Grant seems to moan in frustration. She isn't sure if he is annoyed with her or if he is dreaming, but she figures she might as well get up. It's still dark outside, though she wouldn't have known it with the heavy curtains. The clock reads four thirty in the morning. It took her until three to fall asleep to begin with. Like a person camping in the woods on the first night, every sound she hears has her on high alert.

Rose slips her legs off the bed and creeps to her closet to put on her painting smock. She thinks of Lina's warning. If she doesn't sell in this next art show, that's the end of her career. Another point of stress that will keep her from getting any sleep.

The door to her bedroom opens with a loud whine and she winces, trying to make up for the sound by tiptoeing along the hallway; the creaks are muffled a bit by the Persian-style runner.

When Rose reaches the top of the steps to the studio, she can see a long stream of moonlight stretch across the floor. Out the window, the sky has cleared, and the stars are twinkling against the midnight blue ocean.

Rose flicks on the light, squinting as her eyes adjust. The room looks like a blur now. As she acclimates to the light, she once again scans the room for hidden cameras. She feels so exposed, like being in a fishbowl.

A shudder runs through her as she remembers Evelyn's off-handed comment to her on her wedding day.

I know all about your past.

Did she really? Someone like Evelyn must've had a background check done on her, the same way that Rose had looked up Evelyn and the family, though hers was merely a Google search.

But Evelyn can't know *everything* about her. Rose is the only one alive to tell that story.

Rose thinks of how upset Evelyn was when Harrison was brought up at lunch yesterday. In the evening, Rose tried to look up Harrison Caldwell on the internet. There was a brief Wikipedia page about his accomplishments and career, but other than an obituary, Rose saw nothing about how he'd died. No cause of death or anything. But that's how these rich people survive, right? If it's worth enough to you, you can erase your past.

Looks like Rose isn't the only one with a secret.

Rose pulls the closet door open to find a step stool and a stack of canvases in various sizes.

She tilts her head, afraid to even touch a canvas. She thinks about Evelyn's comment earlier: how Rose is to remember this gesture as Evelyn will want something in return. But at the same time, she needs a place to work. Her career is on thin ice as it is. And truthfully, she's genuinely grateful to have a studio in the house, rather than have to rent somewhere. If that were the case, she'd likely never see James or Grant, which is one of the reasons for his hostility about her work in the first place. At least now Rose can sneak up here at night and try to get her art back on track.

She shakes the thought away and pulls out a canvas to set up on the easel.

Rose tries to get in touch with what she's feeling. It's how she works best. She identifies anxious, displaced, and she ponders the word for a minute. Helpless. Somber tones, she concludes, setting up her palette. She clears her throat and begins to paint.

Rose has her earbuds in, listening to her inspiration playlist, the sun now streaming brightly through the tiny window. What stares back at her from the canvas are impassive and understated tones of blue, blurred shapes of gold and faded purples. She sighs. Lina would hate it. She's going to have to do a lot to fix this up.

A hand grips her shoulder, and she is startled out of her trance.

When she turns around, James is staring at her. He looks so dapper in his sports coat, tie, and tan dress pants. Then her face falls when she realizes that it's the first day of school. She quickly pulls out her earbud.

"I thought you were going to drive me to school?"

Rose checks her watch, eyes widening in surprise. "I'm so sorry. I've been at it since four thirty this morning." She looks between her canvas and James. "I'm almost done."

"It's already seven thirty."

She puts a hand on her forehead, frustrated. "I'm sorry. I lost track of time."

"I'll just have Grant drive me."

Rose hesitates for a minute. She does want to take him, it's his first day of school. But then she hears Lina's regretful voice telling her that if she doesn't do well, she's done for.

James seems to read her face and before she can say anything, he speaks. "It's not a big deal. I'm sure Grant can do it."

"Are you sure?" Rose asks guiltily. "I promise I'll pick you up from school today. I can't wait to hear all about it."

"I'm sure." He turns to leave.

"Come here, give me a hug." She puts her arms out.

He hesitates. "I can't get paint all over my uniform."

Rose looks down at herself. He's right, she is covered from head to toe. She gets so caught up; she loses all sense of things.

"How about a kiss, then?"

James begrudgingly walks towards her, pecking her quickly on the cheek.

"Have a good day. I love you." Once she can no longer hear his footsteps, she starts working again.

Rose continues to paint but after a few minutes, she stops. She should've insisted on bringing him to school. Quickly, she removes her smock and hurries down the steps, bursting through the front door, only to watch as the black Range Rover drives away, dust rising from the gravel.

Rose traipses heavily up the stairs like her feet are made of lead. When she gets back to her studio, she throws the smock back on and takes in a deep, slow breath, trying to get back to the place she was earlier, but after a few more minutes, her paintbrush falls to the side.

She hasn't been a very good mother, she realizes. Rose feels something wet on her cheek and it isn't until she takes a paint-stained finger to her face that she realizes she's crying.

It was tough being a young mother, trying to raise another human when you'd barely been able to raise yourself. To Ian's credit, he'd been a wonderful father to James, but not that great of a husband to her. Despite the fact that it was Rose who was there with her son, twenty-four seven, through the good times and the more challenging ones, she was overshadowed by Ian's presence.

He was the one who featured in all of James's good memories. That was because it was Rose who had to be the disciplinarian when James's grades were slipping. She had to tell him he wasn't allowed to play video games until his grades improved, only to have Ian override her. She felt like she always had to be the bad guy, and it breaks her heart to think that part of James's sadness might be wishing that it was her that had died instead of Ian.

She wonders where she would be right now if she hadn't taken a job at Lina's gallery as a part-time curator. Rose's paintings were not selling as well as they once had and as Ian's drinking became a problem, the quality of his furniture decreased, along with sales, until they barely paid the rent. Rose realized they needed the extra money. On her first day she had been sitting at Lina's desk when Grant had walked in on that brisk fall morning. He was wearing a suit and tie, his thick brown hair brushed back and styled in such a way that Rose wouldn't have been surprised if he had just walked off a photoshoot.

He removed his sunglasses, tucking them into the front pocket of his jacket and smiled at her in a way that caused her stomach to flutter.

"Do you work here?"

Rose nodded, her mouth suddenly dry.

"I'm looking to get educated on art investing. Is that something you could possibly help me with?"

Rose swallowed the knot in her throat. "Yes."

Over the course of the next several weeks, he'd met her as she recited highlights from her degree in art history, only to find out that he had decided he was no longer interested in art investments but wanted to keep coming to see her.

"I'm married," she had told him when she'd learned of his true intentions.

He had looked disappointed, but had taken it gracefully and felt there was no reason that they couldn't be friends.

Obviously, Ian hadn't been too happy that Grant was suddenly everywhere that she was. When Grant had found out that she was also an artist, she found him hanging around the gallery, buying her newest pieces or at the nearby coffee shop where he claimed his office was just around the corner. She had to admit to herself that she liked the attention.

"I don't like that creep hanging around everywhere," Ian had said when they had come back from one of her art shows. His blond hair caught the light of the refrigerator as he pulled out a beer.

"He's just a friend," Rose said cautiously, leaning back on the linoleum counter as if bracing herself for his wrath.

"He likes you as more than a friend." He twisted the cap with his hand and tossed it onto the counter, where it skipped into the sink.

Rose rolled her eyes. "I'm going to bed."

Ian put an arm across Rose to stop her. "He wrote you some weird poem."

Rose looked at him, confused. "What?"

"I saw it in your little mailbox at the art gallery tonight. I knew it was him. Don't tell me you're not screwing the guy if he's writing you poetry."

Rose felt her blood boil. If anyone was stepping out of this marriage it was him, but like always, she swallowed down her rage, doing her best to avoid conflict, and put her hand out.

Ian sneered at her. "Do you actually fall for that crap?"

"Of course not. I just don't appreciate you going through my mail."

Ian pulled the crumpled piece of paper out of his pocket and tossed it to her. "Here, knock yourself out."

Ian was right. Rose wasn't much for poems, even if they were about art, but as she unrolled the poem, she secretly hoped that it would get Ian's attention. She wanted him to realize that she too was desirable to others and maybe he'd stop his philandering and come back to her. But of course, that didn't change his ways.

A few weeks later when they were out to dinner, just the two of them, Ian spotted Grant sitting by himself in the back.

"Just leave him be," Rose urged when she saw Ian stand up.

"Forget that." He stumbled through the gastropub like a rolling steam train. Rose followed, pulling on his arm, but it only seemed to ignite the fire inside him.

"Stay away from my wife, you creep!" Ian yelled, hovering over Grant.

Rose gave Grant an apologetic look and again tried to pull Ian away, only for him to shake her off like she was an annoying fly.

"I'm just having dinner." Grant looked at him incredulously.

"I said, stay the hell away from my wife!" Ian's voice grew louder then, grabbing the attention of other patrons.

Grant stood, his hands up in self-defense.

"Sir, if you don't take your seat, I'm afraid I'm going to have to ask you to leave." A manager with coiffed white hair and leather skin approached Ian.

Ian looked like he was going to acquiesce. He put his hands up in defense before cold-cocking Grant, creating a collective gasp across the restaurant.

The maître d', along with someone from the kitchen, escorted Ian out, while Rose stood there, her shoulders curled over her chest, hands over her mouth. She sat down in the seat across from Grant, scrunching up a white linen napkin to fill it with ice from his water and handed it to him.

"I'm so sorry," she whimpered.

"Don't worry about me," he said, putting the ice to his jaw. "I'm worried about you."

"I'm fine." Rose tore her eyes from him and saw Ian pacing the sidewalk back and forth outside the window.

"I wish you could see you deserve better."

Rose bit her lip.

"Why don't you leave him?"

"I would," Rose admitted. "I just couldn't do that to James."

It was as if she had cursed Ian. The words came out of her mouth and like some horrible prophecy, within a month Ian was dead. Rose woke up that morning treating it just like any other day. Then she got a phone call that Ian had been struck by a car.

Rose had looked up the statistic later when she was trying to make sense of it all. Hundreds of pedestrians in New York alone died that year. They made up half of the motor vehicle accidents. Nothing dramatic had occurred. He was simply another statistic. Rose felt conflicted. She may not have loved him the way she had when she was younger, but she still loved the idea of him. Most of all, though, she loved Ian for the father he was to James, and her heart broke that her son was losing a father figure during the most formative years of his life.

But through her grief, Grant was by her side. Helping her get through it. Suddenly it all clicked for her. She realized she was happier with Grant than she had ever been with Ian. Grant was kind and patient, and she fell in love with him. He was a bit awkward with James, but she didn't blame him; James had been a bit standoffish when Rose finally decided to introduce them.

"Did you ever care about Dad?" James asked her once coldly after she had told him she was seeing Grant.

"Of course I did, and still do," she said defensively. "My relationship with your father was different from yours."

"How so?"

Rose closed her mouth then. She didn't know how to explain it to him. She didn't want to tell James all the horrible ways his father had treated her. His jealousy and anger. He'd been smart enough to keep their fights out of the presence of James, putting on as much of a show as she did. James was younger then, and it was easier for him to accept. Now that he's older, she wonders how much longer they would've been able to keep up the charade until he realized.

Still, Rose wants James to remember Ian as he was to him, not as he was to her.

She remembers all those nights that Ian didn't even bother to come home to them. But when James would ask where he was, Rose would tell him he was sleeping at his furniture workshop because he was in the middle of a big project. Not that he was staying with a woman named Trixie, a waitress who worked not too far from him.

When he did come home, usually drunk, he would barely acknowledge Rose's existence but would wrap James in a friendly headlock, and the two would hole up in the living room playing video games for hours on end, while she supervised like a parent with kids on a playdate.

"I'm doing this for both of us," she said instead.

James rolled his eyes and went into his room, while Rose sat on the couch, still stunned into silence. When it came to communication it was like she was suffering from a disability. No matter how much she tried, she couldn't bring herself to do it, her whole body shutting down on itself.

But now Rose feels like she's caught in a rip tide, the waves churning her in every direction, and she has no idea which way is up. Like she can never make the right choices, with Grant or with James.

Rose shakes her head. These are not the feelings she's trying to channel right now. It will undo her work. She needs to take a step back for a moment.

As she wipes her arm across her forehead, she looks up at the vent in the ceiling. Her stomach pulls in on itself when she sees something inside. She knew there would be a camera somewhere.

Reminded of the step-ladder in the closet, she pulls it out, trying to see what sort of screwdriver she would need for the screws. Only to her surprise, the nails don't seem very secure. The holes seem bigger, as if someone has been going in and out of this vent for some time. She grips the sides of the vent with the tips of her fingers and pulls it down. One of the nails falls to the floor, making a clinking sound. She puts the vent on one of the steps of the ladder, then peers back up into the darkness, realizing she should pull her phone out and put the flashlight function on.

Rose reaches her hand in and feels for whatever it was she saw. A metal box scrapes across the crawl space as she drags it to the edge of the opening before putting her phone away and grabbing it with both hands.

It looks like some sort of cash lock box. Money, Rose concludes. After the Depression, lots of people didn't trust banks anymore and hid money all over the house. Considering how old this place was, she wouldn't be surprised if that's what this was.

Rose steps down, hearing something heavy slide around inside of the box. The weight is no longer evenly distributed. She crinkles her eyebrows, realizing that it clearly isn't money.

Curiosity getting the best of her, she pulls out a bobby pin from her bun and picks the lock, unlatching it with a click.

As Rose lifts the lid, her skin tingles, her hands shaking so violently she nearly drops the box.

I know all about your past.

Bile starts to rise into her throat. She feels as if she's going to be sick. Finding a small bathroom through a side door, she collapses over the toilet, emptying the contents of her stomach.

She crouches against the wall, her face flushed as she tries to keep the room from spinning. Is this some sort of game Evelyn is playing with her?

The night comes back to her in flashes like the still frames from a movie. The blood smeared across the floor, the gun shaking so hard in her hand that she dropped it.

Rose pulls herself up off the floor, her legs so unsteady she needs to lean against the wall for balance. With trepidation, she walks towards the cashbox again, trying to rationalize what she saw. But as her eyes come into focus, she realizes she's not seeing things.

It *is* a gun. The exact gun from that night. The question is, what is Evelyn doing with it and how does she plan on using this against her?

Isabel

Isabel pulls up to the front of the Pelican Academy in her grandmother's silver Camry. Her mouth hangs open like a fish. After triple-checking the address several times, she concludes that this Gilded Age mansion must be the school itself. She has seen pictures of it, but they didn't convey the true level of grandeur. She assumed it was someone's former residence, likely a founder of the area, and was just one of the many buildings on campus, likely the administration office—like that of her former job at Whitmore Prep. But the fact that this building is big enough to house the entire school practically blows her mind.

Isabel knows that the mansion, in its neoclassical Beaux-Arts style, must have been built in the early 1900s, but it appears brand new. The paint of the building looks fresh and as white as the soft cumulus clouds that rest above it. Just then, the sun breaks through as if shining a spotlight on the mansion itself. The sky is bluebird blue and the scene so perfect you would think you were looking at a piece of art, rather than it being real and in front of you. All aspects of the storm are gone; Isabel realizes she didn't see so much as a palm frond on the ground on her way here. Everything has been reset like it never happened. It makes her think how many other unsavory things a town like this would be eager to clean up and do away with.

Although she is confident she knows what she's doing, she can't help the imposter syndrome she's feeling right now. She knows she impressed them with her background. Not only was she working at one of the most competitive schools in the country, but she graduated from Columbia on a scholarship with honors for her degree in mathematics, and a minor in political science and government. Her credentials not only got her the job, but if her political science degree taught her anything, it was how to get what you want out of people. Of course, a school would never accredit themselves for teaching people how to manipulate one another, even though that's exactly what they did. She had calculated strategically what questions they would ask, and she knew how to answer them in the way they wanted to hear. But the several interviews she had via Zoom calls from New York didn't capture the full spectrum of it all. Only now does she realize she is walking into an entirely different world from the one she was used to.

The car line for drop-off snakes around the circular driveway. Each vehicle, from Isabel's perspective, cost at least several hundred thousand dollars, the keys being handed off to a valet who quickly jumps in to keep the line moving. She watches in awe for a moment as these teenagers step out in their uniforms, the boys in blue button-downs with suit jackets, and white polos and pleated skirts for the girls. Yet even all in uniform, you can tell they're a different breed. The boys wear Patek watches and the girls sport accessories from next season's collections or possibly family heirlooms. Even in the way they walk, they carry themselves with a level of distinction. They are among the elite, and they know it.

If James Clark thought Whitmore was hard, this place is going to eat him alive.

A horn blares from behind her and Isabel realizes she is blocking the entrance. She gives a faint wave of apology and follows signs to the faculty parking lot to the far left, relieved to find that she isn't the only one with a modest car.

A nervous jolt of energy surges through her as she follows the students up the front marble steps. She walks between the several Corinthian columns and passes the heavy glass door framed in gold. She feels the eyes of several students settle on her. Isabel is only twenty-three but has a youthful look to her. It wouldn't be her first time being mistaken for a student, by the faculty or by the students themselves. Her silk blouse and black pencil skirt give her the professional appeal she's hoping for, and she's kept it to wedges rather than heels, anticipating she'll be on her feet for most of the day. Her dark hair is swooped up in a bun, which, based on her reflection in the window, has an almost blue shine to it in this lighting. She checks her ears again for her own family heirlooms, a pair of pearl earrings she found in her grandmother's jewelry box. Her first thought was to bury her in them, but she knew her grandmother too well. If she had been given the chance to expect her death, she would've removed them from her own ears, telling Isabel to have them to remember her by. Anxiously, she rubs them once more to ensure they are secure and a part of her, superstitiously seeking good luck.

With confidence, she keeps her head high as she strides towards the front office. A large wooden counter acts as a divide between students and office administrators, though it appears out of place, too utilitarian in a room of such opulence. She stands patiently as an older woman in her sixties, dressed in a pink Lilly Pulitzer shift dress, busies herself around the desks, distributing papers as if she's a bee pollinating various flowers.

Isabel expects that at some point the woman will look up and see her standing there. She doesn't have to stop what she's doing, but a simple "Be right with you" would suffice.

She looks impatiently up at the ceiling, noticing a crystal chandelier, the light casting a twinkle of rainbows that dance across the cream textured silk wallpaper.

A clearing of someone's throat from behind Isabel surprises her. She thought she was alone in the office.

Her breath hitches when she sees Grant Caldwell standing behind her. He gives her a dismissive glance as he stands next to a boy she knows is James Clark, his stepson and a former student at Whitmore. It takes a moment for her brain to catch up with reality. Grant, standing in casual khaki pants and a white linen shirt, notices her staring and smiles at her politely, then cocks his head ever so slightly as if trying to remember if he's seen her somewhere before. She holds her breath in anticipation.

"May I help you?" The woman finally turns her attention to them. Isabel says nothing until Grant ushers her to. "You were here first," he says, gesturing, noticeable sweat stains already below his armpits this early in the morning. Unavoidable in this heat.

She nods a slight thanks. "I'm Isabel Martinez. I'm here to speak with Mrs. McFadden."

The woman nods in recognition. "I'll let her know you're here." Then she turns her head towards Grant and James. Grant puts a hand on James's shoulder, the suit jacket slightly big on him like they hadn't had time to get it taken in. "James Clark. Here to speak with Mrs. McFadden as well," Grant says.

James stands like the insecure teenager that he is. His head is down, with his backpack slung from one shoulder as he shifts nervously from side to side.

Isabel knows she has to say something.

"First day?" Isabel asks.

Grant answers for James, "Yes, actually."

"Mine too." She smiles, more comfortable that they don't recognize who she is.

"Do you work here?" Grant asks.

Isabel nods, watching as the woman disappears into a back room. When she's gone, Isabel turns to James, lowering her body and her voice to a soft whisper. "Sometimes I like to picture people doing silly things. It makes me laugh and then no one notices how nervous I really am."

Grant gives her an odd, curious chuckle, while James goes back to looking down, kicking around a small piece of lint on the floor. Respectful enough not to roll his eyes at her.

Isabel feels sweat bead on the back of her neck. She overstepped and now she's made the wrong first impression.

By now, several other people have gathered behind their desks, some reviewing the memo that busy bee Lilly, which Isabel will forever remember her as, has left for them.

"Something tells me this one sings in the shower," Isabel says, practically under her breath.

James looks up at a tall redhead talking animatedly in a singsong voice to someone on the phone, gesturing as she speaks, as if the person is standing there in front of her.

James laughs, and Isabel does her best to stifle a giggle.

"Mrs. McFadden will see you now." Busy bee Lilly returns, gesturing to James and Grant. Then she turns her head to Isabel. "Just have a seat. She will be with you shortly after them. She'd like to make sure James can start with his class on time."

"I understand." Isabel nods respectfully.

James is still smiling and coughs to compose himself.

"Hey," James calls to her.

When she makes eye contact with him, his face is relaxed, even smiling. "Thanks. I really needed that."

Isabel smiles shyly. A joke at the expense of others was a risk, but it had worked just like she had wanted it to.

She hadn't expected to find James all those months ago, a mere two weeks before the end of the school year. His surname was Clark, and she wouldn't have made the connection if it hadn't been for her colleague Theresa, who had been assigned to handle his transfer.

"Caldwell," she had said out loud, which made Isabel look up.

She peered at Isabel through her round glasses. "Weren't you looking for Caldwell at some point?"

She nodded eagerly.

Theresa tilted her head and looked up in thought. "I'm not sure if this is the same Caldwell or not. But Rose and Grant Caldwell are listed as James Clark's parents."

Isabel tried to play it casual. "Maybe," she said, immediately typing their name into a Google search.

A picture of Rose and her husband, Grant, was displayed in a news article about an art show. Rose had her hair slicked back into a chignon and was dressed in a long black strapless dress, red lipstick against her pale skin. Grant stood beside her in a tux with his arm wrapped around her frail waist almost possessively, smiling coyly at the camera.

It was him. This was who she had been looking for. A smile crept across her face. This was going to be easier than she thought. She was going to finally get to Grant, and she was going to use James to do it.

Evelyn

Evelyn is in a rush, heading towards the garage to check if Renaldo has returned from his errand that she sent him on. He's still not back. She checks her watch impatiently then turns when she hears footsteps and discovers Grant walking into the foyer. He is dressed in one of the pink polos she bought him, with white Peter Millar shorts.

"Grant, Renaldo is indisposed at the moment and I'm going to be late for mahjong. Would you be a d-dear and drive me, please?"

"I was hoping to catch you," Grant says, unfazed by her urgency.

"What is it, darling?" she asks, trying to keep the annoyance out of her voice.

Grant looks around first then comes closer towards her. "Rose could give you a lift, and what do you say about asking her to join you?"

"Is she even familiar with the game?" Evelyn asks skeptically.

Grant pulls his mouth to the side. "You could teach her."

"Maybe some other time. I'm already running late." Evelyn puts her hand on the doorknob.

"Please, Mother." His hand gently grabs her forearm. "It would mean a lot to me. The more time you spend with her, the more you'll see how perfect we are for one another."

Evelyn stops, then smiles. "The problem is, dear, no one is good enough for you."

Grant chuckles then kisses her on the cheek. "While I'm flattered, Mom, I think it's only right that you help make her feel comfortable here."

Evelyn sighs. "If you insist."

In the car, Evelyn sits in the passenger seat, pulling her pill box from her purse, waiting for Rose to say something. Instead, she drives slowly, admiring the hedges and banyan trees that line the street.

"I'm sorry my son forced us into this." She puts a pill in her mouth and washes it down using a water bottle she had sitting in the cupholder.

"Not at all." Rose manages a smile. "I'm happy to spend time with you. It's a good opportunity to get to know each other better."

Evelyn can't help but let out an incredulous laugh at how transparent she is. "You don't have to lie to me. I know I'm no picnic to be around. Not to mention you seem to be on some sort of deadline with your work, right? If you don't sell your art, that will be it for you, won't it, dear?"

Rose turns her head; her brows furrow beneath her sunglasses and Evelyn notices her grip on the steering wheel tighten.

"Spying on me?" Rose tries and fails to sound casual.

"Like I told you before, thin walls."

Rose appears like she wants to say more, but instead closes her mouth, her lips pursed tightly as if actively trying to keep her words from escaping her.

Evelyn can't help but dare her to come out and say what she wants to say.

Instead, Rose's lips part slightly and she lets out a breath of air.

There is a moment of silence before Rose speaks again, her tone lighter, moving on from the previous comment. "So, how do you play mahjong?"

"Well, the goal of the game is to get mahjong. Which means getting fourteen tiles into four sets and one pair. The pair will be two identical tiles, known as a . . . 'chow,' which is three . . ." Evelyn stutters, ". . . consecutive numbers in the same suit."

Rose doesn't say anything, as if she's trying to comprehend what Evelyn just said.

"You'll catch on quick."

Rose's phone dings.

"Can you check that?" Rose asks, keeping her eyes on the road.

Evelyn picks it up from the cupholder, squinting at the small letters. "Grant."

"I'll look at it later. Just wanted to make sure it wasn't from the school." Rose clears her throat. "So, who do you play with at the club? Is it the same people all the time?"

"It tends to be."

"How long have you known everyone for?"

"Some of them going on f-forty years now."

"I thought you only recently moved down here full time?"

Evelyn chuckles. "Palm Beach is a place that people have been coming to for generations. Most of these women, like I did, live in New York. We then come here for the season, followed by summers in either the Hamptons or Nan—Nantucket—although this most recent hurricane messed up the Hamptons pretty badly, so most of us agreed to just stay in Palm Beach."

"So, you all sort of travel together in a pack?"

Evelyn can't help but smirk. "Yes, we do, we are a pack of wolves and you're getting thrown right into the middle of it."

A text message dings on Evelyn's phone and she looks down.

You're late, we're going to start without you.

Evelyn sighs. She ignores the text from Missy and puts the phone back shakily into her purse.

"Look, I know you look down on me because I don't come from anything, but I wish you would give me a chance."

Evelyn scoffs; Rose has no idea what she's talking about. This has nothing to do with her coming from nothing. Evelyn knew all about that. She knew what it was like to be opportunistic.

"You don't want to marry that man."

Evelyn, newly engaged, had been applying her lipstick in the bathroom of the Palm Court when Missy walked in. She stood next to her, fluffing her teased-out brown curly hair. They had never exchanged a word before. Missy was one of these women who came from generationally wealthy families. To Evelyn they might as well have been from another universe entirely. She had no idea how she could relate to them and most of them didn't even seem to want her to try.

"Excuse me?" Evelyn had asked, shocked. "Why?"

"Did you know he was engaged to me when he knocked you up?" Missy stood next to her, staring at her through the mirror as she pulled out her own lipstick from her purse and applied a light pink against her cream-colored skin.

Evelyn looked at her strangely then. Was she lying?

"I have no idea what you're talking about." Evelyn held her head high, ready to walk out of the bathroom when Missy grabbed her arm.

"I'm warning you; you don't want to marry that man."

Missy looked down at Evelyn's belly. Evelyn was still early. Not a lot of people even knew about it.

"Get rid of it and get out while you can." Missy eyed her one last time, then turned around and walked back out of the bathroom.

No, this isn't about Rose's financial struggles, although they are apparent. This is about the threat that she poses to Grant.

"I do love Grant," Rose says as if reading her mind. "You need to trust that I will never hurt him."

Evelyn shakes her head then turns towards the window. "Somehow I doubt that."

"You don't have a lot of faith in people, do you?"

"I don't have faith in humanity itself, let alone individual people."

"What I'm trying to say is that I don't have ulterior motives. I love your son and would like it if we could get along as well."

Evelyn glares at her. "You have to earn trust."

Rose leans back in her seat, frustrated but determined, before giving Evelyn another fake smile. "Then I will do what I can," she replies, as if accepting the challenge.

Rose looks down at her phone's GPS. "Is this the place?" She tilts her head as she reads the sign on the Mediterranean building.

"Yes, we're here." Evelyn sighs with relief as they pull to the front of the building. The valets open the doors for both her and Rose simultaneously.

Evelyn removes her sunglasses, straightening her dress. They step inside, heels echoing against the terracotta tiling. The women are about to head in when Rose's phone beeps an alert again.

Evelyn looks at her, exasperated.

"Grant again," she says apologetically.

"Shut your phone off. I will not have you embarrass me at my own club."

"Mrs. Caldwell," says a blonde woman in a white tennis outfit, standing up from behind a rattan desk.

"Hello, Emily. This is Grant's wife, Rose." She points her sunglasses at Rose, then stuffs them in her purse. "She will be my guest this afternoon."

"Very nice to meet you." Emily extends her hand to Rose. "Welcome to the Coconut Palm Country Club." She looks towards Evelyn. "Everyone's upstairs. Please enjoy."

Evelyn leads Rose through a hallway with white stone walls and vaulted wooden ceilings. After climbing a curved stone staircase, they arrive in a large dining room, divided by arched entranceways with wooden-beamed ceilings and wide rustic black chandeliers. The sound of women's voices fills the center of the room, as they stand around in colorful attire like floral peacocks. In the adjoining room are various tables set up for mahjong.

"Evelyn, what do we have here?" Evelyn recognizes the voice of Missy Fanwood approaching. Her tall brown beehive hairdo gives her five-foot frame another several inches. She grips Evelyn's arm, her bony fingers digging into her skin.

Evelyn's fists tighten. They've barely got in the door before Missy has hunted her down like a dog with a scent.

"This here is Rose." Evelyn gestures to Rose, who appears to still be taking it all in.

"Hello, Rose. I'm Missy," she says, straightening her soft pink tweed jacket.

"Hello." Rose smiles.

"I love your dress." Missy points at Rose's understated white cotton sundress, which is slightly wrinkled from sitting in the car.

"Thank you."

"So, you're the one that just moved here?"

Rose nods.

"Let's get you a drink. You're going to need it surrounded by these old hens."

Missy whisks Rose away, and Evelyn isn't sure if she should be worried. Missy and she have a history, and God only knows what sort of dirt she is trying to extract from Rose or vice versa.

"So how do you know Evelyn?" she overhears Rose asking Missy.

"Oh, we go way back." Missy pulls an olive off the toothpick in her martini. "Evelyn and I shared a fiancé at one point."

Rose looks to Evelyn, her cheeks turning as pink as her freshly poured rosé.

"Ladies, let's get started," a man in a suit with a thick mustache announces.

Evelyn points Rose towards their table.

"What did she mean by that?" Rose says, clearly shocked by the exchange.

"She's talking nonsense," Evelyn says tightly.

"Ah, here we are," she adds, smiling, spotting Marsha and Dorothy at a table. Marsha is dressed in a yellow satin wrap blouse and white pants, while Dorothy is wearing a blue tie-front sheath dress. Both women smile graciously. If there is anyone that will show Rose her place here, it will be them.

"I have a newcomer here," Evelyn says. "Meet Rose."

"So very nice to meet you, Rose." Dorothy puts a frail hand out for Rose to shake, as the decorative hairpiece keeping her white hair in a French twist catches the light off the chandelier.

"What an interesting dress," Marsha adds, her dark hair curled evenly under her chin. "It's so simple."

Rose's smile fades when she finally takes in the elaborate designer clothes these women are wearing. The materials are so refined that Rose can't even dare to guess the price tags.

Rose pats her dress awkwardly and takes a seat. Smooths down her limp hair, which has lost its natural wave with this humidity.

"I love this dress, Evelyn," Marsha says, making a fuss. "Is it new?"

Evelyn smiles and fans out her mint-colored flare dress with cap sleeves. "I just got it at Oscar de la Renta, on sale."

"Absolutely stunning. Perhaps you can let Rose borrow something next time."

Rose shifts nervously in her seat and Dorothy sits down next to her.

Evelyn feels a slight tinge of sympathy for her. "Let's start the game, shall we?"

After an hour, Evelyn can see Rose looks tired. She's not a skillful player, nor has she been great at making a good impression, her glass of wine still untouched.

"I'll get us a drink." Evelyn stands up.

"Should you be drinking?" Rose asks her. The other women stop talking and look at her.

Evelyn feels a flush of embarrassment. "I can do whatever I want, young lady," she scolds her.

"I'm sorry," Rose says nervously, "I didn't mean anything by it, I just meant with your medications."

Evelyn walks away before Rose can finish speaking, hurrying to the ladies' room. That's all she needs, these women gossiping about her. She's angry at Grant for making her bring Rose here in the first place. This is supposed to be her sanctuary.

Evelyn stares at herself in the mirror and swallows hard. How long is she going to be able to keep this charade up? What if someone finds out what she's doing?

Hearing voices outside the door, Evelyn slips into the bathroom stall, not wanting to see or talk to anyone.

She hears a sigh that sounds like Rose. Evelyn can't help herself and peers through the crack of the stall door.

When she realizes it is Rose, she stands up straighter.

Rose is leaning over the sink, taking in deep breaths.

The door swings open again and Evelyn peers back through the slit, watching as Rose tries to straighten up.

"Ah, if it isn't the starving artist." She hears Dorothy's voice. "How was your first day in the lion's den?"

"Just fine, thank you." Rose does her best impression of seeming unfazed, but even Dorothy is not buying it.

"Relax, sweetie, you're going to have to be a lot tougher than that if you want to survive here. Especially when you're going home with the most dangerous one of them all."

"I'm not sure what you mean," Rose says.

"You need to watch yourself with Evelyn," Dorothy says. Her tone is serious. "People that don't get along with Evelyn have a tendency to turn up dead."

Rose

The sun beats harshly down on Rose as she stumbles out of the country club, following signs along the stucco walkway to the tennis courts. She is squinting, and she can feel her skin on the verge of burning, though she doesn't know if it's from the sun or shame.

When she reaches the chain-link fence of the tennis courts, Rose's fingers grip the holes as her eyes scan for Grant, who texted her; he was going to take a lesson and if she needed to bail, she could come meet him. Rose spots him, struggling with a serve the instructor is trying to show him.

People that don't get along with Evelyn have a tendency to turn up dead.

Was Dorothy just trying to scare her? What did that even mean? People die around Evelyn? She thinks about when James found the ring in his desk drawer. The one that belonged to her husband. Evelyn turned white when she saw it and when James asked how he'd died, she didn't answer. Come to think of it, Grant doesn't say much about his father or his death either.

Rose had just assumed it was from either illness or a heart attack, something normal. Nothing as traumatic as with her father.

Rose has tried so hard to move on from that, to forget the flashing light of the police vehicles.

Suddenly, an arm grips tightly around her waist and she lets out a scream.

"Woah, just me, take it easy." Grant steps back with a hand up in mock surrender.

Rose puts a hand over her mouth. "I'm sorry, I didn't realize you had finished up."

"That's okay, didn't realize you had either."

Rose tilts her head towards the second floor of the country club. "Technically I haven't."

"Are you okay?" He strokes her hair.

Rose sees his face fall as his eyes lift to the balcony on the second floor. Some of the women have moved outside with cocktails. She spots Evelyn talking to someone, a martini in hand, and their eyes meet.

Rose turns her attention back to Grant, who now has a hand on the back of his neck.

This is killing him, she realizes.

Rose lets out a frustrated sigh. She should be fine. What is she doing crying to Grant about all this? Whatever is going on is between her and Evelyn, and that's where it should stay. Maybe a lot of this stems from Evelyn's diagnosis and she should be more patient with her.

Rose puts on a brave face and smiles at Evelyn, then waves.

"Everything is fine," she assures Grant. "I just came out to see how you were doing."

"Really?" Grant's lips curve up in a hopeful smile.

Rose nods. "Yup."

"Well," he pulls her close to him, "I have to be on a call shortly so I'm going to head back." He kisses her cheek, and she blushes. "You want me to give you a ride home? I can send Renaldo to my mom when she's done."

Rose tries to keep the relief she feels out of her voice. "I have to pick up James soon anyway, so that would be great."

"I'll go let my mom know you're off the hook."

"Thanks." She smiles.

As he turns, his watch catches the light.

It still weirds her out that he has the same watch that she had given Ian for their wedding. It wasn't very expensive, which was why she was surprised to find Grant wearing the same one.

"I would've expected you to have a fancy Rolex or something," she had told him once, pointing at his watch.

Grant looked at it and shrugged. "It was the first thing I ever bought with my own money," he answered. "I wear it every day to remind myself of that."

Rose remembers that when she bought Ian's, she had used part of her commission to pay for it. She's not sure now what made her pick that watch of all things. Maybe because she saw it advertised everywhere, so naturally she's sure they made thousands of them. It was just an odd coincidence for Grant to have the same one.

Rose remembers the engraving that she chose for Ian's. *May all of our time on this earth be spent together. I love you, Rose.*

She felt foolish now. Especially since she'd started to figure out that he was cheating on her, very shortly after.

As they get closer to the house, Rose realizes there's just enough time for her to switch seats with Grant to grab James from school.

"Did you want to just come with me to get James from school? It's almost time to pick him up."

"Sorry, I need to finalize something with Trexler regarding this warehouse idea."

"What warehouse idea?"

He looks at his phone again and places it back in his cupholder. "I'll tell you about it later. It's complex and I'm not sure if it's going to be a thing yet. I have to see if Trexler comes through on this."

"How come I've never met him?"

"Who?" Grant says, still distracted.

"Trexler Whitehall, your business partner?"

"I barely see him either. He's usually jet-setting all over the world, making deals for us. Most of our communication is by phone or Zoom."

Rose is quiet for a moment. "You know those articles you send me every time Trexler makes a headline?"

Grant smiles. "Yeah, I want to show you what we've accomplished."

"How come you're never mentioned in the articles?"

"I'm a silent partner for a reason."

"Well, don't you want to *not* be silent anymore?"

"No, I like the anonymity without all the exposure."

She contemplates this.

"So, tell me more about mahjong with Mom?"

Rose stiffens a bit. "It was fine. I suck at mahjong, though."

He grabs her hand. "Either way, I'm glad you went. It really means a lot to me that you and my mom get along. You're both the two most important people to me."

Rose smiles, squeezing his hand back.

"What do you say you and I go out to dinner tonight, just the two of us?"

Rose frowns. "I'd love to, but it's James's first day of school and I already feel bad that I didn't take him. Thank you for doing that, by the way," she remembers to say. "How about tomorrow?"

"Okay." He sighs.

She kisses his cheek, trying to smooth things over. Rose knows he gets like this sometimes. It's only-child syndrome mixed in with being rich and spoiled his whole life. It bothered her when she first saw signs of it, but then she saw he recognized it in himself too and would try to correct it.

"When did you get this Range Rover? We already have an Audi." Rose now brings her attention to the car. "Is this your mom's, too?" she questions, though she highly doubts it.

"I thought we needed another car," he answers.

Rose looks around the inside of the car again, as if seeing it for the first time. "Could you have discussed this with me?"

"What was there to discuss? We needed another car."

Rose furrows her brow at him. Sure, it's his money, but if they're going to share a life together, shouldn't he have at least given her a heads-up? Now Rose almost wonders if she's in the wrong for telling him how to spend his money.

Grant appears to ignore her expression as they pull into the driveway. "Are you coming inside?" He opens his car door.

"I have to pick James up now," she reminds him, then extends her hands for the keys.

Grant smiles. He hands them to her. "Take it for a spin. I know you'll like it."

"How was your first day?" Rose opens the passenger door for James as he steps in. His jacket is already off, the collar scrunched in his grip, the sleeves of his button-down rolled up to his elbows. He slings his backpack off his shoulder and tosses it in the backseat, before joining Rose in the front. "It was fine." Then he wipes his palm on his forehead and up to his hairline. "Man, it is so hot here."

"Meet any new people?"

He seems distracted at first, but then realizes that Rose has asked him a question. "Sure, mostly from the soccer team, though. We had a quick meeting with the coach this morning."

"When are tryouts?"

"Tomorrow."

"I'm sure you'll do wonderfully." She smiles, rubbing his knee in encouragement.

He smiles at her then turns his gaze to the window.

Rose bites the inside of her cheek. "Listen, James. I just want you to remember that we are guests in this house, and I want you to be respectful."

"I know," James says, a heavy sadness bringing his voice down like a deflated balloon.

Rose swallows and tightens her grip on the steering wheel. "I know it's a lot of changes, really fast. We just have to take things as they come. But I promise you that I have your best interest at heart. The opportunities at this school are going to do wonderful things for you."

"Sure," James agrees, but sounds noncommittal.

Last year, Grant insisted that James leave public school to join the Whitmore Academy. Wanting what was best for James, she agreed, only she regrets it now considering they had to move, and she had to transfer him, yet again.

"Once things resolve with Grant's mother," Rose tries to be as diplomatic as possible, "we'll move out and have a place of our own. A new life with you, Grant and me."

James scratches his eyebrow.

"I hope you can be happy for me." Rose's voice breaks.

"Are you happy?"

James's comment takes Rose by surprise. There is no real right way to answer this. "It's complicated," she admits. "I can love your father and love Grant as well."

James lets out a huff of air and Rose wonders why she continues to lie to him. She doesn't love James's father. The truth is Ian never loved her. He married her out of obligation and clearly regretted it.

If only she had been brave enough to turn Ian down. It was his parents pushing for it anyway, only to leave and move to another country, offering no help. But she was scared and alone. It was the same reason she'd stayed for as long as she did.

She was afraid of being on her own again. After what had happened to her, all she'd wanted was a family of her own.

Rose shakes her head. The conversation is running away from her. "Just please be on your best behavior at the house, okay? Pretend like there are cameras watching your every move."

Rose walks into the foyer with trepidation as James makes his way into the kitchen. The last thing she wants is to see Evelyn right now. She wishes she had said something to her when they were alone in the car together, but hesitancy overtook her. What if she had it all wrong? Now, Dorothy's comment, as absurd as it sounded, lurks in the back of her mind.

She has a sense that Evelyn knows Rose is aware of the gun. Is she daring Rose to say something?

But then, how *could* she know? Rose hopes she is overreacting, but it was the exact same one she remembers. The one that haunts her dreams almost every night. Is Evelyn planning on using it as some sort of leverage? Rose has never told Grant what happened. Heck, she's never told James what happened. She was planning on taking it to her grave.

Rose smells smoke coming from the office, but it takes a few more sniffs before she realizes that it's a cigar.

Rose opens the door hoping that he's not still on the phone.

When she steps in, Grant is sitting behind the desk with his feet up, blowing smoke rings.

"Oh, I thought you'd be working," Rose says.

Grant checks his watch. "I have to be on a call in a few minutes."

"Oh," Rose says, disappointed. "I was hoping we could go for a walk on the beach."

Rose finds herself scanning this room for cameras. She takes in the built-in bookshelves. A gas fireplace is on the opposite wall, decorated in herringbone tile and fake driftwood behind a wrought-iron metal gate.

A large red oak desk sits catty-cornered overlooking the ocean view. She shakes her head in bewilderment. She still can't believe she's in a position to live in a place with a view like this.

Rose runs her hand along the line of encyclopedias.

"Just give me five minutes," he says. "This call shouldn't take long."

Rose leaves to find James sitting at the kitchen table, his laptop open, with a bowl of popcorn and a glass of water next to him.

"That better be homework that you're working on."

"Mom." He rolls his eyes. "It was the first day of school."

"Right," she says, feeling foolish. "Then what are you doing?"

"I'm setting up my profile for the school. It's like a directory, it makes it easier to find and connect with people based on the same interests."

Rose is familiar with all the dangerous forms of social media, but this one seems out of her realm. It's likely the school's alternative to keep that sort of thing in a closed environment. Plus, the last thing she wants to do is isolate him from an opportunity to make new friends.

Grant walks through the door, taking her by surprise. "That was quick."

"Turns out they have to reschedule. They don't have the files ready that I had asked for."

Rose nods then turns towards James. "Grant and I are going for a walk. Can you show me your profile when I get back?"

"Okay," he says, not looking up.

They step out onto the stone patio. The ocean is flat and calm for the first time since they've gotten here. Grant leans on the stone railing, so thick it would take an earthquake to knock it down.

Rose swallows, looking for any cameras outside. She spots one by the door, but she knows if she tried to point it out to Grant, he'd think she was crazy. Everyone now has cameras outside of their exterior doors.

They descend around ten stone steps before they settle on lush palmetto grass, the edges lined with clusia hedges and palm trees. When she turns around, she sees the overwhelming structure of the estate and she can't help but feel she's in a dream. She never could even imagine a house like this before, and now she lives in one.

She takes off her shoes, leaving them on the grass, then goes down another few steps through a retaining wall onto the beach. The sand feels rough between her toes.

Rose waits for Grant to finish rolling up his pant legs, then they begin to walk on the sand, still a bit hot on their feet even this late in the afternoon. Rose leads them closer to the water, the waves washing up and foaming before retreating calmly like a rhythmic pulse.

"So, what is the deal with your mom and these women?" Rose finally gets the courage to ask.

"Didn't go that well?"

She gives him the side-eye. "They just don't seem to like each other that much."

"Nothing better to do," he says, pulling the cigar out of his mouth. "I'm sure they were all just jealous of you because you're younger and more beautiful."

Rose wishes she had felt beautiful. While she certainly was younger by at least thirty years, she looked haggard, whereas these women spent all the money in the world to age gracefully.

Rose looks up at the house and nervously swallows. While she may not be able to ask about most of the things on her mind, she wonders if she can at least find out what happened to Evelyn's husband. Maybe that would at least clear up what Dorothy at the club might have been saying.

"Grant, what exactly happened to your father?"

He stops walking to look at her, a mixture of shock and confusion on his face. He tilts his head. "What do you mean?"

"After James found the ring yesterday, he asked your mom how Harrison died, and she seemed to get very upset, then she left the room."

Grant's fists clench and unclench and he starts walking again, quickening his pace.

"I'm sorry, it was rude of him. He didn't mean anything by it." Rose seems to be practically sprinting to keep up with him. "Are you okay?"

"Yeah." He stops then, looking over Rose's shoulder at the horizon. He shakes his head and smiles. "It was dumb, really."

"What was?"

"He was allergic to nuts. Somehow, he suffered an attack on the subway when the train was between stops. No one could get to him."

Rose can't help but feel relieved. She was worried his death would be part of some sort of conspiracy theory that would come back to haunt them.

"That's awful," Rose says. "I'm so sorry."

"Don't be," Grant says, picking up a shell and tossing it into the ocean. Rose notes the lack of sympathy in his voice.

"I'm surprised that it wasn't more upsetting for you."

"He wasn't a good father. Put it that way." He rolls his eyes and shakes his head again. "You of all people understand that."

Rose stops walking, her muscles tensing in her shoulders. How would he know about her father?

"What do you mean?"

Grant looks at her, face flushed. "I just meant sometimes we are better off with no parents than bad ones."

"Right." Rose relaxes a little.

"Speaking of which . . ." Grant clears his throat. "My mom is selling the penthouse."

"Is she?" Rose didn't like living there much anyway, but selling makes their time in Palm Beach all the more permanent. Rose isn't quite sure how she feels about that.

Grant doesn't know about the cameras either, she assures herself. Surely he can't be a part of all that. She still wants to tell him but is unsure of how to bring it up. Instead, she ignores the opportunity to stir up trouble.

"It'll be for the best. Then you and I can get a place of our own." She smiles as he pulls her into him.

"Do you have any idea how beautiful you are right now?"

"Sure," Rose scoffs, pulling a strand of wind-blown hair out of her face.

"Really. In this light, I think you are the most beautiful woman in the world."

Rose kisses him.

"Ready to head back?" He tilts his head towards the house, its façade looming over them like a living, breathing thing, watching her every move.

Rose nods, not wanting to press any further, but a thought scratches at the surface of her brain. If Harrison apparently wasn't a good guy, it would be easy enough to kill him with his own allergy, and easy enough to get away with it. And according to Dorothy, people tend to die around Evelyn. As in, more than one. Rose crosses her arms as a deep chill runs through her body.

Isabel

Isabel's eyes flick open with a sudden jolt. She doesn't know what woke her up. She doesn't remember having a dream, and the room is still dark. Nothing but a sliver of light is streaming in through her window from the security lights of the office building across the street. She stretches and glances at the digital clock on her dresser. It is still early for a Saturday, but she gets up anyway. After all, she has a busy day ahead of her. She has to do some reconnaissance.

It had been fortunate for her that James and Grant had gone ahead of her that first day. By the time Mrs. McFadden, the principal, had gotten to her, James's file was still sitting out in the open on her desk.

Isabel's keen eyes had spotted it right away, so when she extended her hand to shake Mrs. McFadden's, she had clumsily knocked her coffee square off her desk, creating a pool of brown on the expensive marble floor. The coffee mug, with the cheesy saying "The Principal Is Your Pal", shattered on impact.

Isabel pretended to be mortified, blaming it on first-day jitters.

Although Mrs. McFadden seemed annoyed, she quickly assured her it was fine and left the room to retrieve some napkins to clean up the mess.

That gave Isabel a few seconds to snap a picture of the file, which displayed their new home address.

Now she knew where to find them.

Isabel takes her time getting showered. Almost a week in, she has added certain items to make the apartment feel homier. She purchased a soft plush robe and terrycloth towels and a lavender diffuser, doing what she can to make the stark, white-tiled bathroom into her own personal spa. She needs a place in her apartment where she can pretend to forget where she is and what she's really doing here. Just a few moments to close her eyes and, with the help of some strong essential oils, just let her mind drift off into nothingness. She imagines being transported to a spa and getting pampered.

Sometimes she lets the shower run for so long that the small bathroom really does become a steam room, making it almost hard to breathe. When this happens, she gives up shortly after, coughing as she turns the shower off, then opening the bathroom door and flipping on the fan.

This time around, she isn't pretending to be anywhere but here. Instead, she daydreams about the various ways that she can try to infiltrate the Caldwells' lives.

Stepping into her room to get dressed, Isabel pulls a bathing suit out of her top drawer, along with a white beach cover-up.

The bedroom is elegantly minimalist. White curtains, a white duvet cover, and a walnut dresser with matching end tables. Isabel sits on the chair in the corner of the room, already covered in the day's previous clothes, and puts on a pair of sandals, broken in and practically falling apart from the previous summer.

After she's made her bed, she pulls her hair into a tight, wet bun, applying sunscreen and a bit of makeup before throwing her newly purchased green beach towel into an oversized canvas bag. By the time she leaves, the sun is up, but the rest of her apartment is still like a dark cave that she can't wait to emerge from.

About an hour later, Isabel has settled herself onto the sand. She parked at the end of some street in the neighborhood at a safe distance, then snuck on through a private path, the door to it unhinged from its lock. Then she walked north towards the private homes until she counted out which one the Caldwells were staying at. By the looks of it, maybe James wouldn't be so out of place at the Pelican Academy after all.

Taking her rolled-up towel out of her bag, she plops it on the sand, further back from the water and closer to the neighbor's house, trying to obscure herself. She doesn't want to look too much like she is setting up camp on what is likely their neighbor's private beach, but based on the construction work being done, she doesn't think anyone lives there now. She wants to see if the Caldwells will come out on such a gorgeous sunny day, especially on their first weekend here.

Isabel isn't in a rush. She crosses her legs out in front of her, twisting her paper coffee cup into the sand so it will stand up straight. Then she pulls another paper bag out and removes a croissant. She bites into the warm buttery flakes and finds her mouth watering. She may not get a bagel as good as the ones in New York, but she does like the Palm Beach croissants.

A seagull squawks from above her and she looks up quickly, making sure it's not making a beeline for her breakfast. Isabel pulls the bag in closer to her, picking up her coffee to enjoy another sip.

She stares out at the horizon. The sun reflects like a blanket of glitter over the calm ocean. The wind is still kicking a bit from last week's storm, catching the outer wind bands, or so she heard on the news this morning behind the counter of the cafe. But it doesn't seem to be stopping the beachgoers. The breeze she finds actually refreshing from the oppressive ninety-degree temperatures. She catches a flash of red in the corner of her eye, and when she turns, she sees several kite surfers, all racing along the coast. Isabel has never seen this before.

She can only imagine how strong and skilled you have to be for it, but she wouldn't mind trying it out sometime.

"Come on, James!"

Isabel comes out of her trance, noticing Grant walking out towards the water, a surfboard in hand. Not too far behind him, James, in a black rash guard, follows him with his own surfboard in tow.

She can faintly hear Grant calling out directions to James on how to duck under the waves with his board to get over the break, but James isn't catching on. He desperately tries to pop over the waves but keeps getting pushed back from the wall of water.

Grant's frustration is evident, until James, after observing Grant's success, finally follows suit. She watches them poorly trying to catch a wave, both being widely unsuccessful.

After about fifteen minutes, Grant appears frustrated. He says something to James, then paddles back in, picking up his towel with one arm while balancing the surfboard in the other and leaves.

Isabel turns to James, who shakes his head, then turns back, making several other attempts to catch a wave.

After about five minutes, Isabel is convinced he's going to give up, when he turns back and lines himself up with an incoming wave. He paddles, a look of determination on his face, then he pops his body up to stand.

He rides it all the way in, an enormous grin across his face. But it's only short-lived when he takes in that no one was around to see it.

He places his board down on the sand, taking a seat on it, his hands pulling his knees towards him.

Isabel takes her cue, throwing her towel and her garbage into her canvas bag before walking over towards him.

"That was some wave you caught," she tells him, pretending to be casually passing by.

"You saw that?" He looks up, surprised, holding a hand up over his eyes as he squints to see her.

"Yeah, you looked like an expert out there. How long have you been surfing?"

"It's my first day." He gives a slight laugh.

"Good for you." She smiles.

"You're from the Pelican Academy, aren't you?" James stands up, facing her. Even at fourteen, he's slightly taller than her.

She pretends to suddenly recognize him as well. "Yes, that's right. How was your first day?"

He shrugs. "It was alright."

"Well, if it was anything like your first day of surfing, I'd say you nailed it."

Then he smiles as if remembering. "How was your first day?"

She mimics his shrug. "Okay, I guess."

"Who's your friend?" Isabel turns to see Rose, James's mother, approaching them. She's wearing a red bikini top with jean shorts. Her skin is so pale, it's almost translucent. She guards herself with crossed arms, streaks of what Isabel can only imagine is paint on her hands.

Isabel pretends not to notice and sticks her hand out. "Hi, I'm Isabel Martinez. I work as a math teacher at the Pelican Academy. I met your son and husband in the front office on his first day."

She watches as Rose's shoulders soften and she releases the grip on her arms, extending a hand to shake Isabel's. "It's so nice to meet you."

"So where did you originally move from?" Isabel keeps the conversation light and casual.

"From New York."

"Funny," Isabel says. "I just started down here from New York as well. I worked at the Whitmore Academy."

She watches as Rose's face beams in surprise. "Really? That's where James went last year." She speaks for him as if he's not there. "Were you a math teacher?"

Isabel shakes her head. "No, I was in the administration office, but I wanted to teach, so that's why I decided to take the job here."

"What a coincidence," Rose says.

"Not to brag, but I'm also a stellar SAT tutor if you need any help." She directs the comment to James to pull him back into the conversation.

"Yes please." Rose takes the bait.

Before she knows it, Rose is pulling her phone out of the back pocket of her torn shorts. "Can I get your number?"

Isabel smiles broadly. "Of course."

Rose punches the number in that Isabel rattles off to her, then seems to hesitate for a moment.

"Is this something that I'll have to clear with the school first?"

"It's completely up to you. I'm not sure what the Pelican Academy's policy is. At Whitmore, they made you take tutoring with their teachers on campus directly after school, which I know for my athletic students was a problem, because they sacrificed practices which usually got them benched during games. I learned eventually with parents that it was easier for them to deal with me separate from the school so we could create our own flexible schedule."

Rose takes a moment to consider this. "We're hoping for James to make the soccer team. He's in tryouts now . . ." She trails off. "I would hate to sacrifice his athletics. I think it would be best if maybe you could come twice a week. Would you be able to help with homework as well?"

"Of course, not a problem."

"Can we do after dinner, Tuesdays and Thursdays? Eight o'clock? Is that too late?"

"Not at all." Isabel smiles. "I'll get my materials ready." She extends her hand again to Rose, who smiles.

"It was so nice meeting you."

"You as well. You don't know how wonderfully this all just worked out." Rose shakes her hand aggressively.

"I'm glad to hear it." Isabel can't help but agree. "Did you catch your son's wave? He's a pretty decent surfer." She nods at James, who smiles appreciatively.

"Nice job," Rose says proudly and wraps an arm around her wet son.

"See you on Monday." Isabel waves to James, then walks away, slinging her bag higher on her shoulder, a smile creeping across her face that this has worked out better than she could ever have expected.

Evelyn

Evelyn is sitting on the patio, enjoying an iced tea under the loggia, when her phone rings. She reaches over to the cream-colored stone end table and picks it up.

"Hello?" she answers, just as the landscaper's mowers from the lower tier begin to whir loudly. She plugs her ear and moves inside to her kitchen.

"Hi, Evelyn, this is Lizzy Fanwood. I'm calling you because we just got an offer on the apartment."

"That's wonderful," Evelyn says. Then continues to listen to her real estate agent give her the offer and the details, as she climbs the steps into her bedroom.

"Did they just do the walk-through now?" Evelyn asks, taking a seat at her desk in her room, opening her laptop.

"They walked through about an hour ago, then just called now."

Evelyn puts the phone in the crook between her ear and her shoulder, pulling up the cameras for the apartment. She rewinds back an hour to see a young family, parents in mid- to late thirties and two small children, a girl maybe twelve and a boy around ten.

The boy immediately climbs the steps, attempting to slide down the metal railing, before his horrified mother pulls him down. She switches cameras, following them upstairs as they walk along the maple parquet floors, peering into each of the bedrooms, each one intricately different, with various colors of silk wallpaper, antique chests and silk duvets that match the curtains.

"It's a bit old-fashioned, but we can certainly spruce it up," the woman says.

Evelyn chuckles.

"Let me call you back, Lizzy. I'm going to think it over."

"Of course, take your time. Talk soon."

She jumps to another camera downstairs, watching as the young girl with blonde hair pulled half up sits at the baby grand piano in the living room playing what Evelyn can recognize as Beethoven.

Impressive, she thinks.

Her father comes in, telling her to stop, that it's not their house and she doesn't have permission to play.

Shame, thinks Evelyn, she was quite good.

"Mom."

Evelyn slams her laptop closed and turns her head to see Grant standing in the doorway. His hair is still wet after his surf, but he's changed into a red performance shirt and gray board shorts.

"Yes, Grant."

"My test drive for the Range Rover is about to expire. They want to see if I'll make an offer."

"Right," Evelyn says. "Give them my number and I'll . . . sort it out."

"You know, Mom, I'm forty years old, I'm pretty sure I can handle it."

"Right, you just need my checkbook." Her tone is harsher than she meant.

"What was that?"

Evelyn builds her courage. "When are you going to tell Rose the truth?"

"What truth?" He looks back, then closes the door behind him.

"How you . . . don't have a job and you never have had one? That you depend completely on me."

"You and I both know that I don't need a job. What I need is for you to allow me to access my trust fund. I'm married now. I am responsible for Rose and James. Is that not enough for you?"

"Marriage can't be based on lies and secrets."

"Right, like you, Mom? You think I don't know the skeletons in your closet?"

Evelyn stiffens.

"Just let me handle it, please."

A shaky breath escapes Evelyn as she pulls out the dresser drawer, retrieving her pen and checkbook.

"How much do you need?"

When he answers her, she writes out the check, trying to steady her hand. "That should cover it."

"Thank you," he says, annoyed; then he pauses, noticing a picture she has tucked away in the drawer where her checkbook was. His face scrunches then he reaches for the picture before she has a chance to stop him.

"Is this Anita?"

Evelyn's breathing begins to quicken. There is no use denying it. "Yes."

"I didn't know you still kept in touch with her," he said accusingly.

"I don't. The picture is very old."

"Anita looks older here than when I last saw her."

"That's because you were younger," Evelyn points out. "That's her and Maria."

Grant stiffens then narrows his eyes at her like daggers, as if waiting to see if she'll break.

"Martha found it somewhere." Evelyn waves her wrists. "I just happened to throw it in the desk drawer. I'd forgotten all about it until you spotted it."

Grant rubs his chin, still looking at the picture, then hands it back to her with a smile.

"You know I love you, right, Mother?"

Evelyn sits up straighter in her chair. "Of course I do, darling."

"Good." He kisses her on the cheek then leaves the room, closing the door behind him.

When he leaves, Evelyn's hands are shaking, and she drops the picture on the desk. Anita, with a beautiful girl with short dark hair around the age of ten, is standing in front of the Statue of Liberty.

Evelyn sighs, her eyes filling with tears. She misses her friend. She was one of the only people that Evelyn can say truly cared about her.

Most people, especially in her social world, found it strange that she was friends with their maid, but she and Anita were more alike than anyone else she was surrounded by. With Harrison away a lot, one day she found herself convincing Anita to stay for tea.

"So do you have a family, Anita?"

"I have a daughter."

Evelyn smiled. "How old is she now?"

Anita blinked her long eyelashes as she raised her eyes to the ceiling. "Thirteen."

"Same age as Grant," Evelyn said, surprised.

Anita nodded. "She is my everything." She pulled out a photo from her purse and handed it to Evelyn. The girl was sweet-looking. She had long, jet-black hair, a wide smile full of braces, and cherry-colored glasses. Evelyn couldn't help but smile. "She's adorable."

"It's a couple years old, I've been meaning to replace it with a newer one. Now that she's becoming a teenager, I'm starting to get kind of protective of her," Anita said. "I don't want her growing up too fast. But she pushes me away."

"I know what you mean." Evelyn sipped her tea. "I love Grant more than anything, but lately he's been making me nervous."

"Nervous?" Anita looked at her, eyes narrowed.

She swatted her hand. "I don't know. I guess like you I'm just overprotective."

"Speaking of which"—Anita stood up—"I have to get back to her. Can't trust what she'll be up to while I'm not home."

Over the next year, Anita and Evelyn started to become close. Anita would tell Evelyn about her relationships with men, and Evelyn found herself admitting to Anita that she suspected Harrison had affairs.

"I'm so sorry, Evelyn." Anita put a soft hand on hers.

"I guess I shouldn't be surprised," Evelyn found herself admitting. "It was how I ended up here. I was the other woman. Only I didn't realize it until it was too late." Evelyn patted her stomach.

"Didn't stop Maria's father from leaving me. I was already expecting. That's what made him run."

"I'm sorry you had to face that on your own. Did you have any family to help out?"

"No. They are all in Mexico." Anita's face seemed far off in another world. "It wasn't a healthy place for me. I can't go back there."

Both women looked at each other, a mutual understanding between them.

"Anyway, I better get back to Maria." Anita stood up, pushing the chair back.

"Maybe next time you can have Maria meet you here," Evelyn suggested.

"That would be great, actually," Anita said appreciatively.

While Anita was a natural beauty, she always appeared modest. She wore little to no makeup, and her black hair was always pulled tightly into a bun. What Evelyn hadn't anticipated was just how beautiful her daughter Maria would be.

The first time she walked through their door, Evelyn couldn't believe this could be Anita's daughter from the picture she had seen. Her eyelashes, like her mother's, were fanned out around her oval eyes, which were no longer covered by her cherry red glasses. Her nose, straight and angular, gave her heart-shaped face a near perfect symmetry. When she smiled, her soft pillow lips parted to reveal a set of straight white teeth. She nervously pulled her long shiny black hair behind her ears. Even though Evelyn knew she was thirteen, her long legs and developing chest meant she could pass for eighteen. No wonder Anita had been so nervous about her.

Maria's eyes caught her mother's, and as if in response to some conversation they'd had earlier, she stuck out her hand to Evelyn. "Mrs. Caldwell, it's so nice to finally meet you."

Evelyn realized her mouth was open, and quickly closed it. "Very lovely to meet you as well, Maria. I've heard so much about you."

As Evelyn gripped her soft hand, she had the overwhelming desire to tell her to leave. This was a bad idea, she realized. She didn't want this girl in her house when Grant got home.

Evelyn was just ready to make up some sort of excuse that she had to leave, when Grant stumbled in through the front door, his lacrosse bag dragging behind him. He was still in his white grass-stained jersey when he spotted Maria standing in the living room with Evelyn and Anita.

"Hi." Maria waved shyly at him, while at the same time standing confidently to walk towards him. "I'm Maria, I'm Anita's daughter." She extended her hand out to him, but he hadn't noticed. He was staring at her face.

When she raised her eyebrows, only then did he look down and notice her hand. He dropped his backpack and lacrosse bag onto the floor. "Oh, sorry." His voice cracked. "Nice to meet you."

"You might want to take a shower, dear," Evelyn said gently.

Evelyn knew just from those few moments of exchange that Grant was infatuated with Maria.

This was going to complicate things, she realized.

Evelyn guesses she should've known better. They were in eighth grade at this point, about to go off to high school, of course a crush might've formed.

Evelyn's eyes fill with tears, looking back on it now. Poor Maria, if only she hadn't had to die.

Isabel

Isabel grips the wheel tightly, palms sweating as she drives over to her first tutoring session with James.

"You're going to be alright," she tells herself. "You can do this."

Grandma did everything she could to prevent this from happening, but Isabel always knew this was inevitable.

When she sees the address on the GPS light up that she has arrived, she's worried she typed it in wrong. She's only seen the house from the back, and here, she can't even see a driveway. But then, through the overgrown vines, she eventually spots a marble stone with the address on a bronze plate.

A horn honks behind her and she checks her GPS again. She pulls off the road onto the private drive. The popping noise of the stone and gravel under the tires seems so loud in her ears. She drives another hundred feet before she finally sees a wrought-iron gate.

Now what? she thinks to herself. But then there is a loud creak as the gate opens, taking her by surprise. Either there is some sort of sensor or there's a camera that she hasn't noticed just yet. She slowly approaches, not knowing what to expect. She enters through a tunnel of banyan trees, their roots and branches outstretched like they could grab you and swallow you whole.

A light appears at the end of the tunnel and before she knows it, an oversized white mansion appears before her. Isabel can't help but think about those fairy tales where you have to battle your way through the trees, fighting off the evil lurking in them in order to make it to the castle.

She pulls the car in a circle around a fountain, stopping in front of the large columns by the front door.

"Isabel!" Rose opens the door in what looks like a paint-stained apron before Isabel even steps out of the car.

"Hi." Isabel smiles at her.

"James is just finishing dinner. He'll be out in a second. Thank you again for making the time work."

"Sure," Isabel says, rolling up the sleeves of her pink shirt, feeling suddenly warmer.

"Have you eaten yet? Can we get you anything?"

Isabel puts a hand up. "That won't be necessary, thanks."

"Well, come on in." Rose smiles, leading Isabel in through the front entrance.

Isabel tries to stay focused, but her eyes widen in surprise at the mere size of the front hallway. She notes the expensive Greek paintings and statues which alone must be worth a fortune, let alone the house they're in.

"So, I think you'll get less distraction in the dining room." Rose points to a room with dark wood doors that slide open from the hall. Isabel stares in awe as she takes in the coffered brushed gold ceilings mapped out into various shapes, squares extending out from the center octagon where a brass chandelier that looks straight out of the eighteenth century is suspended over a long, dark table.

"I'll go get James," Rose says, and Isabel makes a show of putting her bag on the table, pulling out materials.

Rose walks through a swinging door off to the side that Isabel can assume leads to the kitchen. When she disappears, Isabel finds herself walking up to the china cabinet, which harbors what she can only imagine are rare antiques. Her eye catches on a porcelain plate, the only thing in the cabinet that doesn't look like it's worth thousands of dollars. It has a dancing bear on it with the name Grant etched underneath it. Smiling, she opens the cabinet. It makes the slightest squeak, and she winces. She picks up the baby spoon next to the plate, staring at it. It's pristine and polished. She examines it for a moment, before putting it back and closing the cabinet just as James is entering the room.

"Hi, remember me?" She smiles brightly.

He has on a blue Whitmore T-shirt and a pair of white gym shorts. His hair is brushed down, as if his mother made him do so before she arrived. He looks like such a little kid, yet Isabel feels like she was only that age yesterday. Her imposter syndrome creeps up on her again.

"Catch any other sick waves since the last time I saw you?"

"Just a couple." James laughs as he chooses a seat.

Isabel smiles and continues to pull out several folders from her bag. She notes Rose is standing in the doorway, and she wonders if Rose will stay for all of their tutoring sessions, hovering over them like this. It will make it very hard for her to sneak around the house if his mother is there the whole time.

"So"—Isabel pretends not to mind—"we're going to start with some basic questions to get a sense of what areas you struggle with most. Then I'm going to give you a timed test. This will give me an idea of where we should focus our time and I can figure out just how you problem-solve so I can teach you effectively."

Rose smiles, satisfied. "I'll leave you to it," she says finally and disappears back through the kitchen door.

Isabel feels tension release from her shoulders. Now it's just the two of them.

After taking some notes based on her and James's conversation, she pulls out the test.

He groans.

"Relax, it's not a real test, remember, it's just an assessment. I want you to show me your work and when you're done, we're going to go through each question together to break down how you came to those answers."

James nods.

"It's nothing to worry about." She taps his hand with her pencil, then clears her throat. "Okay, so I'm going to set the timer in just a second. Do you mind telling me where the bathroom is first?"

James points his pencil in the general direction of the sliding wooden doors that lead out into the hallway.

"Thanks," she says. "Timer starts now."

She clicks the timer on her phone, leaving it to run on the table.

Isabel quietly slips out of the sliding door, trying to keep the track from making too much noise as she does. A football game is being played somewhere in the house, its commentary and crowd cheers echoing off the tile floor and large ceiling of the atrium. She tiptoes down the corridor and finds what turns out to be an office.

Closing the door behind her, she steps in, knowing she has a few minutes while James works on his test and hopes everyone else in the house is preoccupied. Contemplating the possibilities, she wonders what it would be like for this to be her office.

Then Grant walks through the door, startling her. She smiles sheepishly.

His eyes widen in surprise.

It seems weird seeing him dressed in a T-shirt and shorts. Every image she has of him is so formal.

"I'm sorry," he apologizes, when she was the one who shouldn't be in here.

He continues walking until he gets to the desk. Then he goes behind it, pulling out a cigar and a lighter from one of the drawers.

Isabel realizes she's still standing there dumbfounded. Half expecting to be fired instantly.

"Can I help you with something?" Grant asks, not accusatorially, but wanting to be helpful.

She realizes then she has said nothing, and she's still staring at him. "Sorry." She snaps out of it. "I was looking for the bathroom and accidentally stumbled in here." She runs her hand along the bookshelf. "I just thought this room was beautiful," she says awkwardly.

He smiles, shaking his head like he understands. "Not a problem. My family is pretty ostentatious with their surroundings." He lifts his hands up towards the room.

"Did you grow up here?"

He shakes his head. "No, I grew up in New York. But it's a family home, so in a sense I did grow up coming here."

She nods. She wants to come out with it. Tell him the reason she's here, but she knows now is not the time. She needs more evidence; something concrete he won't be able to deny.

"My wife says that you're from New York as well. Worked at Whitmore?"

"Yes, right." She reflects on the discussion with Rose on the beach.

He waves a finger at her. "I knew you looked familiar, like I had to have known you from somewhere."

"That's probably it," she confirms with a nervous laugh.

"You know, I went to Whitmore myself. Before your time, obviously."

Her throat seems to dry out on her, making her unable to speak.

"You have a tag," she finds herself saying.

"Excuse me?" He looks at her strangely.

"I noticed when you came in, you still have the price tag on your shirt."

Grant reaches back behind the collar of his shirt. "Oh, I guess you're right. It's a brand-new shirt." He smiles awkwardly. "Jeez, that's embarrassing. I've been wearing this all day."

He waves his fingers at Isabel, summoning her over, and goes into the drawer behind his desk.

"Do you mind cutting it for me?" He hands her a pair of gold scissors, so shiny they look like a prop for a murder mystery play.

She takes them from him uneasily. "Um, sure."

"Thanks." He bends his head forward, and holds out the tag for her to take.

Isabel feels her hand shaking. Being so close to him like this, smelling his musky cologne, makes her feel lightheaded.

With the scissors in her hand, she stares for a moment at the back of his neck, contemplating how easily she could kill him if she wanted to. Despite the fact she was a complete stranger to him, he trusted her and placed himself in a very vulnerable situation.

Biting her lip, she sucks in a breath and proceeds to cut the tag.

Grant feels the release of the plastic and lifts his head back up. "Thank you."

She drops the scissors onto the desk. "No problem."

"Anyway, I don't want to keep you. I know you have to get back to James."

"Right," she says. "He's doing an assessment now, and I was just trying to find the bathroom."

He waves his arm. "Come on, I'll show you where it is."

His hand brushes the small of her back as he leads her out of the room. A chill runs up her spine.

"Places like this, it's like walking through a funhouse. You never know what you're going to walk into or what you're going to find."

Isabel laughs nervously as they step out into the hallway.

A place like this likely has a lot of stories if its walls could talk.

A gasp causes both of them to stop. Someone Isabel assumes is the grandmother is staring at them like she's just seen a ghost.

"Mom, are you alright?"

Isabel looks from her to Grant. Grant's right, she doesn't look well. Isabel's worried she might faint.

"Why don't you sit down, Mom." Grant leaves Isabel's side to tend to her. "Sorry, bathroom is that door right there." He points to another wooden door next to the office.

Isabel watches as the grandmother looks at her in horror. It makes Isabel feel uneasy, like this woman knows just who she is and why she's here.

Isabel tries to shake it off, assuming that the poor woman is not well. She heads to the bathroom, the heavy lock making an echoing sound in the hall as she clicks it.

As she looks around, she realizes this is the first room of the house that appears modern. Everything else feels like the turn of the century. But even if you wanted to preserve the look of that time period, you wouldn't want to pass up utilizing the updated plumbing features of today.

There is another door that piques her interest, and she opens it, discovering this bathroom serves also as a cabana bathroom next to their outdoor pool, which is lit up in a green hue.

She quickly closes it before anyone notices and locks the bathroom door to the hall as well. She opens the glass shower door, still wet from a recent shower, small pools of water resting just outside of the drain.

Turning back around, she opens the middle drawers between the large sinks, spotting a hairbrush next to some aftershave and various men's products. Isabel pulls a tissue out of the box on the countertop and pulls a few brown hairs out of the brush.

A knock at the door surprises her. "Just a minute," she calls as she shoves the tissue into her pocket and flushes the toilet behind her.

Rose

Rose tries hard to paint, but her head is spinning. She has so many unanswered questions. When she got back from the beach with Grant yesterday, she looked up Evelyn, trying to see if she was connected to anyone else that might've died besides her husband. But her name rarely came up unless it was to do with a charity event or something.

Then again, Dorothy is Evelyn's friend, Rose realizes. As twisted as it may sound, maybe that comment she made was simply contrived by Evelyn herself, asking Dorothy to relay the message just to intimidate Rose more.

She hates to admit it, but it's working.

Death is not something to joke about with her; she's witnessed too much of it.

Rose throws her paintbrush down on the tarp below her with an angry huff. This is the third painting she's tried to create, and it looks so amateur. She's going to wind up getting pulled from Lina's gallery. She pinches the bridge of her nose, trying to stop the oncoming headache.

She lets out a frustrated sigh, raising her head to the ceiling, and again her eyes are drawn to the vent. The thought of the gun creates a visceral reaction, making her stomach clench.

I know all about your past.

Is Evelyn twisted enough that she'd torture her like a cat with a barely alive mouse? Never putting it out of its misery, but just stringing it along until it begs for a mercy kill?

Whatever her plan is with that gun, she can't do anything with it if Rose hides it herself.

She glances back at the closet with the step stool inside.

Licking her lips, she goes for it and props the stool below the vent. She's on the first step when she hears Grant behind her.

"Need help?"

Rose startles, nearly toppling off the step stool. She recovers and turns around to find Grant standing there. She hates when he does that. The way he always seems to be lurking in a corner somewhere, watching her.

"Just getting frustrated, I can't make this painting work. Thought I'd try painting from a different angle," she lies.

"Why not take a break, come to the beach with me."

"I can't, okay? I have to get this right, or I'm going to lose my spot at Lina's gallery."

Grant shrugs his shoulders. "Is that such a bad thing?"

Rose narrows her eyes at him. "Excuse me?"

"You should make your art for yourself. Not for anyone else. The pressure you're putting on yourself is for no reason. We're going to be fine financially. Don't take something you're supposed to love and make it work if you can avoid it."

Rose inhales deeply through her nostrils. He reaches for her hand and pulls her in. "Come swimming with me," he whispers in her ear.

She understands where he's coming from, but this is her life. She loves making art for the world, she loves it being displayed in Lina's gallery. She doesn't want to lose that. It would be like losing a part of herself. Only he's right. The pressure she's putting herself under doesn't help as far as inspiration goes. Maybe he's right. She needs to reset and come back. Hopefully inspired to paint something better than this pathetic excuse for an abstract.

"Didn't you have a tennis lesson this morning?"

"Turns out I don't really like tennis that much."

"What about work?" she asks him. "Don't you have to be working?"

He spins her around, wrapping his arms around her front and nestling his chin into her neck. "Trexler's got it covered."

"Is he going to fire you?"

"He can't fire me; I finance his investments." He kisses her neck. "Staring at your canvas all day isn't going to accomplish anything, so go get that sexy green bathing suit you have and meet me on the beach."

"Okay." Rose finally gives in, but again her eyes catch the vent, and she suddenly becomes angry. "Where is your mom?"

"Renaldo drove her to a doctor's appointment."

"Is it me, or does it seem like your mom made a big deal about needing your help, and now that we're here, it seems like she doesn't need you at all? I mean, she has cooks, maids and drivers, so why did we have to upend our lives?"

"Because she is my mother, and she is sick. Why have her suffer alone when she can have her family with her?" he says a little more coldly. "I thought you were going to try with her?"

Rose rolls her head. If only she could tell him the messed-up mind games that his mother is playing with her. But she can't risk telling Grant. That would expose her own secrets. "Yes, you're right. I'm sorry."

"You have this idea that she's some rich snob, but she's not like that. She's been through more than you will ever know." Grant pulls away, but Rose pulls his arm back.

"I'm sorry. You're right, okay? I'm not good at this."

"Were Ian's parents so great?"

This stops Rose in her tracks. He's never acted this immature before. "Ian didn't get along with his parents. He became estranged from them after they found out I was pregnant. They forced us to get married, then they moved abroad, and Ian didn't speak to them again."

Grant swallows. "I'm sorry. It was a cheap shot."

It was, but Rose softens. "I apologize for what I said about your mom."

Grant wraps his arms around her shoulders.

"I'm sorry, I'm a bit overprotective of her."

"It's okay. I'll get my bathing suit on, but I need to be back up here tonight to work."

"I understand. I'll be holed up in the office tonight anyway, once Trexler sends me the numbers I've been waiting on."

When Rose's feet touch the hot sand, she notices there is a blue and white striped umbrella with two beach chairs set up already. Grant walks past her and puts down the cooler he was holding then removes his button-down shirt. Rose bites her lip as he bends down to retrieve a sparkling water and hands it to her, his muscles even more defined with his bronzed skin.

They both take a seat, Rose digging her feet into the sand.

"I might go for a dip," he says, standing up, and Rose notices his watch still on his wrist.

"Don't forget to take your watch off."

"It's waterproof," he says.

"Are you sure?" Rose doesn't remember the version she had gotten Ian being.

"Yup." Then he sits. "On second thought, maybe I'll just sit with you and relax."

"I don't know how to do that," Rose jokes.

"It's about time you started. There's less to stress about now."

If only he knew the half of it, Rose can't help but think. She takes a big gulp of her water, allowing the bubbles to fizz in her mouth before swallowing. It's a perfect afternoon. One that will stay perfect if Rose can keep her mind off hidden guns and secret cameras. She looks over at Grant, who is smiling, a hand reaching out to her. She grins and holds his hand, giving it a gentle squeeze.

"I'm sorry I tried to compare our situation to Ian before," he says.

"It's okay."

"It's just that I can't help but wonder . . ." He trails off.

A knot forms in Rose's stomach.

"Did you two know all of each other's secrets?"

Rose frowns. "Considering he cheated on me, no, I would have to say that we didn't."

"I guess you have a point there," he says. "But, like when you first got together. Did you want to tell each other everything? To be able to open up and have someone know everything about you, down to your deepest darkest secrets?"

Rose reflexively pulls away from him. "What good would that do?"

He cocks his eyebrow at her.

"Not everyone has wonderful childhoods or privileged lives. There are parts of my past that are painful and sharing that pain with someone else does nothing but reopen old wounds."

"I didn't exactly have the greatest childhood either, despite what you might think."

"Then all the more reason to lock it away. Why do we need to throw a pity party for each other? We're both stronger people for what we went through."

Grant stares off now at the ocean. His expression is unreadable behind his dark sunglasses. He doesn't say anything for some time and Rose worries that she was too aggressive with her response.

But the truth is, she's never had a desire to share her pain with anyone. How could people, especially the ones she loves the most, understand what she went through, what she had to do to survive.

Rose watches as the waves crash onto the beach, water churning like the thoughts in her mind. She has tried to bury it deep inside her, but this conversation with Grant has just brought it all back to the surface.

Rose was so young; she never really understood the dynamic of her parents. How they'd got together in the first place. Her father was an abusive drunk who would beat up her mom. She always wondered why her mother put up with it. After her father burst through the door one day, her mother rushed her to her bedroom and made her promise not to come out. She sat with her ear against the door, listening to the sound of furniture being thrown around and her mother tumbling to the floor.

That evening when her mom crawled into bed with her, she saw her black eye, as she snuggled up against Rose.

"Mom, why can't we run away?"

Rose could feel something wet on her ear, knowing it was a tear that had dripped from her mother's swollen cheekbone. "One day as an adult you'll understand."

Now Rose understood. Her father didn't like being rejected, and he would've come for them both. While Ian was never abusive physically, Rose wound up following in her mom's footsteps, just trying to hide in the background and avoid conflict. The difference was that Rose stayed for James because Ian was at least a good father.

Images start flashing again in Rose's brain. Her mother rushing her into her room and slamming the door behind her. Rose crouching against the door, jumping every time she heard her mother's cries. But then another sound rang out, one so piercing that Rose had to cover her small ears.

Rose's eyes closed tightly as her ten-year-old brain registered the noise. It was a gunshot. The house was eerily quiet then. She waited for what felt like an eternity, willing her mom to open the door and tell her everything was alright. But Rose knew deep down it wasn't. When she finally did pull the door open, she saw her mother, lying motionless face down, her brown wavy hair covering her face.

"Mom!" Rose instinctively ran to her, trying to shake her awake, but she knew it was too late. The ache inside her was so deep it felt as if she had died as well.

A throat cleared behind her, which pulled her out of her trance. In the other room, she could hear the television on. The gun lay on the floor haphazardly, next to the torn leather couch. Rose's eyes followed the gun to the back of the armchair her father sat in. A few wiry strands of hair appeared translucent against the glow of the television.

Rose knew that her mother had been her only protection against him. With her gone, she didn't know what would happen to her. She leaned down and picked up the gun.

"What do you think you're going to do with that?" His voice was deep and gruff.

Rose stood up slowly, her pink leggings wet with her mother's blood. Her whole body shook like a leaf as she turned around, pointing the gun at him.

His eyes were glassy and bloodshot, his pupils like tiny pinpricks. He smiled at her, his teeth brown and crooked. "You don't have it in you," he said, then extended his hand. "Give me the gun."

"No," Rose said firmly.

His face changed then. Became more serious. His brow was creased. "Give me the gun," he growled.

"No!" she yelled louder, then raised it up, aiming it at his chest.

He charged at her then. The thumping of his racing footsteps was as loud and as quick as her own heartbeat. She closed her eyes and fired.

She stayed like that for a long time, frozen in the moment, trying to comprehend all that had happened around her.

She was still in the same position, on her knees on the floor, her face streaked with tears, when she saw the blue and white flashing lights through the window. Her family had been out on a farm, but the gunshots had clearly been heard by someone.

Rose spills her bottle of sparkling water, the cold causing her to jump up from her beach chair.
"You okay?" Grant asks her, handing her a white towel.
"I'm fine." She rubs the towel down her chest.
"I think you're right," Grant finally says.
"What?" Rose looks at him, confused.
"I guess some secrets are meant to stay buried."

Isabel

Isabel stands in line, deciding on a Greek salad for lunch. She's in the school's cafeteria, walking alongside a decadent countertop with chafing dishes of hot food being served, cold sandwiches, and pre-made salads. She's in awe that this used to be someone's home, although she can be pretty sure that the previous owner never stepped foot into the kitchen. This would have been an industrial kitchen then, built for a hired staff of chefs and bakers preparing Michelin-star-level food each night for them and their guests. And while the appliances have obviously been updated to state-of-the art subzero freezers, ovens and griddles, the bones of the original kitchen are still present. She can picture the potbelly stove, the farmhouse kitchen sink, the wooden cabinets fastened with metal latches. A student bumps her arm as she reaches for her utensils. She turns to see that the girl either doesn't notice or doesn't care. Isabel shakes her head.

"Isabel." Principal McFadden smiles at her, her blonde hair frizzed out by the humidity of the day.

"Hi, Layla," she replies, using the first name that she insisted Isabel call her.

"I just saw your gift on my desk. That was so sweet, you didn't have to do that."

Isabel smiles, shrugging her shoulders. "I broke what was likely your favorite mug. I would never have forgiven myself if I hadn't replaced it."

"Well, it was very kind of you." Mrs. McFadden smiles again. Then she points at Isabel's salad. "That looks good. I might get myself one of those." She looks up. "I'll let you get to it."

"See you around," Isabel says shyly.

Distracted, she looks for a cashier so she can pay for her food, but she forgets that the Pelican Academy has a meal plan. Everyone pays in advance. It's something that takes getting used to for her. That was always an option for students, but never teachers. As she steps out of the kitchen, she finds herself in one of the three grand ballrooms, adorned with actual gold leaf on the walls. The same walls that likely once hosted lavish parties are now absorbing the odor of the students' lunch meat and egg salad sandwiches. Rather than desecrating the beauty of this room and its mural ceilings and crystal chandeliers with conventional cafeteria benches, the school has chosen long wooden tables with legs that look like the shin guards of a Roman warrior.

Isabel sees some of the other faculty wave her over from a table in the back far right corner. It's the least favorable location, but the one with the best view of the whole cafeteria for monitoring the students and reminding them of their conduct. She knows she should be trying to get to know people here, but it seems like a waste. She isn't sure if she'll be sticking around much longer once she does what she came here for. Developing any sort of relationships here would only make it harder.

Isabel gives a small wave. In fact, she does have work to do for her upcoming class, so in any case, she will have to take her salad back to her desk and work on her syllabus. With a smile, she gestures with a thumb behind her to let them know she will be returning to her desk.

As she is getting ready to leave the cafeteria, she suddenly remembers that she left her phone in her car this morning. Not that anyone would call her, but still, when she doesn't have it, it feels like she's missing a limb. More so now that she just rejoined social media. She had become addicted to the lives of other people while wallowing in her own self-hatred, so she removed it from her phone, only to download it again a month later.

By the time Isabel gets to her car, her phone on the passenger seat burns hot in her hand from the sun roasting it all morning. She turns it over and sees the temperature symbol, along with a warning that the device needs to cool down before it can be operated.

Isabel had received that warning in the icy grip of New York City's freezing temperatures, but now, in the scorching heat of Florida, she fears that it might actually be damaged. For her sake, she hopes it isn't.

She closes her car door and heads across the parking lot, her feet crunching beneath the gravel. Already she can feel herself sweating. The last thing she wants is pit stains on her blouse when she is teaching. It would be all the students could focus on, passing notes and making up God knows what sort of nicknames for her. She optimizes that the quickest way back to her desk and out of this heat is by cutting through the football field, which is quiet at this time of day.

The football field rivals that of a college-level playing field. The paint on the grass is pristinely white, with large, looming silver bleachers. Rose squints as she notices a lone student sitting in the middle of them. As a teacher, her first thought is she's about to catch a student sneaking a cigarette or something, but upon further inspection, she realizes she recognizes the sandy blond hair, the posture. It's James.

Isabel knows she should be mindful, especially on school property, about the student–teacher relationship. But her heart goes out to him. She knows why he is sitting there, isolated from everyone else. She literally did the exact same thing moments earlier.

Against her better judgment, she walks towards the bleachers. He doesn't notice her at first, his eyes focused on a textbook. Likely trying to finish some homework right before it's due the next period. When her heels echo on the bleachers, she sees him jump, expecting to be in trouble for being out here, but he relaxes when he sees it's just her.

"What are you doing out here?" she asks as her heels continue to click and scrape along the metal of the bleachers, the noise echoing across the field.

"Just felt like eating by myself," he admits, slightly embarrassed.

She makes a disapproving face at him.

Putting her salad and purse down, Isabel takes a seat next to him and opens up the container of her salad.

He looks at her, confused for a moment, then looks around, even more worried now that they'll get in trouble. He has a right to be nervous. Still, Isabel takes her chance. She needs James on her side.

"You remind me a lot of myself," she starts as she assesses her salad, making sure there are no nuts, before she pokes at an olive, popping it in her mouth and biting down as a salty burst of juice pools around her gums.

"I was an outsider too and an only child, so I know what it's like to feel you don't have anyone, even a sibling, to relate to."

James nods as he scratches the back of his neck.

"I was the smartest kid in public school. That threatened kids who called me a nerd, like it's a bad thing to be smart."

"What did you do?" James asks, leaning his head on his hand that is now propped up on his knee.

Isabel shrugs. "I refused to dumb myself down to conform to their standards. I just didn't let it bother me and eventually, once people realized I didn't care, they stopped caring too and then everyone seemed to get over it."

James nods, reaching for his sandwich that he had on a napkin on the bench next to him, and takes a bite. "Well, as my tutor, you would know that being too smart is not exactly the problem I'm having," he tells her with a full mouth of food.

"So, what is bothering you?" She chuckles a bit, trying to keep the conversation light.

"It's the last week of tryouts for me. I'll find out in the next few days if I made the team."

"I get that's nerve-wracking," she sympathizes, "but why eat out here alone?"

He turns and looks back at the school. Several stately columns support the outdoor stucco deck, where a handful of tables are scattered for an outdoor dining option. From here, you can hear the distant chatter of the students.

"It's just that . . ." he starts, then shakes his head. "Never mind."

"Oh no." She shakes her own head in turn. "Don't do that. I will make it my mission to get it out of you, so you might as well tell me."

He laughs at her persistence. "Well, the only friends I've made here so far are the ones that are on the team already."

"And?" She shrugs her shoulders.

"If I don't make the team, I'm worried that they won't really consider me a friend anymore if I'm no longer a teammate."

"To protect yourself from that rejection, you're isolating yourself now."

"Something like that," he admits, his cheeks flushing red from embarrassment. Isabel remembers when she did something similar after a girl from her soccer team invited everyone and their parents over to celebrate the end of the season. Although Isabel wanted her grandmother to come, she knew she wouldn't agree to it and it was pointless to ask, so she had asked if she could just come herself. The girl throwing the party was nice, but one girl, Tracy— they both competed for the same left forward position—snickered. "Yeah, her grandmother wouldn't come. I hear she's like a gremlin who never leaves the house or something."

Isabel remembers seeing red and just charged at her, the coach pulling her off.

She remembers her face hot with tears later when she knew she had to tell her grandmother what had happened.

Isabel watched as her grandmother's face fell, and to this day, she's not sure if she was scared for her or scared of her.

"You mustn't ever give in to your rage like that," she had said with trepidation.

"I couldn't help it," Isabel defended herself. "It just came out."

"Listen to me." Her grandmother grabbed her by both shoulders then. "I don't care what you have to do, but you keep yourself from ever acting out on urges like that again. Do you understand?"

Isabel felt her grandmother's grip tight but shaky on her. For a moment she felt frightened. What if she couldn't control her urges? What would that mean for her?

She thinks about that now. She let her anger bring her here. When the time comes, will she be able to control it?

Both Isabel and James sit in silence for a moment, eating their lunch, when Isabel clears her throat. "You know, I spent my whole life building up walls out of fear of rejection, fear of abandonment," she says. "Trust me when I say it quickly becomes a lonely world when you do that." She hesitates for a moment. "This may cross the line here, but you are smart, despite what your tutor tells you."

He laughs.

"Don't let the fear of rejection change who you are. You're the type of kid that others would be so lucky to call a friend, and the sooner you realize that, the sooner everyone else will."

She watches as James's Adam's apple bobs in his pubescent throat. "Thanks," he says, and it comes out in almost a whisper.

Now if only she could follow her own advice. Isabel checks her watch. So much for getting on top of her syllabus. "I've got to get back to my classroom," she says, closing the lid to her salad. "I'll see you Thursday for tutoring?"

He smiles now. "Yes."

"I have my fingers crossed for you with soccer. Good luck, even though I don't think you'll need it." She gives his shoulder an encouraging squeeze and makes her way down the steps of the bleachers.

She faintly hears him call her name but isn't sure beneath the noise of her shoes on the bleachers. But when she steps off, she hears her name again.

"Isabel."

She turns and looks back up at him. He's standing now, his backpack slung over one shoulder. From this angle, he looks almost grown up.

He cracks a half-smile. "Thanks. You know, I'm really glad I met you."

She smiles. "Me too." But she swallows hard shortly after, wondering if he'll feel the same when he finally learns the real reason she's here.

Evelyn

Evelyn is lying in bed when she hears her door creak open. A large looming figure stands in the doorway, backlit from the light in the hallway, making it hard for her to see.

"Grant, is that you?"

The figure remains silent. Once they enter, the door closes behind them and the room becomes pitch black again.

She feels whoever it is, hovering over her.

Evelyn's pulse quickens.

She doesn't know who it is. One minute it's Grant, then Harrison. In an attempt to sit up, she presses her hands down on the bed, but her face is forcefully pressed down by something soft yet strong.

Unable to breathe, she begins to struggle, gripping at the pillow and trying to get it off her, but she can't. The person is too strong, pushing back against her.

Panic rises in her chest. She is going to die. She tries to struggle but she can't.

Evelyn screams, sitting up in bed. She's alone, beads of sweat tickling her forehead.

She puts a hand on her chest. It was just a terrible dream.

She falls back onto her pillow, letting out a sigh of relief. She tries to make out her own room in the dark, like a child trying to rationalize a shadow they see. It's not a scary monster, but rather just their robe hanging on the door of their closet.

Evelyn lets out another shaky breath, trying to compose herself, the dream and her memory merging into one. The night that changed everything.

"Give me your goddamn money." The voice was a deep growl, and Evelyn felt a sharp, cold steel object against the small of her back. His breath reeked of a nauseating combination of meat and Southern Comfort liquor.

The city was cold that night, but Evelyn started to sweat. She was a mere block from her apartment, but she shouldn't have cut through the park. She knew better than that, but the traffic had been terrible and after the night she had had, she just wanted to be home. It wasn't even dinner time yet. It was dark early because it was winter, but she had assumed there were enough people around. She realized how terrible of a mistake that had been.

The blood in Evelyn's veins ran cold and her back straightened like a rod.

"I said," he pushed the knife harder against her back, "give me your goddamn purse."

A shrill of panic escaped her. She held her purse out. The man yanked at it, twisting her wrist oddly, making her cry out in pain.

"Shut up!" the man yelled, slamming the butt of the knife down on her, puncturing her nose.

She fell to the ground, the shock of it taking her breath away. She heard his footsteps running, but it still took a minute for her to understand what had just happened to her.

Despite being too shaken to move, Evelyn forced herself to. He might decide while she was still in a fragile state to come back for her jewelry, and then who knew what he might do to her. She half stumbled on a broken heel, her other knee skinned, and reminded herself to breathe. She pulled her coat tighter around herself, breath fogging up in front of her.

When she got into her apartment, Grant and Maria were doing homework in the dining room. Once Maria had started showing up, it had been hard to put a stop to it.

Evelyn didn't want them to see her, so she stumbled through the foyer, kicking off her broken shoe on the black and white tiled floor, and shuffled into the kitchen, through the swinging door. She practically collapsed in a chair, her head falling into her arms as she crossed them on the wooden kitchen table.

"Mrs. Caldwell, are you alright?" Maria came in through the door. Apparently, she had caught sight of her.

She called out to her mom and Anita ran in from the long hallway that led to the living room.

"Mom, what's happened?"

Evelyn picked her head up and saw Grant and Maria looking at her, their faces full of worry.

They were seniors in high school at this point, but seeing the fear in their expressions, she didn't want them to know the truth.

"I just had a nasty spill on the ice," she said. "Why don't you two go back to your homework?"

As she urged them back into the other room, Evelyn saw the light of the streetlamp outside casting a dark shadow from the curtains in the kitchen, stretching ominously across the dark wood and marble countertops.

It made Evelyn think of the dark figure who had assaulted her, and she had to choke back tears.

"Evelyn, what's happened, are you alright?"

Anita hurried to the sink, filling a glass with water, then opened the freezer door, retrieving an ice pack. She grabbed a tea towel hanging off the stainless-steel dishwasher and wrapped the ice pack before gently applying it to Evelyn's nose.

Evelyn winced. "How bad is it?"

Anita pinched the bridge of Evelyn's nose. When she didn't cry out in pain, Anita shook her head. "It's not bad, merely a bruise. There is no break in the skin."

Evelyn took over holding the ice pack with her tender wrist but, remembering the pain, switched hands.

Anita sat down. "What happened?"

"I got robbed," she said in a low, strangled voice.

Anita's eyes widened with concern. "What did they get?"

"Just my purse and my dignity."

Anita put a soft hand on Evelyn's back. "I'm so sorry. Did they hurt you in any other way?"

"Just hit me with the butt end of the knife and I fell."

"Oh, Evelyn, I'm so sorry. Where were you?"

"The park." Evelyn put a hand up before Anita could say anything. "I know, I know. I thought it was still early."

"I don't like going in the park even when it's early. I forbid Maria to go near it." Anita shook her head sadly. "You need something to protect yourself."

"Like what?" Evelyn asked.

Anita stood up and walked into the foyer, coming back with her own small yellow purse. She placed it on the table in front of Rose.

Rose looked at her for permission and Anita nodded her along.

Evelyn unzipped the purse. It wasn't very big, but it was boxy with a white trim and was wide enough that it didn't reveal the contents inside. She opened it up and saw only two items. A wallet, then something metal and shiny. Evelyn reached in and pulled it out, eyes widening.

"Anita," she said in both shock and disapproval. "How did you get this?" Evelyn held the small pistol in her hand.

"I live alone in New York."

"That can't be legal."

"It's not, I bought it shortly after I had Maria. I just went out to New Jersey. I don't plan on using it unless I need to. And if I need to, I'm not going to be concerned if it's legal in New York or not."

Evelyn rubbed the cool steel against her fingertips when the door swung open again and she quickly shoved it back into Anita's purse.

Grant appeared before her. "Are you okay, Mom, really?"

"Yes, Grant, I'm fine. Just a bad spill is all, but I'll be alright."

Grant eyed her suspiciously but didn't say anything. He almost never did. He never questioned Evelyn or Harrison. But she knew he could sense things.

He pulled a glass from the cabinet and filled it with water, looking at both Anita and Evelyn, who had remained silent through this whole endeavor, waiting for him to leave through the swinging door.

Evelyn felt her shoulders relax when he did finally leave.

"Having something like this could've protected you tonight," Anita urged. "Trust me, you'll never know when you're going to need it."

Rose

"Can I come in?"

Rose turns around startled to find Evelyn standing in the doorway of her art studio. Her frail figure in white silk pajamas and her pale skin makes her look like an apparition.

Rose squints as she peers at the clock she put on the wall earlier so as not to lose track of time again.

"Sure," Rose says, the word drawn out in suspicion.

Rose catches Evelyn looking up at the ceiling. Right at the vent where she hid the gun. It was subtle enough, but Rose knew to look for it.

"I was . . . watching you paint for a moment there," Evelyn says. "You paint so smoothly, like some sort of dance."

"Thanks." Rose squints and furrows her brows. There's something different about Evelyn, she notices. She looks small and vulnerable. She has never seen her in this light before.

Evelyn finds a folding chair in the corner and sits down. "Do you mind if I w-watch you paint?"

Rose straightens up. "Not at all," she says, though she feels a little self-conscious. But again, this could be a good opportunity to speak with Evelyn face to face about everything. Things she can't bring up with Grant or in front of him.

Rose dips into her black paint and begins to swirl the brush around the canvas. She has never noticed it before, but Evelyn is right. It is sort of like a dance.

"Couldn't sleep?" Rose asks her.

"Something like that. Do you always work this late?"

"I've had a lot on my mind lately," Rose says a bit stiffly.

The silence between them feels electrically charged and Rose knows whoever speaks first will try to shock the other.

Evelyn shifts in her seat. "Is James struggling with school already?"

Rose bites her lip. "What do you mean?" she asks, worried that Evelyn knows something she doesn't.

"I mean is it really necessary for James to have a tutor? He's only a freshman in high school."

"Absolutely," Rose counters. "The Pelican Academy is a very tough school. I don't want him to fall behind."

Evelyn shifts in her seat. "Well, can he do his tutoring at school? I don't like strangers in my house."

Rose looks at her oddly. The number of people that come through this house on any given day to clean, cook or repair something is staggering, and she can bet Evelyn doesn't know any of their names.

But Rose notices that Evelyn won't make eye contact with her; instead she looks over Rose's shoulder.

"You have a similar style to Jackson Pollock," Evelyn observes, keeping up the small talk.

"He's my favorite artist." Rose cocks her head towards the door. "I noticed you have one hidden in the guest room downstairs. Pretty modern piece of art for a place such as this."

Evelyn sits up straighter. "It was a gift; we didn't know where to put it."

"It'd be better off in a museum than hidden in a guest room."

Evelyn looks her up and down but doesn't say anything.

"You won't because you actually like the painting," Rose concludes, turning back to her canvas to paint again. "I don't really get you, Evelyn. You act a certain way, but I don't think that's who you really are."

"That's something I'd say we have in common."

Rose finds herself looking up at the ceiling. Her eyes home in towards the vent. She can't imagine how Evelyn was able to acquire the gun Rose used to kill her father, but people with money know people in high places. Or it was the exact same make and model just to prove a point or create some sort of scare tactic.

I know all about your past.

Suddenly, something unlocks in her brain.

Evelyn obviously knows for a fact what happened in Rose's childhood. She has the gun to prove it. But for whatever reason, she hasn't told Grant. There is no way he could feign ignorance after learning something like that about her.

Rose's mind slides to the hidden cameras all over the penthouse. Evelyn doesn't trust her. She knows who Rose really is and being afraid for her only son, she planted cameras around the apartment to keep an eye on her, Rose can only assume; to see how she acted behind closed doors. And if Rose so happened to decide to kill Grant, there would be actual video evidence Evelyn could use against her.

Rose wipes her forehead. It all makes sense to her now. Part of her wonders if Evelyn is even really that sick. Or at the very least, has exaggerated her symptoms in order to call her son home to her, selling the penthouse in New York to solidify the move here. Come to think of it, she didn't hear her stutter once when she was at the country club.

"This painting you're doing reminds me of the book *The Picture of Dorian Gray*."

Rose steps back from her work to assess it. "Does it?"

"Oscar . . . Wilde wrote a story about a man, Dorian Gray, infatuated by beauty who sells his soul to ensure that a portrait of him, not Dorian himself, will age and fade, recording all of Dorian's sins in life."

"Is that so?" Rose says, waiting to see where she's going with this.

"I remember the chilling ending when Dorian stabs the picture of himself. The maids rush in after hearing a cry of agony to see a beautiful, intact painting of Dorian, but an old, terrifying-looking man stabbed in the heart on the floor next to it."

"Evelyn." Rose lets out a sigh. "Why don't we cut through the metaphors. What do you really have to say to me?"

"I know you killed your father."

Even though it is what Rose was expecting, it still shocks her system like being submerged in ice water, her throat constricting.

Rose tries to keep her composure. The more even-tempered she is, the better. "So, you've clearly done your research on me." She takes the stool next to her easel and moves it across from the folding chair that Evelyn is sitting in. "So you'll know who he was, and that it was self-defense."

"That's what the police report says." There is a hint of skepticism in her voice.

"I'm not that person. I'm not a cold-blooded killer. I was put in a terrible situation, and I had to do what I could to survive."

Evelyn looks at her with a sort of sadness or pity, Rose can't tell which.

"I'll be haunted by that day for the rest of my life. Looking back on it now, I just should've run. The cops would've arrested my father, and I'd still have gone to the orphanage. But at the time, I thought I was going to die too that night."

Rose can feel the tears building. She shuts her eyes tightly to push them back in.

"It's not something I expect anyone to understand, which is why I won't even tell my own son. I could never bear the thought of him looking at me differently, wondering if he could ever trust me." Rose's voice starts to crack. She pulls in a sharp breath and straightens herself up, bringing her attention back to Evelyn.

"I am not my father."

The moonlight from the window falls on Evelyn's face, hardening her once almost sympathetic expression into something unreadable.

"Your previous husband's death was somewhat mysterious too, wasn't it?"

"He was hit by a car."

"How convenient."

There is a long silence before Rose finally speaks. "What do you want from me?"

Evelyn swallows. "I won't tell your son about your past. But in order for me to keep that promise, you have to do something for me."

Rose leans back and crosses her arms.

"I need you to show Grant that he's too good for you. You need him to want to leave you, not the other way around. It has to be his decision to let you go."

"What?"

"In exchange, I will keep your secret, and I'll send your son to any high school he wants. I have a lot of connections, I can send him to the best ones in the country. I'll happily pay for his education through college. This is, after all, the real reason you're here, right?"

Rose feels as if she's been gut punched. The wind knocked out of her. She can't deny that having this opportunity for her son is wonderful, but she also loves Grant.

Rose's eyes glisten against the moonlight as she stares at the calm ocean below. Does she even know what love is? She certainly has no real understanding of it. No good example that was ever set for her. With James, it's unconditional love. One where she would gladly die for him. But is that what all love is, or just maternal love?

With James, it was instant. This inherent instinct to protect and nurture this tiny human who comes to rely on you and trust that you'll take care of them.

With adults it's a lot harder. You are already your own person. You need to try to see how you fit together, but no two people are perfect for each other in every way. Adjustments have to be made. Each one learns to tolerate the other's imperfections.

With Grant it's his possessiveness, which she knows stems from insecurity. He wants her all to himself. Part of her can't help but wonder if that's another reason he pushed so hard for this move. He took her away from the other people that were taking up her time, like her friends. It's why she has to sneak up to her art studio in the middle of the night. He even gets jealous if she prioritizes painting over him. He seems to want to know where she is all the time and wants her to be at his beck and call, which admittedly she has done more of since they got here, for the sake of making everyone happy.

To be fair, her imperfection is her independence. Hurt so many times before, she's afraid to let others in. So maybe it's not that he's needy, it's that she's too distant, and he's trying to bring her back.

But Grant also seems to have her on a pedestal she doesn't feel she deserves. It's like he has this image of her in his mind that she can't help feeling she can't measure up to. So maybe Evelyn is right. Grant thinks she's someone that she's not.

Her mind flashes back to the beach, when Grant was asking her about sharing secrets. Rose was so adamant about keeping hers, it didn't occur to her that maybe Grant has some of his own, maybe even about his own mother.

Rose turns back to Evelyn, who continues to stare at her, waiting for her to tell her if she'll accept this deal she's making.

"Trust me, you wouldn't want me to take matters into my own hands." Evelyn's voice is low and throaty.

"What are you two doing up so late?"

Both Evelyn and Rose spin their heads towards the door, to find Grant standing there, squinting from the light. His hair is slightly sticking up and his performance shorts and shirt are wrinkled from sleep.

Evelyn and Rose exchange a look, both curious as to how much he heard.

"I just came to admire R-Rose's artwork. I couldn't sleep."

"Yeah," Rose agrees. She can't help but notice Evelyn's stutter disappeared when she was blackmailing her, and now it's seemingly returned.

Grant looks down at his watch. "Well, it's pretty late, don't you think you two should get to bed? Sleep is really important for your health, Mom."

"You're right." Evelyn stands up. "It's time for me to go to bed."

Grant takes his mom's hand and extends the other towards Rose. "Are you coming?"

Rose hesitates for a moment. "Yes," she concedes. "I'm coming."

Grant leads his mother down the steps as Rose shuts off the light. Their footsteps are loud against the aging wood.

"Good night, Mom." Grant kisses his mother's cheek at her door while Evelyn locks eyes with Rose, giving her a threatening stare.

When Evelyn shuts her door, Grant takes Rose's hand and leads her down the hall to their room.

Evelyn's ultimatum sits heavy on Rose's chest as she lies down. Maybe she should just accept that someone with a past like hers isn't meant to be happy. There are just too many deep scars and as much as you try to forget them, they itch until you are forced to scratch them. They never go away.

If James finds out the truth about her, it will break him. He'll never be able to look at her the same way again. His own mother, a murderer.

Rose hadn't realized that when you marry someone, you marry their family. She had no family and Ian's parents moved away, so it had never been an issue for her before.

But marrying into a life with Evelyn is not something she could've ever prepared for. It kills her to think it, but maybe marrying Grant was a mistake and she should just do what Evelyn says.

Rose thinks about her painting upstairs. She does her best work when she lets her subconscious take over. Evelyn's right, the painting does remind her of Dorian Grey. Rose now realizes the smeared, dark, jagged edges are an abstract human. The inside is dark and twisted, much like her own insides. Then with the red, she has smeared what could almost be a puddle of blood trailing from the black paint. Rose has, involuntarily, created death. Something she hasn't done since her first work of art. What she can't decide from the abstract is who she has painted. Who is the subject, bleeding from the heart? Is it her? And if so, is this her past or a premonition of the future?

Isabel

Isabel pulls her car into the driveway of the Caldwells' residence and rings the doorbell.

"Yes?" A voice comes over the intercom.

Isabel steals a look at herself. She is presentable enough after a long day of work, but her eyes are full of trepidation, which gives her away.

"Hi, it's Isabel Martinez, James's tutor."

The gate buzzes and she slowly pulls in. Her breath becomes unsteady, and she grips the steering wheel as tightly as she can, her palms sweating against the leather. She looks down at the passenger seat, the envelope sticking out with the confirmation she was waiting for. The truth, finally.

After she parks, she takes another moment to collect herself, when the door opens. Rose is standing there, confused.

Isabel grabs the envelope and takes one last breath before pushing open the door to her car.

"Isabel, I'm so sorry. I thought we had said Thursdays, and it's usually around eight, right?"

"We did," Isabel confirms. "But there is something I have to speak with you and Mr. Caldwell about."

Rose puts a hand to her chest. "Is everything okay with James?"

"Yes." She puts her own hand up, reassuring. "Everything is fine. In fact, this doesn't concern James at all."

"Oh," Rose says, confused. "Well, of course, come in."

Rose steps aside, then closes the door behind them both with a sickening thud.

"May we all speak in private?"

"James is actually at soccer practice still, so it's just us."

Rose leads her into the living room. More wood paneling, this time in a robin's-egg blue with gold trimming. Two white silk couches face one another in front of a rectangular marble coffee table with a fireplace in front of it.

"Can I get you anything?"

"Some water maybe?" Isabel says hesitantly.

"Of course."

Isabel is still looking around the room when she hears Rose whispering to someone in the hallway.

"Isabel." Grant appears, walking into the room. He's dressed in a white polo and white shorts like he's on his way to a tennis game. There is a look of surprise on his face. "What are you doing here?"

Isabel clenches and unclenches her fist. "I need to speak with you."

"With me?" He points to himself and looks at her, confused. "What is this about?" He takes a seat on the couch across from her.

The grandmother walks by without acknowledgment. The tulle of her dress swishes as she passes. She opens the front door, looking outside. "Someone's car is blocking my garage door. I'm going to be late for mahjong."

She turns to see Isabel, and that same look she gave the last time she saw Isabel comes over her once more.

Isabel tears her eyes away from her and starts to speak. "My mother was Maria Martinez," she says to the floor, then looks up at Grant.

He straightens his posture, looking up in thought. "I'm sorry, I don't believe I know a Maria Martinez."

The grandmother slowly enters the room with trepidation, sitting in a decorative armchair off to the side, her blue dress making her blend into the background.

Isabel makes a point of continuing, hoping to jog his memory. "I was born on 24 September 2003."

Grant squints at her, his look showing he's still not registering what she's trying to say.

She waits for him to say something, but he doesn't. Isabel reaches for her purse on the floor next to her, pulling out the piece of paper.

She pushes it over towards him. "According to this," she starts, "you're my father."

Rose walks in, stumbles and almost drops the water. The glass slams hard on the table, splashing some water onto the marble.

"What?" Rose looks to Grant for answers.

Grant's mouth gapes open. He sits straight, bewildered, and places a hand on his forehead. Then he sucks in a breath through his nostrils. When he looks up at her, Isabel sees his expression has gone from confusion to almost anger. Isabel feels her shoulders pull inward, bracing herself like a child about to be scolded.

"I don't even know a Maria Martinez." He shakes his head. "How long have you had this information?"

She shakes her head. "Not long. I had my suspicions a few months ago. But I didn't have confirmation until today." She gestures towards the letter.

Isabel had gotten home from work, and it was in her mailbox. She had dropped her bag without a second thought, ripping the envelope open with such force that it gave her a paper cut on her index finger. But Isabel hadn't cared. She put her bleeding finger in her mouth, sucking the bitter taste as her eyes scanned the document for the end results. A positive match.

It had been what she had been waiting for her whole life. To finally know the truth. To know who her father was. From the moment she had suspected it, she had been practicing this speech. Isabel had been at work, looking for the last year the school had had a swim team, as parents were arguing they wanted it brought back. Turns out that had been almost twenty years earlier. But as she scanned through the yearbooks, she came to a page that took her breath away. A picture on the prom page of her mother. She didn't think her mom had gone to a fancy private school. When she looked at the credit below, it captioned Grant Caldwell. She double-checked the year: 2002. Since then, she had wondered. Could this man be her father? Was this the reason that her grandmother had pushed her to get this job? It seemed like fate, and she knew then she had to do something. Then, upon seeing the letter earlier today, Isabel got into her car and came here without a second thought. Now she wanted to have this conversation, as she had waited long enough for it. Isabel wanted to confront Grant and demand the explanation she had been waiting for.

"Why?" he starts, then shakes his head as if understanding now. "So, you came to us so you could try to steal some evidence for proof?" He holds up the envelope, putting together that she would've needed a sample of his DNA as well.

Isabel bites her lip. "It's not like that," she starts. "I never knew anything about you. My mother died when I was born, and my grandmother told me she didn't know who my father was. I figured then that I would never know who you are. But then a few months ago, my grandmother died." Her eyes start to tear up, and she wipes them away. "I came to the realization that I was alone in this world now. I had no one anymore." She tries to compose herself. "Right before my grandmother died, she knew I wanted to work in education, and she encouraged me to work at the Whitmore Academy. I got the job and while doing administrative work, I came across an old yearbook and found a picture of you and my mother at homecoming or prom or something. Her name wasn't mentioned because I don't think she ever went to Whitmore. At least I found no record of her. But your name was."

"Prom." Grant drags the word out like he's dredging up the memory. He looks down with a melancholy smile, remembering the night.

Isabel catches the grandmother's eyes and isn't sure what to make of it. It's like the old lady is trying to tell her something, but she doesn't know what. Maybe she's just trying to tell her to stop. But she can't. She's come this far.

"So, then I came across James's file and realized he was your stepson, and he was at the school."

"So you knew the whole time?" Grant looks up, questioning her. "Is that why you came here? You followed us?"

Isabel takes a shaky breath. "I wanted to get out of administration and teach. The Pelican Academy had an offer for maternity leave coverage. This isn't a permanent thing. I'm not sure I'll even have a job in a few more months." She picks at the cuticle on her thumb. "I just wanted to get to know you, to see if I even wanted you as a father. My grandmother said she didn't know who you were, but based on the yearbook photos I found, I think she knew you but didn't want me to." She sighs. "So I had to proceed with caution. Figure out why she didn't want me to know about you. I didn't want to just show up at your door and announce myself. I wanted to see how this all felt." She swallows. "And you all seem like a really happy family."

The room falls silent as if they are all collectively holding their breath.

"I guess I just had forgotten what that felt like." She sniffs. "So, then I thought I'd try to get a piece of hair from a hairbrush or something, just to confirm if I was right. I didn't want to throw around accusations if they weren't true. I wasn't trying to be deceitful, or cause upset; I was trying to figure out the best way to handle this." The tears threaten to spill over like a dam. "If you want me to go away, I absolutely will. I won't stay here, I won't tutor James anymore and when this maternity coverage is up, I'll go back to New York and be out of your life. But I just had to know the truth and I thought maybe you'd want to know too."

She squeezes her eyes tightly, trying to keep it together, trying to quell the rush of nausea in her stomach, the pounding against her skull as she tries to hold back a flood of tears.

"I did know your mother," Grant admits after a long pause. "Her name was Maria Gonzales, not Martinez, and we were never together." He takes a long breath. "Isabel, I hate to be the one to say this to you, but not only am I not your father, but Maria wasn't your mother."

The words explode in Isabel's head like a grenade.

"What?" she snaps, unable to comprehend.

Isabel looks to Rose, who is just as confused, then to Evelyn, who has her head in her hands.

Grant clarifies. "You said you were born in September 2003, right?"

She nods.

"Maria died in March of 2003. Six months before you were even born."

"This can't be right." Isabel's head is spinning. Her grandmother lied to her. She was told her mom died in childbirth and she just took it at face value. She never thought she needed to question it.

"DNA results aren't always accurate," he says gently. "And I'm sorry to say that this must be a false positive."

Isabel feels like she is falling, her mind swirling in a tornado of thoughts.

Rose puts a soft hand on her shoulder. Isabel looks at it, almost confused, forgetting where she is.

Rose seems to look at Evelyn and Grant for something, but both have their heads down. "I'm so sorry, Isabel. I know what it feels like to be alone. I lost my parents at a young age. I'm sorry these aren't the answers you're looking for, but if there is anything we can do, please don't hesitate to ask."

"Thank you." Isabel wipes a stray tear from her eye. "I'm so sorry to bother you all. I should go."

She stands up, everyone else still frozen in place. She hurries across the foyer and slams the heavy door behind her, racing to her car before she bursts into tears.

Her mom wasn't even her mother. All this time, it was a lie. She had sought out the Caldwells for answers and instead, she was left with more questions. Now she had nothing to cling to. She didn't have any idea who either one of her parents was.

Isabel pulls her phone out, googling her mother's name. Nothing has ever come up before that appeared to be about her mom, but this time she tries this new last name, Gonzales. Her head falls back onto the headrest of the car. Right there at the top of the search is a school picture of the woman she thought was her mother. The same picture she stared at on the end table of her grandmother's couch for her entire life. Long dark hair, bow-shaped lips and a sweet smile.

Underneath is a headline: High School Student Shot in Central Park. She scrolls to the date of the article.

Grant was right. She died in March of 2003. She couldn't be her mother.

Bile starts to rise in her throat. She has to get out of here.

Isabel drops her phone to the passenger seat and quickly starts her car, peeling out of the driveway in a rush to get home.

As she does, her mind starts to wander. How could her grandmother lie to her like that for her whole life? What secret was she keeping from her and why?

There is something there, though. Something that the Caldwells aren't telling her either. Isabel sees the envelope sticking out of her purse. The DNA. She knows it connects her to the Caldwells somehow. Someone is lying.

Rose

Rose remains sitting in silence in the living room with both Evelyn and Grant. Everything that was just being discussed felt so foreign to her, like everyone around her was speaking another language, and she found herself having a hard time keeping up.

Rose looks towards Evelyn sitting in a chair by the window. The light cast over her face makes her look sickly.

Grant is staring off in the distance at nothing in particular, his eyes unblinking, but his mind is clearly spinning.

She thinks about Isabel.

Why would her grandmother claim that her dead daughter was Isabel's mother when that couldn't physically be true? Unless Isabel's birthday is wrong altogether?

"So, you were friends with Maria?" Rose asks Grant.

He swallows. "Yes."

"Was it possible she had a baby in secret before she died?"

"No. She couldn't have been secretly pregnant for nine months, then have had a baby without anyone noticing." Grant puts a hand over his eyes like he's battling a migraine.

So maybe this is just a tragedy. Why Isabel's grandmother lied to her is not their business, which means it shouldn't have anything to do with the Caldwells, right?

People that don't get along with Evelyn have a tendency to turn up dead.

Could this be the other death she was looking to connect Evelyn with?

Rose looks at the faces in front of her. Neither of them seem to be writing this off as an unfortunate coincidence. The air in the room sits heavy and still. There is something happening here, like static electricity before a lightning strike.

Rose's mind threads back to the DNA results, still tugging at the corner of her brain.

What does it all mean? Does this DNA somehow pull them into an unsolved murder investigation from over twenty years ago?

Of all the people this news is affecting, she feels the most for Isabel. She's just as in the dark as her.

Rose knows how frustrating it is to have someone ripped from your life like that with still so many questions unanswered.

She catches the light off Grant's watch and finds herself thinking about Ian's death.

Could there have been something more there, too?

There weren't many details to go off. She remembers when she got the call. She had been on her way back with James after he had won his soccer game. He'd done an amazing slide tackle that freed the ball up to score the winning point. A move that Ian had taught James.

It was evening rush hour. Cars and pedestrians all crowding the streets and sidewalks, eager to get home in the dark of the fall night. Ian was one of them, just doing his daily commute.

Rose had climbed out of the subway just outside their apartment when she noticed a voicemail from an unknown number. She didn't bother to listen at first. She was on a noisy street. Instead, she stopped off with James at the bodega to get something for dinner. It wasn't until she was unpacking the groceries that she was reminded of the voicemail and decided to check it.

The regret Rose feels now is still something she'll never forgive herself for.

She had grabbed James, and they jumped in a cab, thinking it would be the quickest way, but the traffic at rush hour was almost impossible.

Nearly in tears, they jumped out and got back on the subway, trying to figure the fastest way to NYU hospital.

When they had finally gotten there, the sterile smell of disinfectant made her nauseous. They were greeted by the somber faces of the nurses, confirming what she feared the most.

Rose's body had weighed heavily with dread. They hadn't made it in time. Rose wonders now if it would've changed anything.

She held James up as he fell into her arms. She felt powerless to help him through what would forever be the worst day of his entire life.

Rose desperately tried to make sense of what had happened for James's sake. But sometimes when there are too many witnesses, it's hard to know what the true story really is.

It was thought maybe someone had accidentally pushed Ian. Too many people on an overcrowded sidewalk. Then there was someone who said he was likely threading between parked cars and the narrow line of moving traffic and slipped. Some said he had fallen so hard that he could only have been pushed intentionally. Likely by someone living on the streets, probably with mental health issues.

But no one ever came forward who'd seen the whole thing. Because New Yorkers keep their heads down and just try to get to where they need to go.

The reality was no one had seen what happened. Even the cab driver that had struck him claimed he truly came out of nowhere.

The look on James's face when he heard his father was dead still makes her sick to this very day. To watch your child torn with such anguish and pain and be helpless to fix it. He was almost a man, but still a boy in so many ways. That became more prominent in those moments when he fell into her, unable to hold up his own weight, the sobs rising deep from within his chest that he tried so hard to keep down. It hurt her more that he was trying to be strong. For a month he barely said a word to anyone. They would merely exchange sad glances, their eyes ringed with dark circles from lack of sleep. A restlessness that wouldn't settle.

Rose looks around the room she's in now. This over-the-top estate that to any outsider might look like if you get to live here, you've hit the jackpot in life.

But as she looks at Grant and Evelyn, both with their heads in their hands, affairs and murders all wrapped into one, it becomes apparent that money can't buy your way out of everything.

She waits a few more moments in silence, hoping for someone to say something. When neither of them does, she decides to speak up.

"Can someone please explain to me what is going on?"

Evelyn lets out a long breath. "Her grandmother, Anita Gonzales, was our housekeeper."

"And her daughter Maria was your high school sweetheart?" She turns towards Grant.

"We were never together." Grant stands up, almost angry now. "I don't know who this girl is. Probably wants money."

Rose is slightly unnerved by Grant's reaction. It's so out of character for him to be this agitated.

Evelyn stands up and puts a hand on Grant's shoulder, trying to urge him to sit back down.

"Whoever she is, she is clearly . . . mistaken," Evelyn agrees.

"So, Anita was your housekeeper. Anita told Isabel that Maria was her mother, but that can't be true because Maria was murdered before Isabel was born." Rose speaks slowly, attempting to process the facts in her mind.

"It appears so," Evelyn says.

"Why would she do that?"

"I'm not sure," Evelyn says. "Anita was a bit cagey before she left us. So there was clearly something else going on, but we were just her employer, we had no idea what was happening in her personal life."

Rose watches as Grant looks over at his mother. She clearly senses it but avoids his gaze.

"Could the death of her daughter have made her so distraught that she adopted?" Rose tries to rationalize.

"Who knows?" Evelyn stands up, done with the conversation, and abruptly leaves the room.

"Grant." Rose turns back to look at him. He's standing at the window, looking out with his hands on his hips. She can't read his expression.

"I'm sorry," he finally says, as if realizing that she's still here. "I need to go for a drive or something. Figure this all out."

"But—" Before she can say anything else, he, too, leaves the room.

Rose decides to pull out her phone and google Maria Martinez, March 2003.

A picture of a woman with dark hair, dark eyes and a soft smile stares back at her. A high school yearbook picture.

Something very strange is going on. Did Maria somehow fake her own death and live another six months to have a baby? Is Grant lying about being with her?

She thinks about the DNA. Yes, Grant was right, there can be false positives. But still, this seemed too odd.

And why would her grandmother Anita lie to her? Why keep her from knowing the truth?

Rose pulls up a search and scans through the headlines. In one of the results, she discovers that someone shot Maria with a Glock pistol. The article then reports how most women who purchase these for self-defense wind up with their assailant using it on them.

Rose's mouth dries up. From what she understands, it's a standard gun that lots of women carry because it's small and easy to use. She remembers when her mom bought the same one to defend herself against her father. The one that, in turn, her father managed to scramble out of her hands and use on her.

The one Rose used to kill him.

She thinks of the hidden lock box with the gun in it in her studio. Does she have it all wrong? Is the gun Evelyn has hidden not the same one from her childhood, just the same model? Maybe this gun is linked to Maria's murder. Rose's mouth starts to dry up as she wonders just how overprotective and controlling Evelyn is of her son and what she is really capable of.

Evelyn

"Anita, what did you do?" Evelyn sits at the desk in her room, her fingers clasped together as she looks up at the sky, tears brimming to the surface.

Anita is gone. Evelyn wanted to ask Isabel how it happened, but she knew it wasn't the right time. She couldn't show sympathy down there.

It has taken quite a level of determination on Isabel's part to get to this point. To find them. But the question now is, what to do about it?

She has always been expecting this, in some ways, but still, it's never easy making a hard decision.

God, Maria. Evelyn was hoping she'd never hear that name again. She wishes she could just wipe her whole memory of that time.

Maria was beautiful. Too beautiful for her own good.

Evelyn would catch Grant looking at Maria when he thought she wouldn't notice. But of course, she did. Women always notice when men are giving them attention. They know the power they hold over them. Grant had been more on the shy side at this point, but his feelings for Maria hadn't been as subtle as Evelyn would've hoped. One day Evelyn had been in Grant's room when he had gone to take a shower. She was helping Anita and picking up dirty clothes when she spotted Maria's name on his computer screen. He was drafting an email to her. Checking she still heard the shower running, she found not just the one, but what looked like at least a hundred emails sent to Maria. They were mostly quotes from poems, sonnets and song lyrics. She then saw his instant messenger chats to Maria, asking her why she hadn't responded to him. Evelyn winced, embarrassed for him. Maria was completely ignoring them, pretending they didn't exist.

This had been Evelyn's fault. Anita had been her friend, and she'd desperately needed someone to talk to. Her life had been so lonely back then. So it had only made sense that if she wanted Anita to stay, she'd let Maria come over after school. After she had allowed it once, she didn't know how to say no after that.

Even Harrison, who had once frowned upon her for her friendship with their maid, started to come around. Not only would he come home earlier but he would insist they both stay for dinner. It seemed as if Maria's presence was, in fact, a good influence on her family. At least that's what she'd foolishly thought at first.

After discovering the emails, Evelyn tried not to say anything to Grant, and stayed out of it while Maria teased him playfully. Of course, it was all just a form of flirting. Grant tried on several occasions to ask her out, but she'd say things like, "Well, we're already here at your house, why do we need to go anywhere?"

Evelyn sensed Maria seemed embarrassed by Grant. She walked a fine line of trying to keep his attention while ignoring him in public.

One night, Evelyn walked past his bedroom and overheard him talking to himself in the mirror. He was trying out different ways he could ask Maria to prom. Overprotectiveness gripped Evelyn, but she could do nothing but shake her head.

She wanted to burst into the room and tell him, Maria is not interested in you. She's stringing you along until she can find someone better. But she knew Grant wouldn't listen.

It was like witnessing a car crash slowly happening, knowing there was nothing you could do about it.

To Evelyn's surprise, Maria did say yes to prom, likely through the insistence of Anita. That night, she was sure that Maria was going to stand him up somehow, make some lame excuse, but, maybe thanks again to Anita, Maria and she both showed up at the apartment. Maria and Grant exchanged corsages, and pictures were taken.

Just after Anita had left, Harrison pulled Maria aside, calling her into his office.

Grant's relationship with his father had become harder at this point. Evelyn had only been able to hold the wool over his eyes for so long before he realized that Harrison had been cheating on his mother this whole time.

The time Harrison spent with Maria in his office had been longer than anyone had expected and Evelyn could see Grant getting agitated.

Grant had finally knocked on the door. "Dad, we're going to be late." Grant pulled on the door, but it was locked.

Seconds later, Harrison appeared on the other side. "A little jealous, are we?" he mocked. "I was just having a chat with Maria about the dangers of men and gave her some pepper spray in case she needs to fend you off."

Grant's face hardened to a scowl as his father patted his shoulder and walked past him like he didn't matter at all to him.

As soon as they left for prom that evening, Evelyn knew it was all over. Maria was going to rip Grant's heart out.

"You know Grant really likes Maria," Evelyn had said the next day to Anita.

"Yes, I know. Maria says they're great friends. I'm so happy for them."

"I just don't want to see anyone get hurt."

"They're just friends. How could anyone get hurt?"

Evelyn tried to urge Anita to read between the lines, but Anita seemed to feign ignorance.

Evelyn would have to do something about it.

Evelyn paces her room back and forth now. By any means necessary, she must protect herself.

Dialing her bank, she pulls her phone out of her purse to arrange discussing some items and acquiring a safe deposit box. She had considered getting a deposit box a while back, but she was aware that when she passed away, Grant would be able to access it. He'd know the truth for sure. But now, with everything boiling to the surface, she can't risk anyone finding it.

"Rose!" Evelyn hangs up the phone and climbs the steps to the studio, surprised to find for the first time that Rose isn't there.

"Rose!" She comes back down the stairs, finding Rose emerging from the closet in her bedroom.

"Yes?"

"I need you to run to the store for me, will you?"

Rose looks at her, surprised.

Evelyn rolls her eyes. "I have a migraine after all of this business, and I need some aspirin or something."

"Grant just left. Would you like me to call him to pick it up?"

"No," she says, louder than she means to. "Just take my . . . car. The keys are in the foyer."

The two women stare each other down for a long moment.

"Fine, Evelyn." Rose goes back into the closet and retrieves her brown cross-body purse. "I'll be back shortly."

Evelyn waits by the window until Rose is out of the driveway. When she is sure that she's gone, she goes back up to Rose's art studio, pulling out the step stool from the closet. She has no concerns about getting paint on her blue dress. If she needs to, she can throw it out; this is important. Pulling down the vent, she extends her hands. A wave of relief hits her when she feels the lock box. She pulls it down, then puts the vent back.

Something doesn't feel right, though. She shakes the box. Quickly, she pulls the key out of her dress pocket. Shaking, she struggles to get the key into the lock to open it. When she does, panic consumes her.

The gun is missing.

Rose

Rose storms down the aisle of the drugstore, a feeling of queasiness churning in her stomach. She can't believe how just last night Evelyn had the nerve to threaten her, when she is clearly hiding something as well. Rose comes to an abrupt halt when she reaches the aisle labeled pain relievers, staring between the different brands.

"You look like you're in a hurry. Can I help you with something?" A man in a white pharmacy coat with short dark hair and black glasses smiles at her.

"Yes, actually." Then something occurs to Rose. "Do you happen to know Evelyn Caldwell?"

He nods. "Yes, very well."

"Great," Rose says, relieved. "She asked me to come to the pharmacy because she has a headache. Only with her Parkinson's, I'm worried if one of these might mess with her medications. Do you mind looking her up on your computer to see what I can give her?" The last thing Rose needs is to buy the wrong aspirin and accidentally kill her.

The man looks at her quizzically. "You mean as a preventative measure?"

It's Rose's turn to look confused. "I'm not sure what you mean by that."

"Well, ibuprofen is associated with a lower risk of getting Parkinson's."

"But she already has it," Rose clarifies.

He shakes his head. "No, I think you're mistaken."

"Evelyn Caldwell. She was diagnosed about six months ago with it." Rose pulls out her phone and googles Evelyn's name. A stately picture of her on the board of some local charity pops up. "This is her."

The pharmacist pushes his glasses closer to the bridge of his nose. "Yes, that is the same Evelyn Caldwell."

Rose is stunned into silence. She starts replaying all of her interactions with Evelyn. Evelyn has perfected a stutter and a bit of a shake in her hands from time to time, but then Rose remembers her at the Coconut Palm Club. Her speech had no hint of a stutter. Then there was when she was threatening Rose. Her voice was clear as a bell, making sure Rose heard every word.

Rose sucks in a tight breath. She knew it. She knew Evelyn was faking her sickness all along. The whole act was made up to pull Grant away from Rose. She slams the ibuprofen onto the counter, then musters a smile for the man. "Thank you so much for your help."

As she storms out of the pharmacy, she quickly hurries into the car before letting out a frustrated scream. How manipulative is this woman? What is her sick, twisted relationship with her son that she will stop at nothing to keep him all to herself?

Rose stamps on the gas as her arms tingle with what feels like tiny drops of acid. She needs answers and she knows just where to go for them.

Ten minutes later, her tires screech to a stop in front of the Coconut Palm Country Club. Something very strange is going on and she knows these women will have some idea about it. Evelyn had planned to go to mahjong before hearing the truth about Isabel. That means the rest of them will be here.

She's going back into the lion's den.

As Rose pulls Evelyn's silver Rolls-Royce up to the valet, they are surprised to see her and not Evelyn. "I'll just be a minute," she explains, wincing at her own intrusion. "Evelyn left something she needs me to get for her."

"Of course." The dark-haired valet smiles his bright white teeth at her. As she walks in, it dawns on her that she is not wearing the right clothes. Suddenly feeling very self-conscious, she looks down at her jean shorts and pink spaghetti-strap tank top with no bra.

But it's too late to turn back now because she's already here. "Hello," Rose says almost apologetically to the blonde woman behind the front desk. "Emily, right?"

The woman nods, but eyes her suspiciously.

"I'm terribly sorry for my appearance," she starts. Then points at herself. "I'm Rose, Evelyn's daughter-in-law."

Emily's face feigns mild recognition.

"She had to cancel coming to mahjong because she has a terrible headache, but I believe Dorothy has something of Evelyn's that she wants me to pick up."

Emily assesses her disapprovingly and clicks her tongue.

"If it will only be for a moment, then for Evelyn, of course." She gives a forced smile.

"Thank you," Rose says appreciatively.

She is snaking her way through the hall when she runs square into a man lugging a pair of golf clubs on his shoulder.

"Sorry about that," Rose says apologetically.

"It's okay." He smiles, looking oddly familiar to her somehow.

"Good game, Trexler." Another man in a golf uniform fist-bumps him walking past.

"Catch you next time," Trexler says back.

"Mr. Whitehall," Emily calls. "There's a message for you at the front desk."

"You're Trexler Whitehall?" Rose asks. She recognizes him from pictures that Grant has of the two of them on his desk in their apartment. Trexler is the face, and Grant is the silent partner. She has been trying to meet him for a year at this point.

He stops for a moment, lifting his white baseball cap as if to get a better look at her, then smiles. "I'm so sorry. Do we know each other?"

"Oh, right, I'm sorry." Rose feels foolish. "I'm Rose Caldwell, I'm married to Grant Caldwell."

"Oh, Grant Caldwell." He shakes her hand formally. "Right. I haven't heard that name in a long time. How is he doing?"

Rose looks at him strangely. "What do you mean?"

Trexler shrugs his shoulders. "I just haven't heard from the guy in, what, maybe a decade. I was just curious what he's been up to."

"Oh, I'm sorry," Rose says. "I must be confused. Grant told me he's your silent business partner, or at least that of *a* Trexler Whitehall. Maybe I'm thinking of the wrong person."

He clears his throat. "Not too many people I know with my name, but yeah, it's not me." He looks at her curiously, then shrugs his shoulders again as if brushing her off as a confused housewife. "Either way, it was nice to meet you."

"You too," she says, avoiding eye contact as she slinks away.

What was that about?

She scans the hallway for the nearest bathroom. Walking further down the hall, she spots a ladies' room and ducks inside, pulling her phone out of her back pocket. She goes to her inbox and searches for Trexler Whitehall's name, then reads the email that Grant sent her less than a month ago.

We did it! it reads.

This is the guy. The one that Grant has been talking about since they've been together.

All of that was just an elaborate lie?

Rose thinks back on their relationship. When they first met and kept running into each other, he claimed his office was near her gallery.

She had seen it, hadn't she? She thinks back on it now. They stopped there once; she's sure of it. The receptionist recognized him, but not in a way like she saw him every day, and when they got to his office, the name on the door wasn't his.

"I just moved offices; facilities have to update the nameplate."

Rose thinks of all the times she walked in on him with a phone to his ear, talking about "work," probably hearing her coming. Was he ever talking to anyone or was it a ruse?

Someone walks into the bathroom and startles her out of her trance. She can't think about this now.

Instead, she leaves the bathroom and heads up the stairs, seeing the familiar flock of women in their bright colors. She cranes her neck, trying to spot Dorothy, but not before several women eye her up and down.

She tries to ignore them, until her eyes finally land on Dorothy, at the bar with her martini and bright pink dress talking to a slightly plump woman in a floral pantsuit.

Dorothy catches her eye, and Rose awkwardly waves her over.

Dorothy cocks her eyebrow in intrigue and excuses herself from the pack.

"Making an even bigger impression this time, I see." She looks at Rose's torn jean shorts and back at the women. "You'll be the talk of the party now."

"I need to speak with you for a moment." Rose looks around, then points her finger towards the outdoor balcony.

Dorothy takes a sip of her drink. "Of course."

She holds it up to Rose. "Need one of these?"

"I'm fine," Rose says dismissively.

Rose leads the way, bringing them out to a stone balcony that overlooks the beach club. Green and white umbrellas speckle the sand, shading white loungers. To the right is a large pool surrounded by personalized cabanas with open wooden doors that reveal private bathrooms and showers, seating areas indoors and out, and a small kitchenette and television.

Rose is hoping for a slight breeze of relief from the hot sun burning her skin, but even the ocean is still.

"I'm sorry to say, dear, but here at the Coconut Palm you should make more of an effort to blend in."

Rose rolls her eyes. "You know, it's odd calling this place the Coconut Palm Club."

"How so?"

"Well, I mean, coconuts are an invasive species to Florida. A trade ship carrying them sank, they washed up on the shores, and grew into coconut palm trees."

Dorothy smirks. "Pretty clever on your part. How do you know so much about coconuts? Aren't you from New York?"

"I have a curious teenager. He likes to look things up." Rose shrugs and leans her elbows on the stone balcony. "I mean, most of the women here are invasive species. You show up seasonally and are threatened by anyone who doesn't conform to your lifestyle."

Dorothy smiles, leaning on the railing. "So, in regard to invasive species, what did the old bag do to you? I see she's not here." Dorothy spots Missy through the glass door with a concerned look on her face, trying to make her way over to them, but Dorothy makes a point of shooing her away before turning back to Rose.

"No, she's staying home today."

"Must be something big, because Evelyn never misses a mahjong game."

Rose hesitates for a moment. She doesn't want to stir up gossip, but she needs some information and is convinced that Dorothy is the one that will give it to her.

"Dorothy, what can you tell me about Anita Gonzales?"

Dorothy squints at her, confused, cocking her head ever so slightly.

"She was Evelyn's maid back in New York, early 2000s, when Grant was in high school," Rose says.

Dorothy's face floods with recognition. "Oh my goodness. Anita, of course." She takes another sip and looks out towards the ocean. "Her daughter was killed tragically." She shakes her head. "What a horrible ordeal, and then, of course, Harrison died shortly after that." She looks up at Rose and Rose can tell she isn't all that upset over it. "It was quite the scandal."

"What do you mean, scandal?"

"It's just that no one really believed it was a random hit. First Maria, then Harrison. It all seemed too coincidental."

"So, what exactly are you trying to say?"

Dorothy shrugs her shoulders and takes another sip, making Rose second guess whether this was a good idea or not. Dorothy doesn't seem to know anything aside from the rumors she clearly stirs up.

"Maria was what, seventeen, eighteen at the time? What does that have to do with Harrison?"

"Well, there was gossip that the two might have been having an affair. Maria was over at the Caldwells' a lot because Anita worked there and who knows, maybe someone walked in on something?"

Rose thinks back to her conversation with Grant. He doesn't think his father was a good man, so it would make sense if he was a philanderer. But still, it was a hard pill to swallow.

"Was Harrison known for cheating on Evelyn?" Rose asks this before remembering that Missy said they had shared a fiancé at one point. But she doesn't know if that was necessarily at the same time or not.

"Oh, he chased anything with a skirt." Dorothy swats her hand. "Evelyn just turned a blind eye and pretended it wasn't happening. But everyone has their breaking point, don't they?"

"Is that what everyone believes?"

Dorothy props her elbow on the stone railing. "I wouldn't doubt it for a second."

Isabel

"Hello, is this the NYPD?" Isabel asks through her car speaker.

"Yes. Is this an emergency?"

"No, it's about a cold case that happened back in March 2003. Maria Gonzales. Is the person who worked the case still there?"

"Do you have additional information that would help the case?"

"No," Isabel says sadly. "I'm her daughter and I just wanted to have a better understanding of what happened that night." It felt strange asking about a completely different version of her mother's death to the one she'd always believed to be true.

"What is your name?"

"Isabel Martinez."

"And can you please provide me again with the name of the victim in the investigation?"

"Maria Gonzales. March of 2003."

"Let me get your number and we can call you back."

"Thank you." Isabel hangs up.

Isabel bites her fingernail, thinking about Grant rejecting her like that, when she had hard evidence that he was her father. Was he thrown because maybe he is her father, but someone other than Maria is her mother? But who? And why would her grandmother raise Grant's child?

She pulls out a notebook, the one she uses for James's tutoring sessions, and tries to write it all down. There are more questions than answers, which frustrates her. There isn't any way to really dig up her grandmother's past, right?

When it comes to her grandmother, she ponders what she knows. Born in Mexico, she worked as a maid in New York, for some of that period for the Caldwells. Nowhere is there a record of her other clients. Her grandmother never told Isabel who her grandfather was, either. It was just secrets on top of secrets. She literally has no other family anywhere that she can talk to.

What about friends?

Isabel thinks about her own schooling at Columbia. She had gotten a scholarship that paid for some of the tuition, but her grandmother had urged her not to worry and she'd come up with the rest of the money. And she had, but how? Had she been saving the whole time?

After Maria died, she'd moved out to the suburbs of Pennsylvania.

Her grandmother dated no one and while she was friendly with some of Isabel's friends' parents, she can't think of anyone her grandmother might've divulged her secrets to.

Her grandmother hadn't had a lot of trust in people. She knew her grandmother had loved her, but the harsh reality was she hadn't trusted her, which was why she'd chosen to keep her in the dark.

Then again, look at her. Look where she is. But did her grandmother really expect that she would sit back and just accept things as they are?

One thing she has to admit to herself is that her grandmother had her reasons. But was she lying to Isabel to protect her? Or to protect herself?

Isabel thinks about a fight she had with her grandmother one day. She had come home from school, slamming the door behind her, prompting her grandmother to come out of the kitchen to see what the matter was.

"I don't understand. How could you not know who my father is?" Isabel had come home angry after she had heard several of her friends were going to a Yankees game with their dads. Isabel was upset over feeling left out, but more about the awkward conversations she'd had to have over the years when people asked about her father.

Was he dead? Were her parents divorced? All of these questions that she didn't know how to answer.

"Because I don't," her grandmother had told her, matter-of-factly.

"You were her mother, weren't you?"

Her grandmother had looked at her then, eyebrows raised, but Isabel was only getting started.

"Of course I was."

"Then was she a slut or something?"

"You watch your mouth, young lady." Her grandmother's voice was tight with warning.

"If you were her mother, and she wasn't sleeping with lots of guys, then why don't you know? Did she hide him from you?"

"You listen to me." Her grandmother stood up and gripped Isabel's arm, hard. "It doesn't concern you."

"It's my father, of course it concerns me." Isabel pulled her arm away. "My only guess is that you don't like him, and therefore I'm never allowed to see him. You can't just control me like that, it's my life too. I have a right to know who my father is and if you're not going to tell me, then I'll simply find him myself."

"Don't you dare!" Her grandmother's voice roared through the apartment. Isabel had never heard her use her voice like that.

"If I don't want you to know who your father is, it's for an important reason. They are dangerous people."

When Isabel pulls into her parking garage, her phone rings again. She looks down, not recognizing the number, but assumes that it is the police calling her back.

"Hello?"

"Isabel Martinez?"

"Yes?"

"This is Detective Swanson."

Isabel jumps at the abrupt voice but recovers quickly.

"I just pulled up my files for that case." The voice is more sympathetic now. "It was terrible. I'm sorry for your loss."

Isabel's throat constricts. Is it her loss? She wasn't even alive at the time. Maria may not even be her mother. What she can grieve, though, is the loss of the life she thought she had.

"Can you walk me through it?"

"We have little to go off. From what we gathered, she was walking in Central Park at night alone. Someone came up and shot her in the chest."

"Was it a robbery?"

"They didn't appear to take anything. She still had a purse."

"What type of gun was used?"

"We would need both the gun and the bullets together in order to confirm the analysis, but based on the bullet, we believe it to be a Glock, fired at close range."

Isabel wonders how horrible that must've been. Someone hit her in the chest, which means she saw her assailant, maybe even looked them in the eye. Those last few moments of terror she must've felt, a gun pointed at her, her life over in seconds.

"Is there anything else you can tell me?"

"Unfortunately, that's all we have to go on. Do you have any information that you think could assist with this case?"

"No," she says. "I don't think so."

"Then is there anything else I can help you with?"

"No," Isabel says again, almost on the verge of tears. "Thank you."

She hangs up, and a cry escapes her throat. So it's true. Maria was not her mother. If the police can confirm that the body was indeed Maria Gonzales, then she couldn't have had Isabel.

Why the lies?

An alert goes off on Isabel's calendar, startling her. She looks down at her phone and curses. She forgot she was giving a test tomorrow, and she hasn't compiled it yet. All her materials, including her work laptop, are still at the school.

Her grandmother's words echo in her mind once more. *They are dangerous people.*

The Caldwells initially appeared to be far from dangerous. She has spent time with them, and they seemed nice enough. Grant was especially friendly, which was why she thought she could confront them about the information she had learned.

Isabel's face hardens. That was before she knew the truth. That someone shot and killed her mother—or the woman she thought was her mother.

Was that what her grandmother meant by dangerous people? She had thought she only said that to keep her away.

Did the Caldwells have something to do with Maria's murder?

Isabel's head spins again. She can't really concentrate on this right now. She's simply circling the drain. She's not going to get any bursts of inspiration to help her at this moment.

Isabel needs the distraction of some actual work. Maybe once she's cleared her head, she'll be able to figure out what her next move should be.

She pulls out of her parking spot and turns around to head back to the school. Her heart feels as if it's beating faster than normal in her chest. What does all this mean now? Should she try to get her job at Whitmore back? She assumes she will no longer be tutoring James. It's a shame. She liked him and the idea that they possibly could've been siblings. With him growing up as a lonely child just like she did, she had sought comfort in having someone else in her life she could look out for.

The drive back to campus seems to take longer than normal, but she's in such a daze she finds herself missing turns and going below the speed limit. When she does finally arrive, the sun has settled behind the trees, offering a sense of relief from the day's heat, but then she takes in the rolling dark clouds. It's going to storm soon.

The school is quiet. Not too many people left other than some administrators. The fields are starting to clear of soccer and field hockey players, walking away from her towards the athletics building on the opposite side, a wave of fading black shadows over the hillside.

With a deep breath, she opens the classroom door and stumbles towards her desk, where she finds her forgotten laptop.

Urging herself to focus, she sits down so she can get this done and go home. Part of her is still wondering what she's doing here in the first place. Though she has to admit, she does like teaching. It's more interesting than admin work. She's even started to appreciate the quietness of the campus. No loud city noises, just the chatter of students and the birds outside.

She looks around her classroom, although it's hard to call it that. It's just one of the many rooms in this mansion. At least once a week, her parquet floors are shined. Elaborately hanging on both sides of the window are oversized yellow drapes. On the ceiling is a painting of a blue sky and pink and white clouds, framed by gold leaf, with a white crystal chandelier suspended from the center.

It's certainly a long way from linoleum floors and painted brick walls.

She likes it here, but how can she stay after all of this?

A loud thunderous roar rattles the windows. It's dark outside now, and within a few seconds the rain starts tapping the windowpane.

"Great." Isabel realizes she left her umbrella in her car. Then again, she's just going home after this. Not seeing anyone. She's all alone. Just like her grandmother was. Maybe it was their destiny to be loners.

Another clap of thunder makes her jump, and she startles when she sees a dark shadow standing in the crack of her doorway.

She puts a hand on her chest, feeling her pulse quicken. The door swings open abruptly.

"Excuse me, miss, it's okay if I take your garbage?" The janitor smiles nervously at her, his English a bit broken.

Isabel feels stupid. "Of course." She reaches under her desk and pulls out her trash can. She waits patiently as he takes it from her and dumps the contents into a bigger garbage can on wheels. Then he hands it back to her.

"*Gracias*," she tells him, thanking him in Spanish.

"*De nada*," he answers. You're welcome.

Thirty minutes later, she finishes her tests and prints out the copies she needs. At least now, if she doesn't get any sleep over this whole mess, she doesn't have to worry about scrambling to do all this. She is thankfully now prepared for tomorrow.

Once she wraps up and sets everything on her desk, she shuts off her classroom light and locks the door behind her. As she swings her key from her lanyard, her footsteps echo through the hall and down the grand staircase that spills into the main lobby.

She's about to open the door to leave when she decides to stop and look into her mailbox. Something she has been forgetting to do, missing important meetings she was supposed to attend as a result. She wishes they would just send emails, but then she guesses busy bee Lilly would be out of a job.

She reaches in to grab a stack of papers from her cubby, her name on a sticky label below it.

On top of what looks like standard school memos is a folded note.

She picks it up curiously with one hand, then puts the other papers back so she can open it up.

As she reads it, her hand starts to shake.

Run. Get as far away from here as you can.

Evelyn

"Can I get you anything, Mrs. Caldwell?" Martha startles her from behind.

Evelyn has been spinning her diamond ring on her finger nervously, standing next to the window in the kitchen and watching the storm clouds on the horizon, a clear metaphor for her own situation.

"No, Martha, I'm fine, thank you." She gives a faint smile.

"Another bad storm coming?"

"Looks like it," Evelyn says, transfixed by the lightning strikes she sees hitting the water. She turns back to Martha. "Feel free to go home."

Martha nods appreciatively and leaves the dining room.

The gun is gone. Has Rose discovered it? Or worse, has Grant? What's even more troubling to think about is what would either of them plan to do with it?

Evelyn checks her watch. Rose still isn't back yet. It doesn't take that long to go to the pharmacy.

Did she go to the police?

Is she coming back with someone who will bring Evelyn in for questioning?

Evelyn feels as if she's going to be sick.

She doesn't know what she'll do if that happens. Either way, it will be the end of her life as she knows it. There's no getting around it.

Missy was right all along. She should've never married Harrison.

Forty years later, Evelyn still thinks about that day with the same emotion she felt when Missy confronted her. She had been angry and flushed with shame. Evelyn had never wanted to steal someone's fiancé. But she looked down at her belly and knew this was her ticket to a life she needed. She didn't have other options like Missy did. All she knew was she didn't want to go back to Nebraska, to a family that neglected her. She was young and alone in a big city, with nothing but her work and Harrison. If she left Harrison, she wouldn't have a job either, as she had been his secretary. Fear had prevented her from deciding. Now, she had to live with it.

She has to get out of here.

The front door opens, and Evelyn can hear Rose sigh as she closes the door to the garage behind her.

Evelyn meets her in the foyer, relieved to see she's alone. Still, Evelyn steals a quick glance out of the window to be sure.

"Can I have my keys, please?" Evelyn extends her palm to Rose.

"Should you be driving, with your Parkinson's?" Rose asks, pulling the pharmacy bag from her purse ready to hand it to her.

"I'm fine."

"I thought you weren't feeling well?" Rose counters.

"I'm going to the doctor," Evelyn answers, frustrated. Disregarding the pharmacy bag, she snatches the keys from Rose's hand. She struggles to open the door to the garage before it finally gives, and she pushes it open. Even though she knows she looks hysterical, it's how she feels.

"I know the truth, Evelyn."

Evelyn stops abruptly and turns around. Rose is standing there with a smug expression on her face.

"I know you're lying about having Parkinson's. The pharmacist confirmed what I had already suspected about you."

Evelyn turns quickly around and pushes through the door into the garage. Her whole body is shaking as she fumbles to get the key into the ignition.

This is bad, she thinks. This is really bad.

Evelyn remembers holding the gun in her hand. She was shaking with the realization of what had happened, what it all meant. She found it hard to breathe. Harrison found her on the floor, wails of agony escaping her body. He had pulled her up then, trying to get her to get a hold of herself. That's when he heard the loud thud of something falling from her lap onto the wood flooring, his eyes widening in fear mixed with shock.

They didn't say anything to each other after that. Then, there wasn't anything to say. Their exchanged glances said it all. Harrison knew and he would die because of it.

Now, as she grips the steering wheel so fiercely her knuckles are white, she realizes her day of reckoning has finally come.

Rose

"Damn it!"

A loud crash of what sounds like glass shattering brings Rose downstairs from her son's computer. For the first time, she hasn't heard from Grant this afternoon. He hasn't answered her calls either.

Rose pushes through the dining-room door, eager to talk to him, but stops when she finds him rummaging through the liquor bar, pouring a brown liquid into a rocks glass, another glass shattered into pieces across the floor, picking up the light like diamonds.

Rose finds a dustpan in a nearby utility closet and returns to clean the mess up.

"Sorry," he says apologetically.

"You okay?" Rose looks at him, trying to get him to make eye contact.

"Fine." Grant throws his head back, finishing the contents in one quick motion. Then he pours himself another.

Grant has never been much of a drinker, so it's off-putting to her watching him down Scotch the way he is. It makes her think of Ian and her father, what they became when they drank like this.

As he brings the glass to his lips, she notices blood on his wrist right above his watch.

"You're bleeding," she tries to tell him, pulling his arm towards her. "You look like you might have some glass in your wrist. Take your watch off and I'll get it out."

"No." He pulls away abruptly.

She rolls her eyes at him. "Seriously, Grant, I need to look at it, just take your watch off."

"Leave it alone," he says, his voice now angrier and more serious.

Rose takes a deep inhale through her nose. "Fine."

She cleans up the rest of the mess and dumps it into the garbage, her thoughts still spinning about Trexler Whitehall, and the elaborate lies that Grant told her about the two of them working together. If he hasn't been doing that, then what exactly has he been doing? Were there any real work calls at all or was it all made up? She desperately wants answers, to know what sort of pathologically deceitful family she has married into.

She suppresses her upset, worried that piling this on top of Isabel's claims will only provoke an overreaction, which won't get her anywhere. Instead, she tries to remain calm, for now.

"Do you want to talk about it?"

"Not really." He looks down into his glass.

Rose swallows uncomfortably. She feels totally lost in all of this and has no idea how to navigate it. It's like walking through a minefield in the dark.

Rose rests her hands on the back of one of the chairs. She knows she'll have to fire Isabel now. It's a shame. James has been doing great with her as his tutor, and they seem to get along really well.

But at the same time, this woman followed them down here and found a way into their home to steal a DNA sample. She can't help but feel freaked out over the whole situation.

"Where's James?" Grant asks, checking his watch and finally noticing the blood Rose pointed out. But he only wipes at it with his finger, leaving a smudge of blood across his arm.

"At a friend's house for dinner."

He rolls his eyes. "Good."

Rose stands there for a few moments, waiting on some sort of sign from Grant about what she should do. Should she leave him alone? Try to talk? She decides on the latter. His mind is on Isabel right now, so she'll just stick to that topic.

"Do you know why Isabel would think you're her father?"

"No," he answers quickly. "Other than the fact that Maria and I were friends, and her mom cleaned our house, that's all she has to go on."

"That and a DNA sample," Rose adds gently.

Grant glares at her in a way that makes her hair stand on end.

"It was a false positive. They get those things wrong all the time. Innocent people have gone to jail because of it."

"There's still something else going on here."

"What do you mean?" Grant seems to grow impatient.

Rose swallows hard. "Your mother." The words catch in her throat. How is she going to say this? That his mom lied about her Parkinson's? That Maria was killed with a Glock and that Rose coincidentally found a Glock hidden in the vent in her studio but didn't bother to tell him about it until now? "I don't think she's who you think she is."

"Think very carefully about what you're about to say." His voice is edged with warning as he pulls the dining-room chair back and takes a seat.

Rose turns to see heat lightning flashing over the water and heavy clouds of rain already approaching.

He crosses his ankle over his knee and puts his drink down. "Maria, you haven't slept since we got here. I know you've been sneaking to your studio at night to paint. You're paranoid and exhausted, and I think you're spinning a bit."

"You just called me Maria."

He pauses. Mouth open, unsure what to say. "Sorry, I clearly have a lot on my mind."

Rose raises her voice in frustration. "You know something, just tell me. I'm your wife."

"I don't know, okay?" Grant's voice is loud and it startles her. "I never slept with Maria. Maria is not even her mother. I don't understand any of it."

"Okay." Rose gives in. He doesn't know, so her hounding him won't help. "I'll leave you be," she says more softly, putting a hand on his shoulder.

He puts his hand over hers, stopping her from leaving.

"I love you very much. I'm sorry to put you through this."

She rubs her thumb over his hand before pulling away and leaving the room.

Rose feels a rising sensation inside her and she takes the stairs up two at a time. Returning to James's room, she closes the door behind her, locking it. She picks up her purse that was resting on the floor and pulls it onto the desk while looking around once more before flipping the screen of the laptop open to the ATF's e-trace website that she was researching earlier. She pulls the gun from her purse, the sound heavy on the desk.

Filling out the form, she provides the gun's type, and the serial number etched on the side.

Then she presses enter. If she can't get answers from anyone, she will simply get them herself.

A notification comes up that the ATF will answer her inquiry in twenty-four hours with the manufacturer and wholesale gun dealer. Once she knows who the gun dealer is, she can call them and identify the owner of the gun.

Rose puts the gun back in her purse, then erases her search history on the computer. Time to find out once and for all whose gun this is.

Her cell rings, startling her. She looks down at the caller ID. James, likely calling for a ride home.

"Hey." James climbs into the passenger seat of the car twenty minutes later, wet from the rain and still in his T-shirt and gym shorts from soccer practice. A faint smell of salt and sweat emanates from him. God bless Taylor's mother for offering to have a bunch of smelly boys at her house. He tosses his backpack and gym bag, likely with his uniform crumpled inside it, into the backseat.

"Hi, sweetie. How was Taylor's house?"

"It was great. He was throwing a little celebration for all of us."

Rose looks at him, confused. "What do you mean, celebration for all of you?" The rain is getting heavier now, and she increases the speed on her wiper blades.

James's smile is wide. "I made the team. They announced it this afternoon."

"Oh, sweetie, that's wonderful!" She hugs him. "Why didn't you tell me when you called to say you were going to Taylor's?"

He shrugs. "I just wanted to celebrate with the team first."

Rose feels guilty but relieved at the same time. Given the information that came to light this afternoon, no one at their house would have been in a particularly celebratory mood.

"Well, I'm glad you had fun." Rose starts the car up and pulls out of the driveway.

"Can you text Isabel that I made the team? She was eager to hear if I made it, but I didn't see her after school today and I don't have her number."

Rose's heart drops. Part of her doesn't want to tell him all this now. She wants him to enjoy his victory. But at the same time, if she doesn't, then he will look for Isabel at school tomorrow and she'll be the one to tell him. It should really come from Rose.

"About that . . ." Rose lets out a breath. "I don't think Isabel can be your tutor anymore."

James looks at her oddly. "Well, why not? I've been doing well at school thanks to her. She actually gets how I think and she teaches me in a way that makes things easier than with any other teachers I've had before."

"I get it—" Rose starts.

"So, what's the problem?"

"Isabel came to us under false pretenses."

"What does that mean?"

"It means that she followed us all the way from Whitmore in order to try to become your tutor."

James scrunches his face. "Why would she do that?"

"She was convinced that Grant was her real father, but it doesn't look like that's the case."

James creases his brows as if he's having a hard time believing it. "So, she's not Grant's daughter."

"No."

"Then what's the problem?"

"She lied to us."

"About what?"

Rose hesitates for a second. Did she lie to them? She told them she'd worked in administration at Whitmore, and she had. Rose had verified that when she called Whitmore.

Isabel wanted a teaching position at the Pelican Academy, and she is currently working there. She is a good tutor; the results are showing with James. So, he's right. What did she lie about?

Rose contemplates for a minute.

"She lied about the reason she came here in the first place."

"What was she supposed to do?"

Rose becomes flustered. "I don't know. It's a lot more complicated than I currently understand. Maybe Isabel can tutor you at school, at least. I just don't think it would be a good idea for her to come over to the house anymore."

"This is ridiculous. When am I ever going to have a say in my own life?"

Rose is taken aback. "What do you mean?"

"No one ever listens to me about what I want."

"Honey, of course I do. Everything I ever do is for you."

"Is that why you got over Dad so quickly and married Grant?"

"Things between your father and I were very complicated."

"Sure, like you were likely having an affair with Grant?"

Rose's cheeks flush red like she has been slapped. "How dare you speak to me that way. I never cheated on your father; it was the other way around."

James looks at her, stunned into silence.

"I'm sorry." Rose shakes her head. "I never meant for that to come out. I want you to remember your father and who he was to you. But as far as your dad and I were concerned, it'd been over for a long time. I stayed with him for you."

"So now it's my fault."

Rose shakes her head. "Nothing is your fault."

"I didn't even want to go to that stupid Whitmore prep school. I didn't want to move out of our apartment. I didn't want to go to the Pelican Academy, and I didn't want to move here."

Rose looks at him, flabbergasted. "I know it was hard, but it's what's best for you."

"No, it's what best for *you*. You wanted to erase Dad's memory, so you agreed to move out of the one place that reminded me of him and move us into this alternate universe or whatever. But it doesn't make anything better.

"Isabel is the only one that seems to get me. She comes from the same background. She's an only child, and she gets how much that sucks. And now that I've finally found someone who understands me, you're telling me that I can't see her anymore."

James slams his hand on the window.

"James." Rose is at a loss for words. She's never seen him act like this and she feels as if she's on the back foot.

She pulls slowly into their driveway, unsure if they should even go in right now. There is enough going on with Grant and Evelyn; they don't need James coming in this hostile as well.

James shakes his head angrily and points at the house. "These people." He looks at her. "These people are the ones you should be worried about. Not Isabel."

James gets out and slams the door, leaving Rose stunned, the rain pelting hard on the windshield now as she realizes that her son is probably right.

Isabel

"Isabel."

Isabel turns her head and spots James standing in her doorway in his school uniform and his backpack hanging at his side.

"James." She sits at her desk, coming out of her daze. She's had no sleep and has been staring out the window; everything is still damp from the storm, much like her thoughts.

"Sorry, James, classes start soon. You have to get going," she urges. "We can talk later."

He ignores her, closing the door behind him.

"My students are going to be coming in any second and you're going to be late for class," she repeats.

"This is bullshit," he says sternly.

Isabel's eyes widen in surprise. She can't tell if he is mad at her. She wouldn't blame him if he was.

"James, I'm sorry."

"Don't be. This is not your fault, it's them." He points away from her, in the imagined direction of his house. "It's not fair that just because you wanted to know who your father is, that I'm not allowed to have you as a tutor anymore."

"Look, if you'd like, I can continue to write out exercises for you to do." She stops herself, now thinking about the note she found. *Get as far away from here as you can.* "Listen, I agree with your parents—"

"They're not my parents," he says angrily. "Grant is not my father."

"Right," she says softly, trying to calm him down.

"It wasn't about the tutoring sessions," he says, more upset. "I think it would've been cool to have you as a stepsister." Half his mouth rises into a smile.

She nods. "I would've liked that as well."

His edge finally softens. "I made the soccer team."

Isabel smiles. "Congratulations, I knew you would."

The bell rings, causing James to look up at the clock above her door.

"First bell." He points his thumb behind him. "Better get going."

"I'll see you around," she says in a hopeful tone to soften the blow.

"See you around," he says more sadly, as her classroom door opens and teenagers start to file in. He gets swallowed up by the crowd of students piling in and, before she knows it, he's gone.

"Okay, class, test day," Isabel announces, wiping her sweaty palms on her black pants. She can feel her underarms prickling with sweat beneath her blue button-down shirt.

A collective groan ripples across the room. "I know you all will do well, just trust yourselves." She stands up from her desk and counts out the number of tests she needs to hand out to each row.

"You have the entire class time to work on it."

The second bell rings for the start of class. "Begin now."

Isabel circles back to her desk and lifts her laptop. She thinks about James's words just now.

It would've been cool to have you as a stepsister.

There was a thought.

She googles false positive DNA results, trying to get an understanding of how common it is.

Isabel clicks on random articles that come up. There are a lot of factors that can cause a false positive. She could've used a not good enough sample, or somehow contaminated it. Maybe there were lab errors that were out of her control, like human error in the testing, or they simply mixed her results up with someone else's.

She pulls out the envelope from her purse in her desk drawer. She reads it again and again. They used the hair follicles that she had provided. She scans how the test was done and the results once more.

Isabel isn't a scientist, but she doesn't think this is a mistake. She could demand another sample from Grant. After all, the lab couldn't get it wrong twice, right? But something tells her that the way Grant responded, he has no interest in being her father, and would most certainly not agree to another test.

Isabel keeps scrolling when she comes to a DNA diagnostic site. Maybe this will help her better understand her results, she figures.

The website is very straightforward, on the verge of clinical, but Isabel can understand it pretty well.

Her eyes scroll across a sentence that makes her ears prick. She hadn't thought about it before, but it makes sense.

There are sixteen markers for a paternity test. There is a possibility that the person who is not the father can match that of the child when the DNA matches other family members.

Other family members.

Isabel waits until lunchtime, staring at the clock, urging it to move faster. When the bell finally rings, she is the first one up. "Tests on my desk, please," she calls out as she opens her classroom door.

"Someone has to pee," she hears one of the student joke.

She doesn't care how it looks; she needs to understand this better. She searches the sea of students filing out into the hallway, staring at the tops of their heads, until finally she spots James.

"James!" she calls out and waves to him.

He turns his head from the boy he is talking to and looks at her, concerned. She watches as he tells his friend he'll be right back and he follows her to her classroom, where the last of the students are putting their tests on her desk.

"Time's up, Mr. Walker," she calls to the last student in the back, sweating out the last few test questions.

He looks up nervously at her.

"I'll give extra credit points, if need be," she tells him. He has been trying but is struggling. She isn't looking to fail anyone. She also wants him out of her classroom now.

He stands up, putting his test on her desk, and walks out just as James is approaching her door.

James notices the look on her face and closes the door behind him.

"What's up?"

Isabel circles around to the front of her desk, leaning back on it and crossing her arms. James takes the cue and puts his backpack on one of the chairs and sits on the desk.

"What can you tell me about your step-grandfather?"

He shrugs his shoulders. "What do you mean?"

"So, I'm not sure how much you know," she starts.

"Assume I don't know anything. My mom thinks she's protecting me, though from what, I don't know. Tell me everything."

"Well. My grandmother raised me. I was told my mother Maria died during childbirth with me. But yesterday, when I confronted Grant about the DNA results, he told me that not only was I not his daughter but also that Maria couldn't be my mother because she didn't die in childbirth; someone killed her in Central Park."

James looks at her curiously.

"Six months before I was even born."

His eyes widened. "Whoa."

Isabel wonders if she's making a mistake telling James. He's only fourteen. But she has no one else to bounce these ideas off and she's going out of her mind. She decides to keep going.

"Maybe Grant's right. He's not my father, but that doesn't mean the DNA was wrong, necessarily."

"So, you think . . ." he starts but then trails off.

Isabel pulls on her bottom lip. "Maybe Harrison is my real father. And because he shares DNA with Grant, that's why it came up positive."

James looks down at the wood floor, tapping his shoe nervously.

Isabel homes in on him. "You know something, don't you?"

"I don't know what I know," he says, more nervous now.

"James, please."

James sucks in a breath. "There was also this weird thing that happened . . ." He trails off again.

Isabel crosses her arms, her head forward, urging him along.

"I found Harrison's wedding ring in the desk drawer in the room I'm staying in. Evelyn kind of got weirded out because I guess he was supposed to have been buried with it. I don't know if it means anything, but everything got really awkward when I asked her how he died."

Isabel turns around and grabs her phone off her desk. She googles Harrison Caldwell. She finds results of him as some sort of oil tycoon, but nothing written about his cause of death.

Isabel bites her lip in thought then googles conspiracy theories around Harrison's death. Someone that important with no cause of death mentioned would definitely draw some attention, though she has to remind herself that any theories were still hypothetical. Sure enough, more articles start to pop up. She clicks on a few until she draws a conclusion based on what most of the articles are saying.

"It says here that he died from anaphylactic shock on the subway." Isabel feels a heavy weight resting on her chest. "I'm allergic to nuts as well."

James looks at her oddly. "Really?"

Isabel nods, her mouth now dry. She reads on until she finishes the article she's alighted on. "Do we think he was poisoned?" she asks.

James shrugs. "I don't know."

Isabel scans the article again. "Why would someone as well-off as him take the subway?"

James shrugs. "Maybe there was a traffic jam, and he was running late?"

"People wait for a man like Harrison Caldwell," Isabel rationalizes. "This reads like an unfortunate freak accident, but I think these people might be on to something. I think he was poisoned."

"Who would poison him?"

"For Harrison Caldwell, that's the million-dollar question," she says. She scrolls back up to the top of the article. Her grip around the phone tightens. She swallows the lump in her throat.

"What is it?" James asks, noticing the look on her face.

She notes the date of his death. "Harrison died within a week of Maria."

"What does that mean?" James asks, not catching on.

"It means that I think their deaths might be connected in some way."

"Are you sure?"

Isabel nods, slowly remembering the note in her office mailbox. "I got a note."

"What do you mean, a note?"

"I got a note in my mailbox here." She points downstairs in the direction of the front office. "It said, *Run. Get as far away from here as you can.*"

"Did you report it?"

Isabel shakes her head. "I haven't been able to make sense of how to even convey this to the police."

"You have to do something," James says.

"You're right," Isabel agrees. "Whatever this is, we are on to something, and someone is worried we're too close."

Evelyn

The smell of wet pavement from the storm last night fills Evelyn's nostrils as she parks her car at the Sailfish Yacht Club. This is the second time she's driven herself in a very long time. Yesterday she just tried to clear her head, but it didn't work. When she got back to the house, she overheard Grant and Rose in the dining room and took the opportunity to sneak up to her room for the night.

The moisture in the air is thick, making it hard to breathe, but Evelyn doesn't care. She might only have a few more days of freedom left, and she wants to go for a walk and try to figure out her next move.

The Lake Trail is a walking path that runs along most of the island facing the Intracoastal. From the parking lot Evelyn walks down a narrow jungle-like path until she reaches the open trail. It's a paved walkway, so not exactly a nature walk, but it's beautiful. Large houses of all different styles line the trail, with tall privacy hedges and a gate that allows them to cross the trail over to their private docks, some with boat houses and yachts that drift in the water.

She's unsure of Rose's intentions, but more afraid of Grant asking questions. Only, he's never been like this before. It's almost worse in some ways. Instead of questioning her and allowing her to defend herself, he instead makes his own assumptions, which can be inherently worse.

But would he know she was lying? He's always been able to see right through her. It's how he's gotten away with everything he has. He, on some level, knows the truth about her and he holds it over her like a guillotine, threatening to drop it down on her whenever he wants.

Evelyn is suddenly taken by surprise when she hears the urgent ringing of a bell and a cyclist flying past her so fast, she almost gets knocked over.

She leans against a bench and sits for a moment, trying to slow her speeding heart rate. She needs a drink.

By the time she walks back to her car, it's almost lunchtime. She drives the few blocks over to the Coconut Palm Country Club, relieved that mahjong was yesterday. Most of the women she knows will be at tennis today, which means at least the club will hopefully be empty this afternoon.

Evelyn pulls up, the valet smiling at her well-known silver Rolls-Royce.

"Mrs. Caldwell," he greets her and opens her door.

"Thank you, Patrick." She slips him a twenty-dollar bill from the pocket of her white cropped pants and removes her sunglasses to put them in her wicker purse.

"Mrs. Caldwell." Emily smiles from her usual spot at the front desk.

"Hello, Emily." Evelyn smiles.

"Did you get what you needed yesterday?"

Evelyn looks at her curiously. "No, I couldn't attend yesterday. I had a splitting headache."

"I'm so sorry to hear that." Emily's face falls into a sympathetic frown. "But I believe you sent your daughter-in-law to retrieve something for you. She stopped in yesterday. I was just confirming that she was able to retrieve for you what you needed?"

Evelyn stiffens but doesn't want to let on that she has no idea what Emily's talking about. "Yes, of course, thank you."

She quickens her pace down the hall.

What the hell was Rose doing here?

She couldn't possibly know anything. Did Grant send her? And if so, what did they expect to find?

Evelyn climbs the stairs and sees the maître d' is already waiting for her at the top.

"Mrs. Caldwell." His round puffy cheeks swallow up the edges of his mouth as he smiles. "Will you be dining with us today?" His hands are clasped together in front of his white button-down and black pants.

"Yes, Emilio, that would be wonderful."

He extends a hand. "Right this way."

Emilio leads her through the dining room, already reset after yesterday's mahjong tournament to its rightful elegance of cream-colored tablecloths with green porcelain plates and silverware with bamboo handles.

"Is this table suitable?" Emilio asks. "It has the best view, but if there is too much sun next to the window, let me know."

"It's fine, Emilio, thank you."

Evelyn sits down, putting her purse on the table to retrieve her sunglasses yet again.

"Can I get you started with a drink?"

"Martini, please." She puts her sunglasses on. "Extra dirty."

"Of course," Emilio says in a way that shows he knows her order all too well.

Evelyn sits stiffly, staring out at the ocean, until another waiter, Stephan, a young man in his late twenties with a sleek quiff of hair, makes an elaborate gesture of sweeping the martini from his serving tray to her table.

"Thank you, Stephan."

"And the menu." He removes it from his tray to place it in front of her.

She doesn't take it. "I'll just have the Cobb salad as usual."

"Right away, Mrs. Caldwell." He takes the menu back and disappears.

Evelyn takes a shaky sip of her martini, wondering how Grant is taking all of this, what he might suspect. She never knows with him.

As if her thoughts have summoned him, she hears someone call, "Mom."

She looks up to see Grant coming in through the side door, catching her off guard. She puts on a smile.

"Hello, Grant." She puts her hands up on his shoulders while she tilts her cheek towards him to kiss. Grant sits down, his hair still wet from his shower, and pulls his chair in closer to her.

"I wanted to talk to you, but you snuck out. Renaldo was home so I didn't realize you'd left. Did you drive yourself?"

"I was . . . fine to drive," she dismisses him.

He doesn't argue. "Listen, I have a business proposition for you, or rather, us," he says fairly light-heartedly, which makes Evelyn shift in her seat.

She drums her fingers on the table. "What is it?"

"I'm doing what you've been asking of me. I'm finally going to get myself a job." He smiles.

"That's . . . wonderful, sweetie," she says, though she doesn't quite believe it. It's as if he's putting on some sort of performance. But then, Grant has always been able to compartmentalize his emotions. Maybe he's chosen to put the whole situation with Maria on hold for now.

"I'm going to invest in a warehouse business."

"What sort of w-warehouse business?"

"I've been speaking with investors about a business model storing people's cars. They want them to be cared for and attended to all year. Not only that, but they need to build something that's hurricane proof to protect their investments. We're going to expand that into wine collections, and any other items that people value and want stored properly.

It can include a wine-tasting or car-viewing room where clients can hang out."

"Sounds like a man cave." Missy comes up behind Evelyn, making her jump at the sound of her voice.

"In a way it is," Grant says politely, but she can sense that he feels annoyed by the intrusion into their conversation.

"Where is it located?" Missy, in her tennis whites, pulls out a chair from the table.

Grant looks uncomfortable but clears his throat and proceeds. "It's in Riviera Beach."

"What's it called?" Missy continues to fire off questions.

"Right now, it's just an empty warehouse building that was formerly used as a storage unit for shipping containers over by the docks, but we're looking to move in."

"Well, good for you," Missy says, tapping his shoulder approvingly.

Evelyn's fingers tighten around the stem of her drink.

Grant looks at Missy and then to Evelyn, realizing he's not going to get any further in this conversation. "There will be a few sheets of paper that I'll need you to sign later."

Evelyn nods.

"Well, it was nice seeing you, Missy. I'll be getting back to Rose."

They both watch as Grant leaves.

"What do you want, Missy?" Evelyn takes a sip of her drink, not having the energy to deal with her.

"We were sorry to have missed you yesterday," Missy says in a sarcastic tone.

Evelyn lets out a laugh.

"We did get a visit from your daughter-in-law, though."

Evelyn stops, her drink suspended halfway to her lips. She puts it back down. "What do you mean, exactly?"

Missy shrugs her shoulders. "So, what happened that we missed you yesterday?"

"I had a headache," Evelyn explains.

"Evelyn, I've known you for forty years. You don't get headaches, you give them."

"Well, what did my daughter-in-law have to say?" Evelyn steamrolls over the interrogation.

"She did mention that you were feeling under the weather, but from what I heard from Dorothy, she asked to know more about Anita."

Evelyn's eyes flick from the table to Missy.

Missy cocks an eyebrow. "I was wondering, why?"

"I'm not quite sure," Evelyn answers, drumming her fingers on the tablecloth.

Missy clearly doesn't believe her. "It's just so strange to me that Rose would have any sort of interest in your old maid. Perhaps it has to do with that salacious scandal twenty years ago. Has something happened that would bring attention back to all that?"

"Why would you say that?"

"Well, unfortunately a lot of women here have an opinion on the whole affair. It would only take the slightest hint of smoke for a fire to start again."

"They don't know any details, Missy. You weren't there, and neither was I."

"Rumors don't just come from nowhere, Evelyn. They come from the belief that there is an essence of truth to them. Just because it couldn't be proven, doesn't mean everyone is unaware of what happened there."

"Your Cobb salad." Stephan places the plate in front of Evelyn. Neither woman looks up at him.

"And can I get anything for you, Mrs. Fanwood?"

"I'm alright." Missy stands up. "Might need to get her a to-go bag. I don't think she's going to have much of an appetite."

Missy gives a wiggle of her fingers and turns to leave the restaurant.

Evelyn reaches for her water, trying to bring it to her lips as it shakes in her hand. Eventually, she gives up and places it back down, spilling it across the table.

Stephan approaches quickly with a napkin to clean it up.

"I've got it, Mrs. Caldwell," he tells her reassuringly as she places a hand on her forehead. "Are you alright? Can I get you anything?"

"I'm fine, thank you," Evelyn says, trying to keep the strain out of her voice.

"I'll be right back with more water," he tells her.

Evelyn holds her breath. Missy is right. It could never be proven before, but given the gun is now missing and Rose is asking questions, she realizes that soon it will all come to a head. And she's going to go to jail for murder.

Rose

Sorry to have snuck out, I had a last-minute business meeting. I'll be home shortly. Miss you already.

Rose can't help but roll her eyes as she shoves the phone back into her pocket. Part of her wonders if there is a meeting at all. Like the situation with Trexler, he might just be blowing smoke. But as mad as she is, she doesn't have time to interrogate him. She's upstairs stressing about her most recent painting, though it's impossible to try to work with everything that's been going on. She looks around at the rest of her canvases, stacked against the walls, and shakes her head. They're terrible and Lina is going to see that. How is Rose going to survive this show if even she doesn't like her own work?

Rose checks her watch. Lina will be landing in Miami shortly and she's going to meet her for lunch. She'll want to see pictures of what Rose has been doing, but Rose knows she doesn't have anything good to show her. She's nowhere near ready.

She hears the faint ring of the doorbell downstairs but continues with her work.

Moments later, she hears Martha behind her.

"I'm sorry to bother you, Mrs. Caldwell."

Rose turns around and smiles. "Please, call me Rose. There's only room for one Mrs. Caldwell in this household."

Martha smiles, agreeing. "Rose. There is a Lina Prose downstairs to see you."

Rose narrows her eyes, looking at her confusedly. Lina is supposed to be in Miami.

Rose follows Martha downstairs to find Lina in a black dress and heels with a large white pearl necklace draped across her collarbone. She's standing in the atrium, admiring the freshly cut roses on the hall table.

"Lina!" Rose calls from the stairs, causing Lina to pick her head up. "What are you doing here? I thought I was going to be meeting you in Miami?" she says in an upbeat way while trying to suppress the nervousness in her voice.

"You were, but my flight got canceled. Something is going on at Miami Airport and I thought, why not change my flight to Palm Beach International? That way I can meet up with you, see what you've been up to and then just get a car service to drive me the hour to Miami."

Rose still stares at her, dumbfounded.

"Did you not get my text?" Lina holds her phone up.

Rose jumps and pulls her phone out from her smock. Somehow, she completely missed it. Then again, to say she's been a bit distracted is an understatement. A nervous knot forms in her stomach. Her head's on the block, and now it's all up to Lina.

"I'm so sorry, Lina, I didn't see it, but I'm so glad you're here."

"What a place!" Lina gives a twirl with her arms extended. Her black hair is still perfectly straight and curls neatly around her sharp chin. "So, where have you been working?" Lina asks.

"Evelyn was nice enough to turn her old sewing room into an art studio for me." Rose reaches the bottom of the steps and points back up.

Lina clasps her hands together. "Oh, how wonderful. I can't wait to see it."

Rose tries stalling. "Can I get you anything to eat or drink first?"

Lina flicks her red fingernails. "No need. Let's see your work." She points her finger up the stairs. "Then we'll grab lunch somewhere afterwards."

"Sure." Rose tries to smooth back her own hair, with strays popping out from her ponytail.

Lina eyes her. "You know my routine. That gives you time to shower while I have a look and see what you've done."

Rose's jaw clenches as she nods. "It's right this way." She leads Lina up the several flights of stairs, leaving her at the open door below her studio.

Lina huffs. "More steps? How does your mother-in-law handle this place?"

Rose shrugs her shoulders. "I'll be ready in ten minutes."

Lina eyes the upstairs curiously and waves her hand at Rose, signaling for her to go.

Rose rushes to get showered, but this time, catching a glimpse of herself in the mirror, takes a minute to care more about her appearance. She twists her wet hair into a bun, applies makeup—basic foundation, mascara and red lipstick—then puts on a sleek black romper.

Rose's heart is beating out of her chest as she drags her feet up the back stairs to the studio.

When she reaches the top of the steps, Lina is standing in her trademark stance: one leg jutted out, a finger pressed against her cheek.

"You're not quite there yet," Lina says without turning around.

Rose's stomach drops. "I'm trying, Lina, I promise. There's been a lot going on and I can't seem to get back into it the way I normally can."

"You have something here, though." Lina points towards her canvas still sitting on the easel. "It's not quite done, but I can feel the energy of this one." She turns back to Rose. "So, what are we calling it?"

Rose crosses her arms, staring back at her painting. Again, she is reminded of Dorian Gray, from Oscar Wilde's novel. The same crimson red dripped from the shadow figure's fingers, though Rose has added a spray of red down from the heart, the heaviness of the paint sliding down the image.

"Rage," Rose finally says.

"I like it." Lina smiles. "If you can produce more of this," she points, "then you should be good, but remember, you don't have much time."

Rose nods obediently. "I know. I'll work on it."

Lina nods then checks her watch, her bracelets clinking against one another. "Then let's go to lunch."

After lunch, Rose pulls back into her driveway and checks her phone, discovering an email from the ATF. Her forehead tingles with sweat.

She opens it, feeling her heart racing. As promised, she has the information about the manufacturer and the wholesale retailer.

Outdoor Sports and Co.

She knows them as a common chain across the country. She googles the number and calls them, still sitting in her car.

"Outdoor Sports and Co."

"Hello, I'm looking for the name of the owner of a certain gun that was purchased from one of your stores," Rose says shakily.

"Just a moment."

Rose drums her fingers rapidly on the steering wheel.

"Outdoor Sports and Co. hunting department."

"Hello, I'm looking to find the previous owner of a specific gun?"

"Can you provide the type of gun and serial number?"

Rose reads off the information.

"Let's see," he says after Rose hears the typing on the other end stop. Now she imagines he is scrolling the information on the computer.

"It appears that the gun was registered to Anita Gonzales, purchased on August seventeenth, 1985."

Anita's gun?

"Is there anything else I can help you with?" the person at the other end says when Rose doesn't respond.

"Um, no, sorry, that's it. Thanks."

Rose hangs up the phone, staring out the front windshield in confusion. She watches the palm trees sway in the breeze against a pale blue sky. The essence of calm, yet her mind is anything but.

Why does Evelyn have Anita's gun?

The possibilities swirl around Rose. Did Evelyn use Anita's gun to kill her daughter, Maria?

Did Anita kill her own daughter, and Evelyn hid the evidence for her? But why? Was it all just some horrible accident?

"What are you doing out here?" Grant knocks on the door, causing her to jump.

"You scared me." She opens the door and steps out.

"Why are you sitting in your car?"

"I just had my meeting with Lina today. She surprised me and showed up here."

"What did she say?" he asks cautiously.

"That it's not quite there yet."

He rubs his hand up and down her arm. "I'm sorry."

But Rose can't help but feel his sympathy isn't that genuine, like he's almost glad that's what happened. It infuriates her.

"Grant, you and I need to talk."

"What's wrong?" His face is serious now.

She exhales. "I ran into Trexler at the Coconut Palm Country Club."

She watches his face register where this is going, his mouth twitching slightly. "Did you?"

"He told me he hasn't heard from you in ten years. I thought you were his silent business partner?"

Grant scratches the back of his neck. "We were."

"Ten years ago?"

"Not exactly that long ago. We had a falling-out."

"Grant." She looks at him, confused. "Why would you lie to me like that?"

"Because I didn't want you thinking less of me because I didn't have a job."

She takes a moment, trying to find her words. "I wouldn't think less of you. But I wish you'd been honest with me."

"I'm sorry."

"So this whole time, it's always been your mom's money we've been living off?"

"It's our money." He holds her hand. "She just likes to be in control. It gives her a sense of purpose, I suppose."

"But wouldn't you want to get a job and break free of her?"

"That's what I've been trying to do."

"Okay," she says, but there is a hint of skepticism.

"Come with me." He takes her hand and leads her inside, into the office. He flips open his laptop. "Do you see this?"

Rose peers at the screen. "It looks like a warehouse."

"Not just any warehouse," he starts. "It's a new kind of storage facility. It's going to store wine and cars and it's going to have a wine-tasting room and a car-viewing room where you can display your collection to your friends."

"So, like a man-cave storage unit?"

"Exactly," he says, excited that she gets it. "It's a couple-million-dollar idea. I'm going in on the ground floor."

"With your mom's money?"

His face falls. "This is how I get my money out of her. I'm not going to start working at a corporate nine-to-five job where

I make fifty thousand dollars a year grinding it out." He shakes his head. "No, this is how you do it. You make money with money. With this investment, I triple our worth in five years. It's not about working harder; it's about working smarter."

Rose asks him a couple more questions but becomes skeptical when his answers are that they will iron out the details later. Ultimately, she decides to keep her opinion to herself.

"It looks amazing," she smiles faintly, still shocked that he lied to her about it all. Was this the secret he wanted to share with her, when she stopped him on the beach? It couldn't have been the Maria thing. He seems to not be able to comprehend it himself, unless of course he's lying about this as well. Now she's not sure she can believe anything he says.

"I still can't believe you've been lying to me this whole time."

He stares at her for a moment, then his face falls. "You're right. I'm sorry." He brings her in tightly for a hug. "I just want all of our time on this earth to be spent together and not wasted on meaningless jobs. You understand that, right?"

Rose freezes. She knows what he means. Instead of spending his days in an office, he wants them to be together, but it's the wording he chose that irks her. It's oddly close to the inscription that was on the watch she gave to Ian. Those were her words to him.

May all of our time on this earth be spent together.

They are her words, but hearing them from Grant's mouth feels somewhat chilling.

Isabel

Isabel sits by herself at a pizza parlor five blocks from her apartment. The smell of basil and heated cheese fills her nostrils as she hungrily waits for her slice to heat up.

She drinks her soda, flicking her eyes to the TV that is on in the corner of the restaurant, showing a soccer game.

She thought getting out of her apartment would help her get her mind off things, but it isn't working. Instead, she pulls the note out of her bag and plays with it between her fingers.

Run. Get as far away from here as you can.

She searches for clues, but it's just a typed-out message in typical Times New Roman font.

Could it be possible it's a prank written by one of the students here?

Maybe, but given what's going on in her life right now, she doubts it.

Is it a threat or a warning? Is someone going to hurt her if she doesn't leave? Or is this someone else warning her that someone is trying to hurt her?

But why? What has she done that she deserves this? All she wants is to know the truth about her father. But now, after realizing her entire family is a lie, she has even more of a reason to find out what's going on.

"Number 79," a man in a white T-shirt, apron folded at his waist, calls out.

Isabel stands up, making her way to the clear countertop, grabbing her slice of plain and bringing it back to her seat.

As she places it down, she finds herself looking out the window again. Since getting that note, she's had this strange feeling like she is being watched or followed. She knows she's being paranoid, though. Still, she examines the cars along the street.

She has to break away from the note. Focus on the connections first.

She takes a bite of her pizza, then realizes she needs to write this all down.

Still chewing, she grabs her blue notebook from her bag and a pen. She begins to scribble as she thinks.

If Maria is not her mother, that means that Anita, her grandmother, must be. And if Grant isn't her father, it's because Harrison is. Harrison and Anita had a cliché affair that resulted in her giving birth to Isabel.

Isabel sits for a minute, letting that realization wash over her like a tidal wave.

She thinks back to when she asked for her birth certificate since she needed it for her driver's license. When she had gone to the DMV, they almost wouldn't issue her a license, telling her this wasn't the original birth certificate. Her grandmother stepped in then, saying she'd lost the original, but they could confirm it was real.

Isabel had thought nothing of it. People lose documents all the time. But now she wonders if hers must've been doctored.

Was her birthday even her real birthday?

She's so overwhelmed with everything that she can't even process it. The only thing she can do is continue to treat this investigation like she's an outsider. She starts to write out more questions.

But then why did Anita lie about being her grandmother?

Isabel twists it over in her brain some more.

Because then Anita would obviously have to know who the father was. By claiming that her dead daughter was Isabel's mother, she could claim to be ignorant about who the father might be.

Okay, she thinks. It's starting to make more sense. But why lie about not knowing who the father is?

They are dangerous people. Her grandmother's warning echoes again in her head.

Someone opens the door to the pizza parlor behind her and a rush of heat hits her back. She looks around nervously, as if someone can read her thoughts, but no one is even looking in her direction. Just some regular college kids and her, enjoying their pizza.

She turns back to her notebook, chewing on the edge of her pen.

Was Harrison so powerful that, wanting to keep the scandal out of the papers, he paid Anita off? Or maybe, after his death, Evelyn paid her off?

Isabel remembers her grandmother, or rather her mom, cleaning the occasional house. But she really didn't work that much and yet they remained comfortable. Isabel went to an Ivy League school, and yet money never seemed to be an issue.

But then there is the unsolved murder of Anita's daughter, Maria.

Isabel sips her soda, the bubbles tickling her tongue. She reflects on when she was trying to teach James algebra last week.

"It's too hard," he told her, scratching his neck.

Isabel looked over his assessment. Equations filled almost all the free space underneath the problem.

"James"—she pointed—"you're making it way too complicated. It's a simple problem." She took the pen out of his hand. "All you have to do is this."

She circled the one simple equation he had written that summarized everything. It had been directly underneath the problem.

She smiled. "You had the answer in front of you all along. You just tried to overcomplicate it."

Was she overcomplicating this?

Isabel's heart sinks and her pen, limp in her hand, falls to the side.

Was there no connection at all? Was it just a terrible tragedy? Maria was just in the wrong place at the wrong time and ended up dead because of it. Was her connection with the Caldwells that she was the daughter of Harrison Caldwell and after years of paying off Anita, they just wanted her to go away?

Maybe that was all the note was. Go away. We want nothing to do with you.

Isabel can't help but feel the sting of it. Being alone is hard enough. Being rejected, as viscerally as she has been, just feels like the knife being twisted.

She doesn't want more money from them. It's never been about that.

Is she just making this into something it isn't?

James, she realizes. *Shit.* She's pulled poor James into this. An extreme overreaction and she's just hyped up this poor kid into thinking he's part of some major scandal.

Isabel feels like an idiot. The note is right: she should leave and go back to New York. Although she has enjoyed it here, it's a small town and once word spreads about all of this, she'll appear insane. It's time to move on. Today, she'll begin her search for a new job.

God, she feels ashamed of herself. All of this is probably just a big stupid misunderstanding. A flush of anger hits her. Why couldn't Anita leave her some sort of note? Something that told her the whole story. Told her that she was Isabel's mother, and Harrison was her secret father who had been paying them off all these years and that when she died, don't bother finding them. They want nothing to do with you.

It would've saved her the mystery and heartache.

Tomorrow she's going to go back to the Caldwells' one last time. She's going to apologize for everything and agree never to see or speak with them again.

It's time to tear the Band-Aid off completely and start over.

Isabel finishes the last of her slice and throws away her trash by the door. She pulls her tote bag up onto her shoulder, her head slumped down in shame.

She walks along the street, which is much quieter than New York. Not nearly as many people. No horns honking, just the hum of engines as cars drive by. She reaches a crosswalk still in her own head when she steps off the curb.

Suddenly she hears the loud screech of tires and a horn blaring. Isabel is caught off guard, but quickly recovers and runs out of the way just in time. She falls between two parked cars on the other side.

Her heart is thumping as adrenaline courses through her veins. She manages to stand up; thankfully there isn't a scratch on her. She takes in a deep, shaky breath, trying to stabilize herself.

She didn't even bother to look when she stepped off the curb. She could've gotten herself killed. She shakes her head, rubbing her eyes in disbelief.

"Are you alright?" An older man approaches her, gently touching her arm.

"I'm fine," she says, realizing that her bag is still on the ground. She quickly picks it up, trying to avoid a scene.

"Here, I think this fell out of your bag." The man hands her a folded piece of paper.

"Thank you." She smiles.

He nods, walking away as she opens the paper. It's the note from her mailbox. Isabel eyes the corner where the car disappeared. She knows what happened just now was an accident, but she wonders if it was some greater sign. As logical as she has tried being, she can still feel the pull in her stomach. There's something darker going on, she can sense it. But the question is, does she leave it all behind or stay to find out?

Rose

"Mom, I've got to talk to you." James gets in her car quickly after practice.

"What's wrong? Are you okay?" Rose looks at him, worried.

"I'm fine."

"Everything okay with practice?"

James rolls his eyes. "Practice is fine. It's about Isabel."

Rose feels her stomach tighten. "What about her?"

"We were thinking that Harrison might be her dad."

We were thinking. Was Isabel really bringing James into this? Rose is not sure how to feel about this, but it appears it's too late now.

"Maria was murdered, right?"

Wow, so Isabel really did tell him everything. Rose doesn't want to engage; she wants to tell him not to worry about it, it's something the grown-ups are handling, but of course she knows it's no use. He already knows too much, and she can't shield him forever.

"Right," she finally agrees.

"And Isabel thinks that Harrison was poisoned—"

"He wasn't poisoned," she cuts him off. "He suffered an allergy attack."

"That's bullshit."

"Watch your mouth," she scolds him.

He falls back into his seat, realizing he got too worked up. "Sorry. What I mean is, Isabel and I were talking, and why would a guy like Harrison take the subway? I suggested that he was running late, but Isabel said that people wait for a guy like Harrison. He wouldn't ever normally be on a subway in the first place."

Rose raises her eyebrows. Isabel had a point there.

"And he didn't have his pen on him," James points out. "Isabel is allergic to nuts as well. She knows you don't go anywhere without your EpiPen. Someone must've taken it from him. And I think it proves that Isabel is Harrison's daughter."

Rose is still wrapping her head around all this. "What?"

James rolls his eyes impatiently at her. "Rose got a positive DNA match with Grant. But that can happen if the DNA is from the same gene pool. Which means if it isn't Grant, it's Harrison who's her father."

Rose tries to take in this information. It all makes sense.

"So, back to the murder." James sits up, holding out his hand. He grabs one finger. "You have an important guy. Way too important to need to take the subway. He's in a place where no one can get to him if he goes into anifa—"

"Anaphylactic shock," Rose corrects him.

"Right. Then, he doesn't have his pen on him, which someone with that sort of allergy always would. They also would be careful enough to make sure they don't have any sort of nuts in their food or drinks."

"You have a good point," Rose admits.

"Here's the really weird part." He edges closer to Rose. "Harrison died, like, within a week of Maria being murdered."

A chill runs up Rose's spine.

"I mean, there's got to be a connection, right?"

Harrison, poisoned. Maria, shot. There's something very wrong here and as Rose grips the wheel for the first time, she's worried that she might've not only put herself, but also James, in danger.

She pulls off onto the side of the road.

"What is it, Mom?"

"James, listen to me very carefully." She rotates her whole body towards him. "This isn't some fun crime show. This is real life, with real people, do you understand?"

James looks at her oddly. "I do, Mom."

"We are dealing with two unsolved murders that we seem to be dangerously close to. Do you know what I'm getting at?"

He nods at her, but his face still shows confusion.

"I don't want you talking to Isabel about this anymore."

"What do you mean? She needs help to solve this. I'm helping her. She got a note threatening her. She needs our help."

"What?"

"Someone left a note in her mailbox at school telling her to get out as fast as she can or something like that."

Rose's eyes widen. "You're not helping her; you're endangering yourself. Do you get that?"

"No," he says angrily.

"I want you to pretend that you know nothing. Do you hear me?"

"Mom, I can't just—"

"You can and you will." Rose puts her hands on James's shoulders. He looks at her hand as it visibly shakes.

"Mom," he says more carefully. "What's going on?"

Rose regains her composure. "I'm not sure. But I'm worried that whatever it is, we don't want to be tangled up in it."

She struggles to pull her seatbelt over, tugging on it several times in frustration. "Tell me you understand now."

"I do," he says, looking at her more seriously. Finally, getting the weight behind her demands.

Rose starts up the car. "I need to get us out of here." Before we become the next victims, she thinks.

Evelyn must know Rose has the gun by now. Rose saw that the grate of the vent had been put back sloppily, not at all how Rose had left it.

While she feels safer knowing the gun is in her possession, she doesn't know what else Evelyn might be hiding within these walls, or more importantly, what she's capable of.

Rose thinks she's waiting. Waiting to see what Rose's next move will be.

Rose feels strangely powerful, but she also knows that one false move could put not only her, but also James at risk.

As Rose pulls into the driveway, a surge of energy runs through her. She can't wait any longer, she has to tell Grant about the gun. It's now or never.

"James, can you please go into your room and lock your door?"

James looks like he's about to question her, but given their conversation, a simple stern look gets him to agree.

As they enter the foyer, Rose pulls James in towards her and whispers. "I'll knock on your door when you can come out."

James nods, making his way up the steps.

"Grant." Rose storms into the office.

Grant looks up from his computer, squinting at her in confusion.

"Rose." He closes his laptop and walks over to her, almost stopping her at the door. "What's going on?"

"We have to get out of here." Rose rushes to the couch to sit before her legs collapse beneath her. She puts her head in her hands.

"What do you mean? What's happened?" he asks calmly and assertively.

"Where is your mom?"

"Upstairs in her room? Why?"

"You need to come with me." She finds the strength to stand up and walk. She grabs her purse and Grant by the hand, leading him outside, back towards the beach.

When she feels far enough away from any sort of cameras, she stops, the sand grinding between her toes.

"Rose, you're scaring me a bit," Grant says. It's only then that Rose realizes how shallow her breath is. As they walked, she was practically gasping for air.

Rose's face tightens in worry as the panic starts to rise in her chest. She can't let James be put in the middle of whatever this is.

She decides to start off slow. "Your mother has been lying about having Parkinson's."

"What?"

"It's true, Grant. The whole thing with the shaking and stuttering has been an act."

"Parkinson's comes and goes; just because she's fine sometimes and struggling other times doesn't mean she's lying."

"Did a doctor ever tell you she had it? When you were flying back and forth all the time to help her, did you ever speak to anyone other than her about her condition?"

Grant goes to open his mouth, but then stops himself.

"I spoke to her pharmacist."

"You did what?" He is angered.

"It wasn't like that," Rose says defensively. "I didn't dig into your mom's medical history. She asked me to go to the pharmacy and get her something for her headache. I asked the pharmacist about her, because I didn't want to give her something that could harm her if it was mixed with her medications."

Grant's eyebrows are still furrowed. "Why would she lie about something like that?"

"To keep you close." Rose holds his arm. "And to push me away."

Rose watches as Grant stares out towards the ocean, trying to make sense of it all.

"Your mom isn't who you think she is." Rose swallows. "I think she murdered Maria and your father." The wind is blowing her hair in all sorts of directions. She pulls a strand out of her mouth.

He looks at her incredulously. "What?" Then he laughs like he can't believe it's true. "My mother may be a liar, but she didn't kill anyone."

"I think you're lying to yourself, Grant. Think about your father. He wasn't a good man, right? I heard rumors that he cheated on your mom all the time. I think she finally snapped."

"We discussed this," Grant says, frustrated. "He died from anaphylactic shock."

"Why was he on the subway? He was a powerful man. Why would a man like Harrison Caldwell ever take the subway?"

Grant runs his hand down his face. "I don't know." He seems to agree. "Maybe because he was trying to be discreet about meeting another woman he was having an affair with."

Rose stops herself for a moment. That did seem probable. "But his EpiPen?"

"Dropped it. He lost it all the time."

Rose is silent for a moment, mulling it over. They were reasonable explanations.

"My mother didn't kill anyone."

"Then I need you to answer me this." She reaches into her cross-body bag and pulls out the gun. "Explain to me why your mother would have this?"

His eyes narrow in on it. He looks at her accusingly. "What is this?"

"I found it hidden in the vent in the art studio."

He runs his tongue along the top part of his lip as if that helps him figure out the reasoning.

"Are you sure it's even her gun? This house is old, generations of my family have lived here."

"Look at it." She hands it to him, and he rubs his fingers along it. "It isn't exactly an antique. But you're right, it's not your mom's gun."

His head jolts up from the gun to her.

"I ran the registration on it. The gun belongs to Anita."

"Anita?" he says, like he's still playing catch-up.

"Only why would your mom have Anita's gun? I know I don't know much of the story, but I doubt that Anita killed her own daughter and then gave your mom the gun for safekeeping."

He lets out a slow exhale. "No, I suppose you're right."

"Which can only mean that your mom killed Maria and hid the gun all these years."

"Why wouldn't she just get rid of it?" he asks.

Rose realizes this is a fair point. "She was holding the gun as insurance on someone?"

Grant swallows.

"Your father?"

Grant shakes his head. "He died shortly after. Why hold it this long?"

"Anita?"

Grant nods. "It's the only thing that makes sense. My mom didn't know Anita was dead until recently. Maybe it was insurance against Anita."

"But what was she getting out of Anita? The only reason you'd hold this over someone's head would be if you were getting something in return. What could Anita have possibly had that Evelyn wanted?"

"I don't know," Grant says, puzzled.

He looks out onto the ocean. For a moment, Rose thinks he's going to throw the gun into it, but instead he seems to stumble backward and sits down on the sand.

Rose wipes her hands on her black yoga pants and sits next to him. She wraps an arm around him and puts a hand on his shoulder.

"Are you okay?"

"My mom is not a killer."

Rose lets out a sigh.

But then who is? A deep uneasiness takes root in the pit of Rose's stomach, so much so that she pulls away from Grant.

"Hey." Grant runs his hand softly along Rose's cheek and faces her towards him. "I promise you, I will talk to my mother. There has to be a perfectly good explanation for all of this. I will get to the bottom of it."

Rose nods. "Okay."

He kisses her gently, then pulls her in for a hug. "As long as you and I are together, nothing bad will ever happen."

Rose swallows, thinking of the two deaths within his orbit already, and wonders if even he believes what he says.

Evelyn

Evelyn's heart is racing so fast her whole body is vibrating. She is walking around her room, unsure of what she should be doing.

Should she run? Pack her things and leave? But where could she go so that no one would find her?

Then again, it wouldn't be her first time in hiding. She did it twenty years ago after everything happened.

She knows it was cowardly. As soon as Grant graduated high school, she shipped him off to a summer camp before he began his freshman year of college, while she went to Geneva and hid.

Maybe Grant is the way he is because of her reaction. She never gave him much love, and it wasn't like Harrison was ever there.

She's played this blame game with herself before. One too many times. The problem is her, but it lies further down in her subconscious, so deep that it would likely take years of therapy to dig out of her what led to her inability to love or trust anyone, even her own son.

No one has ever cared about her. It's why she longed for a new life and why she had to leave her family. It's what made her so desperate and determined to crawl her way to the top. But the problem with success is once you have it, you're so afraid to lose it. And you'll stop at nothing to keep it, even if you have to kill for it.

Evelyn's mind falls back onto Anita.

Evelyn had walked in on Anita, throwing up in her toilet that she had only cleaned moments earlier.

"Anita, are you alright?"

"I'm fine," she said, trying to stand up quickly as if nothing had happened.

"You should go home if you're sick," Evelyn said, concerned.

"Really, Evelyn, I'm fine."

Still, Evelyn made her go home. But then as the next few weeks progressed, Anita's sickness continued.

"Do you need to see a doctor?" Evelyn asked her, taking a pen and paper from the kitchen drawer. "I have an amazing doctor you should see. Dr. Warren is the best. He'll be able to figure out whatever it is that's going on with you."

"No," Anita said harshly. "I'm fine."

Evelyn didn't believe her, but after that, she never heard her being sick again.

But there was something going on with Anita. Evelyn noticed she looked paler, her cheeks fuller. She started to withdraw from interactions with Evelyn.

"Anita, you don't have to run off, stay for tea," Evelyn would call from the kitchen, the kettle already boiling with a high-pitched whistle.

"I really must be going," she'd say. Making up excuse after excuse.

"What is going on with you?" Evelyn had finally confronted her. "Did I do something wrong? If I have offended you in any way, I'm truly sorry. You're my friend, Anita. Please talk to me."

"I'm not your friend." Anita seemed to laugh absurdly at this.

The words cut into Evelyn like a knife. "Anita, I . . ." But she was at a loss for words. "What's changed?"

Anita's eyes met hers briefly, then flicked back down at the floor. Evelyn realized that she hadn't made eye contact with her for several weeks now.

Anita wasn't mad at her, she realized. She was ashamed. If it wasn't what Evelyn had done, then it was what Anita had done.

Evelyn swallowed the lump that was rising in her throat. Everything started to come together.

"Are you . . . ?" Evelyn watched as Anita pulled away. That's when she saw it. The protruding belly that Anita had been trying to hide under her oversized tops.

Evelyn gasped. She didn't love Harrison, at least she didn't anymore. She knew he was cheating on her, but she had accepted it, as long as he was discreet. She had even taken a lover herself. But this? This was Anita, her only real friend.

"How could you?" Evelyn's voice was hoarse.

Anita put a hand protectively on her stomach. "I didn't mean for it to happen."

"You didn't mean to get pregnant or you didn't mean to get caught?"

"I . . ." she said, her voice fading.

"I thought we were friends. How could you do this to me?"

"We were never friends," Anita responded, more upset now. "How can you be friends with someone when you clean their toilets every day? I'm your employee. I work for you for money."

"I guess it wasn't enough. You wanted to get pregnant so you could get what, child support? Get more money out of us?"

"I did not want this." Anita pointed to her middle. The bump was now so obvious that Evelyn couldn't believe she'd missed it. Of course Anita had been trying to hide it with flowing tops, but still, it had been there for a while now.

"Of course you did." Evelyn was bitter now.

"No, I did not. I did not even want your husband." Anita's voice broke, and she covered her face with her hands, a cry escaping her throat.

"You disgust me," Evelyn said, her voice deep and hot with anger. "Get out of this house. I never want to see you again."

Evelyn was so angry in that moment, she felt deep rage like she never had before. She wanted to hurt Anita, in the worst way possible.

Just thinking about it now, the pain grips Evelyn like a vice. Her heart tightens like it could turn to stone at any second. Everything about that day she wants to forget. That's when everything became different. In the heat of her rage, her world and Anita's were both ripped apart and changed forever.

"Mom." Evelyn almost jumps out of her skin. She turns around from her desk to face the door. "God, Grant, you scared me."

"Are you okay?"

"I'm fine."

He looks at her quizzically. "You seem a bit jumpy."

"I'm just . . . tired." She turns to the mirror above her desk, noticing that this entire ordeal seems to have aged her ten years. She tries to compose herself by smoothing her hair into place.

"Listen, I need you to come co-sign this deal with me."

"Now?" She turns back around. "Grant, listen, I—"

"Now, Mother." His voice is stern, making Evelyn sit up in her chair. Then his face relaxes, and he smiles. "You and I haven't really had much time together since you so graciously took us all in, and we have a lot to discuss." He tilts his head. "How about after the signing we go to lunch, just you and I?"

This is it, Evelyn realizes. It's finally happening, but she knows she can no longer run. She's tired, and it's too late. It's time for the truth to come out.

Isabel

Isabel writes several math problems on the whiteboard in front of her.

"Who wants to come up here and solve this equation?" Isabel puts the cap back on the marker and holds it out to the class. As is generally the case, there is an exchange of glances before someone in the first row raises their hand.

"Mr. Walker!" She calls on someone in the back row. The boy sinks down in his chair, dropping his head so his black hair covers his face. "Come, show me how you break this problem down."

She knows she's putting him on the spot. But the way he struggles with his tests, she wants to make sure he is paying attention.

Isabel hands off the marker. Without making eye contact, he takes it and approaches the board with heavy shoulders. Nervously, he turns back to her, only to be met with an encouraging smile.

As he begins to write, he looks back at her once more.

"You're on the right track." She nods at him.

He hesitates a few more moments, then lets the marker drop.

"It's okay," she says, grabbing a red marker and helping him along. "See," she steps back, "there you go. Do you understand it now?"

He shakes his head. "Not really."

"Okay, what are you struggling to see?" she asks patiently, looking up at him and realizing just how much smaller she is than him.

He shrugs his shoulders again. "I guess it's hard to focus, because I'm not sure how this is actually going to help me in the real world, you know?"

"Fair point," Isabel says, looking at the algebra equations.

She grabs the eraser and clears the board. "You've made a good observation, Mr. Walker. How can we try to solve something without motivation, right?"

She writes across the board: "Importance of Math Modeling in the Real World."

"Okay," she announces to the class as Mr. Walker sits down. "Who can give me an example of some math models used in the real world?"

The class remains silent.

"I'll start." She writes a number one and next to it, the word "Epidemiology." "This is the spread of diseases. During the pandemic, mathematicians and scientists used models to predict the spread of the virus. This helped in planning the government's healthcare response."

She turns around. "Anyone else?"

A girl with brown hair raises her hand. "Climate change?"

"Exactly." Isabel turns back to the board to write it down. "What else?"

"Sports?" a boy calls from the middle row.

"Yes, sports analysis. It's how they do draft picks, right? What else?"

"Investments and stuff?" someone else calls out.

"Yes, investment strategies. Which stock will do well." She scribbles across the board. "Transportation, understanding the flow of traffic so you can time the traffic lights correctly." She turns back around to face the class. "The universe itself is one big math problem. Scientists and mathematicians have spent hundreds of years trying to understand the meaning of life. All of this is math. Does it make sense now why we need it?"

The class nods at her.

"Good."

She erases the board again, returning to their math problems.

Isabel trails off as she writes out the last equation.

Math is used in everyday life, she thinks.

"Ms. Martinez?"

Isabel turns. "Yes?"

"I think you got lost in thought for a second," a girl in the second row tells her. She turns around and realizes she hasn't finished the math problem and has just been standing there.

"Right." She finishes it quickly, calling the girl in the second row to come up and solve the problem while she stands off to the side with her arms crossed.

What is the probability of Anita's daughter and lover dying within a week of each other?

To some extent, a problem does need logic, but the odds are low. Isabel tells the girl she's correct and calls on the next person while Isabel pulls her blue notebook out of her desk drawer. She looks at it, assuming that most students will think she is looking up more math problems for them. But as she continues to scan the notes she took when she was at the pizza parlor yesterday, she realizes that not only were the deaths close to one another in time, but also in location.

Harrison died on the subway a few blocks from his house. Not exactly a big stretch. But Maria, Maria also died near the Caldwells' residence. In the park right outside their apartment. That fact makes this whole situation less random and more calculated.

Isabel is trying not to spin off course. She wonders if the cops had their suspicions, only they couldn't prove it.

"Is this right, Ms. Martinez?"

Isabel blinks herself out of her trance again and looks at the board. "Yes, correct, Ms. Stance, thank you."

When the bell rings, Isabel is frustrated with herself. She thought she had talked herself out of all this, but she keeps getting sucked back in as if into a tornado.

As the students pile out, she opens her desk drawer to put her notebook back when she sees a notification on her phone. A voicemail.

She picks it up to look at the number.

"The Whitmore Academy?" She looks around her classroom like the answer might somehow be in there.

Why are they calling me? she wonders.

She listens to the voicemail.

"Hi, Isabel, this is Theresa. Dan asked me to reach out and see if you could give him a call back at your earliest convenience."

Isabel's throat dries and she feels a surge of fear in the pit of her stomach. Did the Caldwells call and tell the school that she used their resources to stalk them? Could they penalize her even if she had already resigned from Whitmore? At the very least they could inform the Pelican Academy, who would likely fire her. That would be the end of her teaching career. Then what would she do?

Isabel lets out a shaky breath. There is no point in putting it off. It's lunchtime now, so she might as well get it over with. Otherwise she's going to walk around with this feeling of trepidation all day.

She dials the number.

"Whitmore Academy," a bright, cheery person answers the phone. Isabel knows immediately who it is.

"Hi, Theresa, it's Isabel."

"Isabel . . ." Theresa drags her name out. "How are you?"

"I'm doing well." Isabel decides to keep the exchange simple.

"Let me put you through to Mr. Lopez," says Theresa, before the line is quiet.

"Dan Lopez," a voice answers a few moments later.

"Dan, it's Isabel Martinez." She tries to keep her voice upbeat, not wanting him to sense how scared she is right now.

"Isabel." His voice matches her tone and it throws Isabel off. Why is he happy to hear from her?

"How are things at the Pelican Academy?"

"They're great," she lies, but not really. She is enjoying the job. Just everything else in her life is a mess. "I really love teaching."

"I heard you've been doing wonderful at it."

"You have?" Isabel tilts her head curiously.

"Listen, I know that it's only a temporary position you have there, so I wanted to let you know that if you would like to come back when that term is over, we do have a maternity leave coming up in our school as well. We'd love it if you would come back, and we could work on a permanent teaching position for you."

Isabel is stunned. "Really?"

"Yes, really."

"Wow, I don't know what to say. Thank you so much."

"You're welcome. We loved having you. Just take some time to think it over, and get back to me."

"Of course, Dan, thank you again."

Isabel hangs up the phone, shocked into silence.

Has Dan been keeping an eye on her?

It's a great opportunity. Especially if she's planning to leave soon. She'd have a job to return to. She's kept her apartment. It would be an easy enough transition. She could go back to her old life.

But still, something irks her. It all seems too easy.

She remembers how she saw in James's file the donation that Evelyn gave to the school to get James down here. Did Evelyn do the reverse to get *her* out?

Is this some sort of consolation prize for being rejected by the Caldwell family? Or is this their way of assuring themselves that Isabel will go away and not look further into this whole business with Maria and Harrison?

Rose

Rose and James are setting the table when she hears Grant walk through the garage door. She has been nervous about how Evelyn would react when Grant confronted her and on some level has been hoping that he's right, and it's all some misunderstanding. But to her surprise, it's only Grant standing in the foyer.

"Where's Evelyn?" Rose asks Grant, who, noticing the dinner table is set, sits down with a long exhale.

"She's in New York, finalizing the close on the apartment."

James and Rose exchange glances and sit down as well.

The sun is setting, making the sky a swirl of pink and orange that reflects on the plates in the dining room as they pass each other servings of steak, seasoned vegetables and mashed potatoes prepared by Martha.

Rose scrunches her face. "It's odd that your mom just left like that."

"Why is that?"

"One minute she was going to lunch with you and then, what, did she leave right from lunch to the airport?"

"What do you mean?" Grant saws into his steak with his knife.

"I didn't see her come back."

"She came back," he says, putting the cut of meat into his mouth and chewing. "You must've been upstairs painting or picking James up from school."

"Then where were you?" She tries not to sound accusatory.

"The bank, finalizing this warehouse deal."

Rose tries to hide her skepticism. Anything work-related now just seems like another fabrication.

"Okay. But, given what we were talking about earlier"—she signals to him, raising her eyebrows, regarding the gun that she found—"I find it strange how quickly she left without much of a word to anyone."

Grant wipes his mouth with his napkin. He looks at James and then to Rose.

"The truth is, I spoke to her about what we discussed. I think that's why she was eager to leave."

Rose raises her eyebrows. "Oh."

James looks from Grant to Rose, but Rose avoids his look by cutting into her own steak.

"How are your studies coming along?" Rose says, still not looking up.

He sighs. "Not so great. I got a C on my algebra test."

"You can do better than that, James," Grant says.

"I could when I had Isabel." His tone is accusing. "Now I'm not allowed to see her anymore."

"James, that's enough." Rose's tone is sharp. Then she sighs. "Is your homework done?"

"No," he answers, spearing the last of his broccoli.

"Then why don't you take your dinner into the kitchen and finish working on it? Grant and I have some things we'd like to discuss. When you're done, I'll come check your work, then you can play your video games."

"Fine." James stands up, all too eager to leave.

"Bring your plate in the kitchen," Rose reminds him. "And tell Martha she can go home. I'll clean up."

Once the door is closed, she turns back to Grant. "So, what happened?"

240

"I took Mom out to lunch and told her that we found Anita's gun and wanted to know why she had it."

Rose waits in anticipation. "And did she tell you why?"

He shakes his head. "She told me it was none of my business, which leads me to believe something I don't want to come to terms with."

Rose's shoulders slump. "I'm sorry, Grant." If she's being honest with herself, she doesn't want this all to be true either. She wanted Evelyn to have a reasonable explanation that would make sense. But it had to be done. Rose is scared of Evelyn. She's not only a liar, but a powerful person with money and connections. If she had something to do with what happened to Maria and Harrison twenty years ago, what stops her from harming Rose or James?

Evelyn knows that Rose is on to her. Exactly how close has she come to becoming Evelyn's next victim? Then, of course, James is starting to get involved; what if Evelyn has caught on to that? The thought sends a shudder through her. She pushes it away, along with her dinner.

"So, what happened next?" Rose asks. "What did she do?"

"She pretended her phone rang, said it was Lizzy and that she needed to fly up and close on the apartment in New York."

"So, you let her come back, pack her things and run?"

"She's not running."

"Of course she is, Grant." Rose lets her silverware drop onto her plate. It clunks loudly, echoing off the dining-room walls.

"Where is she going to go, exactly?" Grant asks.

He has a point. She sticks her tongue against the inside of her cheek. "So, what happens now?"

"Well"—Grant wipes the corner of his mouth with a napkin—"it pained me to do it, but I called the NYPD today and I sent them the gun."

Rose swallows as her eyes go wide. *He actually did it.*

"Now it's in their hands."

Rose reaches across the table. "That must've been so hard for you."

"Yes." He lets out a sigh. "Unfortunately, it had to be done. All of these years, she's been hiding this." He sniffs and rubs his nose. "If you'll excuse me, I have to do a little more work tonight." Then he stands up and leaves the dining room.

Rose doesn't argue. She can tell he's upset and how could he not be? He just turned in his own mother. It's a lot to take in.

Relief spreads across her chest. The police will handle it, and Evelyn won't be able to harm anyone else again.

There is a part of her that is also incredibly guilty. But why does she feel that way? After all, she has to do what is necessary to protect herself and her son.

Still, she can understand how conflicted Grant must be. Evelyn may be a liar and a manipulator, but as much as she dislikes Evelyn for what she's put her through, she can't see her as a killer. But then again, how well can we really know a person? No matter how close they are to you, how can you possibly know their deepest, darkest secrets?

Isabel

Isabel is walking out of her classroom when she feels her phone vibrating in her back pocket.

She pulls it out, noting that she doesn't recognize the number.

She opens the text.

Isabel, this is Grant Caldwell. I got your number from my wife's phone. I apologize for my reaction the other day. It was a lot to take in. Listen, we just learned some new information, and I wanted to discuss it with you. Is there a place we can meet?

Isabel stops, her body frozen in place. She can't believe it. She's finally going to get some answers.

A student knocks into her, and she stumbles.

"Sorry," she hears. But Isabel doesn't look up. She's still staring at her phone like she can't believe it's true. Finally, after all this time.

She starts to type. *Let's meet at Cafe Paris, it's right by my apartment off Clematis Street. I'm leaving school now. When can we meet?*

She starts slowly walking, urging her body to move. She feels excited and terrified at the same time.

Her phone buzzes and she pulls it out, this time bumping into a crowd of students.

"Sorry," she says without looking up, then stumbles around them and looks at her phone.

We can meet at five.

This is it, Isabel thinks. She feels as if she might throw up. Does she want to hear what he has to say? Will it shatter everything she's ever known about her grandmother? At the same time, she argues in her head that her image of Anita was already destroyed when she learned that Maria wasn't her mother.

There is no turning back now.

Isabel sits idly in her apartment, staring at the clock. She waits until 4:55 then leaves, walking to the next block over. She finds Grant already sitting there, waiting for her at one of the outdoor bistro chairs. He interlaces his hands on the table, but she can see from here that his knee is bouncing up and down.

He's nervous, she can tell. Is that a good or bad thing?

Grant looks up and smiles. "Isabel." He stands up. "I'm glad you could come."

"Me too," she says awkwardly, pulling up her purse that was falling off her shoulder.

"Can I get you a coffee?"

"Sure," she says.

"How do you like it?"

"Just black."

"No milk?"

"I'm allergic to nuts. So, I don't risk a mislabeled dispenser that might have almond milk in it."

He looks at her oddly for a moment, but she can't figure what he's thinking.

"Got it. I'll be right back."

Isabel drops her purse to the ground and waits patiently, twiddling her thumbs and trying not to draw any conclusions before he even speaks with her.

A few moments later, Grant comes back out with two drinks and puts one in front of her. "Here you are."

She lifts the lid. "This has milk in it."

"Oh." He looks down. "I must've given you the wrong one." He reaches for it quickly, almost spilling it and replacing it with his. "Sorry, you just told me your allergy and I promise I only have cow's milk in mine, but sometimes I overthink something so much, I confuse myself. I thought I had put yours in my left hand."

When Isabel opens the lid of the second cup, she sees it's black and takes a sip.

Noticing him staring at her, she begins to feel self-conscious.

"So, what is it that you wanted to tell me?" Isabel then takes a sip to slow her urgency, even though she can barely sit through the suspense anymore.

"Right." He clears his throat, leaning forward, and drinks from his cup. "I feel there's something you should know."

Isabel leans in towards him. She wants to know exactly what he has to say, and she wants to hear it as clearly as she can.

"I'm sorry to say that I think Anita and my father were having an affair. But I fear that my mother suspected it was Maria who was having an affair with my father, and she stole Anita's gun that she kept in her purse and used it on Maria. Shortly after, my mother poisoned my father, with his own nut allergy." He points at her coffee. "Again, I should know better. I feel like an idiot." He rolls his eyes and shakes his head.

"It's okay." She puts a hand up.

"I don't think she realized it was Anita all this time because she thought Anita was her friend. After everything happened, of course we never saw Anita again, so she must've been pregnant and went on to have you."

Isabel takes a moment for it all to sink in. She suspected as much, but confirmation from Grant seems to solidify her theory into a fact.

245

"How did you know that it was my grandmother's?" She stops to correct herself. "I mean, how did you know it was Anita's gun?"

Grant lowers his eyes to the table, tracing the holes of the bistro table with his finger. Once he's figured out how to say what he wants to say to her, he stops and looks up.

"I found the gun. It was hidden in our house, in a vent in the ceiling, specifically. I recognized it as Anita's because I had seen it before, and we confirmed the registration."

Isabel falls back into her chair. It's all so much to take in.

"What do you mean? When did you see it?"

"As I said, Anita kept it in her purse. She was nervous, I think, as a single mother living in the city, and she kept it for protection. One night, someone mugged my mother in the park right outside our apartment, and she ended up getting pretty beaten up. Anita pulled out her own gun to show my mom, insisting that she get one herself because she never knew when she would need it."

A loud ringing takes over Isabel's hearing. No wonder Anita held so much guilt. It was her gun. A gun she had shown to Evelyn herself. And Evelyn used that gun to kill her only daughter.

Isabel wants to cry. No wonder Anita was so tortured all those years.

So, Anita had to have known that Evelyn killed Maria. That was why there was this elaborate backstory to prevent Isabel from finding out who her father was. Because it would lead her back to the family that killed Anita's daughter. She was worried Evelyn would find out who Isabel was and finish the job she started.

A deep chill causes Isabel's whole body to shiver.

It all suddenly becomes so clear. Everything before was in black and white, and now she sees colors and contours.

Grant puts a warm hand on hers as she takes in a shaky breath.

"I am so sorry for everything that you have been through, Isabel. On top of it, none of it is your fault. I know that we were all in a bit of shock when you first came to us with the news, but the truth is I'm really happy that you did. It's nice to know that I have a half-sister." He wiggles her hand encouragingly before pulling his own back.

"Look, my grandmother—Harrison's mother—she had this beautiful family heirloom necklace. It probably makes the sapphire heart from the *Titanic* look small."

Isabel laughs awkwardly, wiping a tear from her eye.

"She always wished for a daughter or granddaughter to pass it down to, but it's been a family of men." He scrunches his face. "She never did like my mother."

Isabel looks at him quizzically.

"I know it doesn't make up for everything. But as a sign of apology, and for everything, really . . ." He looks around as if it's all the universe's fault. The world against her. "I want to give it to you."

"Wow," Isabel says, stunned. Is he really trying to give her some consolation prize? What about justice for Maria? "I don't think I can accept something like that. I really don't want anything from you or your family. All I ever wanted was the truth."

"I understand. And that you shall have. I sent the gun to the NYPD. My mother is on her way there now."

Isabel feels a weight taken off her shoulders as if she is suddenly lighter somehow.

"So, it's over?"

"It's over," he assures her.

The stress of this secret she has worked so hard to uncover is finally over. She really can move on now.

Isabel lets out a slow breath.

"Can you at least come look at it? It would mean so much to me to be able to give it to you."

"Okay, but really, I don't think I can accept it."

"But you'll come see it?"

Isabel hesitates for a moment. She really wants to just be alone with her thoughts. But then she sees this necklace as an olive branch. Grant wants to get to know her more. She's sure he has questions for her as well. Her face softens. "Sure."

"Great." Grant pushes his chair back. "Can you follow me there, then?"

"Now?"

"What better time than the present?"

Rose

"You look a mess," Rose says, shocked, as James climbs into the front seat. His hair is slick and sticking up all over the place, and he looks like he sweat through his entire shirt. "And here I was going to take you for pizza."

"We can still go."

Rose licks her thumb and tries to settle the cowlicks in his hair.

"Ew, Mom." He pulls away.

"Guess you'll have to go dirty."

"Where's Grant?"

"He said he had a client meeting." She hesitates, still hurt over his lies about working with Trexler. But of course, this is not something she wants to share with James. "So, I figured since we're on our own, we'll take it easy."

"Can't go wrong with pizza." James pulls his door closed. "But you have to go to the one on Clematis Street. It's apparently the only place in Florida that is even close to New York-quality pizza."

"How do you know that?"

"Isabel told me about it. It's right by where she lives."

Rose looks it up on her phone, then pulls out of the parking lot. "Okay, let's do it."

Rose drives the next five minutes over the bridge to West Palm Beach. She slows as her GPS tells her she is one minute away.

"Is this it?" Rose cranes her head, looking up at the sign.

"Yeah," James confirms. "I see a spot up there." He points.

Rose pulls into the parking spot, and they make their way to the restaurant.

"Smells promising," James says as they pull open the door.

"Why don't you grab a seat by the window? I'll get our usual."

"And a lemonade, please," James calls.

Rose nods and heads to the counter.

"Two slices of pepperoni and one plain, please."

"Anything else?" the teenage boy behind the counter asks as he logs it into their system.

"A bottle of water and a lemonade," Rose adds, handing over her credit card.

"Number 47, and drinks are behind you."

She turns and approaches the industrial glass fridge behind her, pulling out two bottles, the cold air refreshing.

"Here you go." Rose drops the lemonade in front of James. He barely lets it touch the table before he takes it from her, removing the cap and gulping it greedily.

"I'm so thirsty," he says, wiping his face after.

"Heck of a day?"

"Hey, is that Isabel?" James points out the window to a cafe across the street.

Rose looks up to see that it is her, sitting outside at a bistro table. She appears anxious.

"I want to go say hi," James says, standing up. Just as he does, Grant comes out of the coffee shop with two cups and hands one to Isabel.

She smiles at him gratefully. Grant takes a seat across from her as they begin talking.

Rose's face sours. Once again, she's caught Grant in a bold-faced lie. If he was going to meet with Isabel, she wouldn't blame him. Why does everything have to be a secret in this family?

She grabs James's arm. "Let's leave them be."

"What do you mean?"

Rose hesitates for a minute, but already knows there is no getting around it. She decides to tweak the narrative to avoid her involvement. "Grant found the gun used in Maria's murder. He turned the gun and Evelyn in."

"Woah." James's jaw drops.

"They need their privacy for this, okay? When we get home, we can ask Grant what the conversation was about, but Isabel has been waiting her whole life for this. Let her hear the truth."

James sits back down. "You're right."

"Number 47."

Rose turns around and spots their pizzas sitting on the counter. Steam is still rising from them. She takes the tray over to their table, along with several napkins from the dispenser on the counter.

When Rose comes back, James is still focused on Isabel and Grant, and admittedly, so is she. Both are trying to get a sense of what's happening, based only on body language and poor lip-reading.

Grant puts a hand on Isabel's in a supportive gesture.

After about five more minutes, Grant and Isabel both stand up.

James jumps up as well.

"We're going to leave Isabel alone," Rose instructs him. "We'll talk to Grant when he gets home. I don't want it to look like we were stalking them from across the street, okay?"

James's face falls, but then he thinks better of it. "Fine."

They watch as Isabel and Grant both go into some sort of residential garage. Rose and James look at each other oddly, but Rose tries to shrug it off and urges James out of the restaurant and into their car.

By the time Rose has swung the car back around in a U-turn, she sees Grant's car up ahead.

"That's Isabel's car." James points to the silver Camry, following Grant's Range Rover.

Rose realizes he's right. Where are they going?

"Maybe they're heading back to the house to tell us," Rose suggests, but then both cars make a right, opposite from the way home.

"Follow them," James suggests.

"No," Rose says instinctively, but then before she even realizes it, she has turned the car too and starts following them.

"Nice, Mom."

Rose knows this is not a good example to be setting for her child, but the way Grant has lied to her about his job, she just wants to know if she can really trust him at all. They make a right onto Dixie Highway, tailing them. Rose makes sure to stay several cars behind them to avoid detection.

"Where are they going?" James asks, after they've followed them for fifteen minutes.

"I'm not sure," Rose says before spotting a water tower that says Riviera Beach on it.

Is he showing her the warehouse he bought? Why?

She continues driving, watching as they eventually pull into a parking lot. She sees a gray building not far from the ports.

Well, at least he didn't lie about the warehouse, she thinks. She's about to turn around and leave, but then something catches her eye that stops her.

"What is it, Mom?"

Rose squints. "It looks like Evelyn's car."

But then what is it doing in this parking lot? Evelyn went up north to close on the house. Rose would've assumed her car would be at the airport or back in the garage at home.

Her interest is piqued now. She pulls into a parking spot just as the door to the warehouse closes behind Isabel and Grant.

James jumps out of the car quickly.

"James, wait!" Rose calls out, opening her car door. "I don't know what we do from here."

"We check it out." James points to the building. "We've come this far."

Rose gets out of the car and follows him to the front door. He pulls on it. "It's locked."

Rose stands there for a few more seconds, contemplating.

Finally, she pulls two bobby pins from her bun. "Not anymore." She inserts the pins and flicks her wrist a few times before she's able to open it.

"Woah, Mom, that was awesome."

Rose tilts her head to the side, trying to hide her smirk.

"Can you teach me that?"

Rose pulls the door open. "Absolutely not."

She closes the door softly behind them. They are now in what looks like a small office building with various halls and large metal grates.

"Did you see where they went?" James asks.

Rose pricks her ears, trying to hear the sound of footsteps, but she can't make out anything.

"We would've heard them if they'd pulled up one of these gates." Rose motions towards the heavy metal doors.

"Didn't use the elevator either." James points to the screen above it. It says L for lobby.

Both of their gazes fall down a long hallway towards a single regular-size gray door.

They start to walk down the hall when suddenly the loud crack of a gun being fired echoes through the building.

Rose instinctively grabs James and throws herself on top of him.

There is silence again. They both look at each other, wide-eyed.

Was that really what she thought it was?

"Isabel!" James yells, then stands up, running as fast as he can towards the gray door.

A surge of adrenaline runs through Rose's veins. "James, no!" she calls, running full sprint after him.

Evelyn

Evelyn squints at the sudden brightness of the room. She puts a hand up as a shield until her eyes have adjusted. Rising from the squeaky cot she's been on, she sits up. She has no idea where she is. It's a plain gray cement block room, with no windows and up until a moment ago, no lights. Other than the metal cot she's on, an empty desk and metal chair pushed up against one of the walls is the only other furniture in the otherwise sparse room.

How did she get here? Is she already in jail?

Evelyn thinks back to what she can last remember.

"Where are we going?" Evelyn had asked nervously when Grant pulled into a parking lot.

He pointed up at a sign for a lawyer's office.

"I figured we'd stop here first to co-sign the lease."

"Oh," she said, somewhat relieved.

Evelyn remembered signing the lease, but not much about what the lawyer had to say. Evelyn knew her hands were tied. Where Grant told her to sign, she did.

"That wasn't so hard, was it?" Grant said, bringing her to her car afterwards, the intense heat making her nauseous. "Let's say we go to lunch and celebrate."

"Sure," Evelyn said, unsure how she would be able to muster up conversation.

"Where are we going?" she asked again as she sat up straight in her seat, realizing that the area wasn't familiar to her.

"On second thought, I figured I'd show you the warehouse quickly. Just so when I give you the details about it at lunch, you'll get the full understanding of what we're looking to do."

"Right, that makes sense." Evelyn picked nervously at her cuticle.

"What do you think?" Grant asked as he pulled into the parking lot ten minutes later.

The warehouse was set further back on its own from the other buildings. The gray stucco block, while looking like a rather standard warehouse, appeared ominous to her against the darkening clouds that were hovering over them.

"Let's go to lunch. I'm rather hungry and I need to take my m-medications soon," Evelyn told him.

"Right, of course you don't want to skip your medication," Grant said. "But why not come inside? We came all the way here."

"I'd rather not," Evelyn said. "On second thought I'm not feeling . . . well. Maybe we skip lunch, and we can just go home."

Grant seemed not to hear her as he climbed out the car and came around to open her door for her.

"It'll only be for a minute."

The loud creak of the door causes Evelyn to jump. Grant walks in, this time with Isabel, and he's holding some sort of box.

Isabel sees Evelyn, haggard-looking on a cot, and turns from her to Grant with confusion as he puts the box on the desk.

It happens so suddenly that Evelyn doesn't even process it correctly.

Grant pulls a gun from his pocket, firing it at Isabel.

Evelyn opens her mouth to scream but nothing comes out as Isabel falls to the floor.

She runs over, collapsing next to her.

Isabel looks woozy and confused. Her eyes look to Evelyn's in terror before they roll into the back of her head. Evelyn turns, looking for anything to help her. She spots the sheets from the cot and scrambles to drag them over, tying a tourniquet of some sort around Isabel's bleeding stomach.

"It's going to be okay, Isabel." Evelyn's eyes tear up as she runs a shaky hand along her cheek. "I'm so sorry about this." Her voice catches in her throat. "I tried to warn you to run."

She pulls the sheet as tightly as she can.

"Have a seat, Mom, we need to talk." Grant gestures with the gun towards the cot.

Evelyn's body runs cold. She turns to face him, now realizing it's Anita's gun he's holding, the one she had been hiding all these years.

"I love you so much, Mom. You know that, right?"

Evelyn begins to cry as she turns to Isabel bleeding out in the corner.

"And I thought you loved me too."

"I do, I—" Evelyn's voice catches in her throat.

"I thought I was doing both of us a favor by killing Dad. He spent your whole marriage making a fool out of you. He didn't care about us. And Maria . . ." He trails off. "That was a horrible mistake. I really did think that she and Dad were having an affair. It wasn't until Isabel showed up that I realized how wrong I was."

Evelyn's teeth begin to chatter, the temperature of her body dropping rapidly.

Grant looks down at the gun in his hand. "I always knew that you had figured it out. And all these years, I thought you were protecting me. But then"—he picks up the gun—"why keep the gun?"

Evelyn tries to speak, but no words come out.

"When I went back to my closet to get rid of it, it was gone. I thought you had gotten rid of it for me, but it turns out you were using it as insurance the whole time. The only thing keeping you from going to the police was that you didn't want to see Anita take the fall for Maria's murder, and now, Anita's dead."

Grant heads over to the desk and the box he put on it when he first walked in. Evelyn notices that it looks like a promotional box for some vodka company.

Grant opens it, pulling out a shaker, a bottle of vodka, a jar of olives and a martini glass.

He pours the ingredients into the shaker and begins to mix it up for her, adding a drop of something unidentifiable, but which looks like it came from a brown bottle in a chemistry lab.

"What was Maria doing near our neighborhood, anyway?" Evelyn asks. "Anita had quit that afternoon."

"Anita had forgotten her purse," he answers, pouring the martini into the glass. "I thought now that Anita had gone, Maria didn't have to think it was awkward that her mother worked for us. That we could just be together."

Evelyn already knows how that must've gone down. Maria had never been interested in Grant.

"Anita's gun was in her purse." Evelyn comes to the horrible, obvious conclusion.

Grant nods. "I gave her back the purse, but after she rejected me, I assumed it was confirmation that she was having an affair with Dad. I followed her to the park. When I confronted her, she denied it, saying I was delusional. Then she tried to run away from me. Do you know how humiliating that was?"

Evelyn grips the metal side of the cot for support.

"I lost it then, and I ripped the purse back from her, taking the gun out. I didn't intend to shoot her at first, I just wanted an honest answer. I thought showing her the gun would show her how serious I was." He starts walking in a circle. "Then she called me crazy, and I guess I was, because I snapped."

Evelyn swallows hard. She knew the moment she'd found the gun in the back of Grant's closet several days later what he had done. She remembers when Harrison came in when he heard her crying and discovered the gun in her lap. He took it from her, making the decision that he was going to handle it, placing it in their safe.

Two days later, Evelyn hid in her room while Harrison confronted Grant about Maria. They were in the kitchen together, Grant had been making coffee for the two of them. She couldn't hear much, other than raised muffled voices followed by the slamming of a door. Harrison called out Grant's name, then she heard the door slam a second time. Grant stormed out of the apartment towards the subway, obviously knowing Harrison would chase him. It wasn't until after, that Evelyn discovered a jar of peanuts hidden in the back of the cupboard. They had never kept nuts in the house because of Harrison's allergy. Evelyn opened the jar, the residue on the lining wiped clean on one side like a finger had run over it.

Now, Evelyn looks around the room for any way she might escape, but she feels helpless. Grant is stronger than her; there's no way she'll be able to get out or save Isabel. All she can do is keep him talking and pray for some sort of miracle.

She builds up the courage, but the words seem to stick on her tongue, and she has to force them out. "You didn't kill your father for me. You killed him to cover your tracks, because he knew about the gun and likely threatened to send you to prison. Your father cheated on me for years and took advantage of God knows how many other women, including my best friend, Anita. That was never your reason."

"Enough was enough." Grant's voice is high-pitched now, becoming unhinged.

"Why did you shoot Isabel now? Is it because she was snooping around and getting too close to the truth about what happened?"

Grant pushes his palms hard into his eye sockets. "Poisoning her would've been easier, since she's allergic to nuts like Dad, but Isabel is too smart. Too smart for her own good."

The room is deathly silent except for the wheezing shallow breath coming from Isabel.

He glares at Isabel with a hatred that Evelyn hasn't seen in him since he saw Harrison with Maria the night of prom.

"This is all her fault." He points the gun at her. "If she hadn't come into our lives, this wouldn't have to happen like this."

Evelyn swallows hard. "Happen like what?"

Grant gives her a regretful look, then picks up the martini. "You co-signing this warehouse means you have rights and access to the building. Isabel confesses to being the child of Harrison's lover. You already killed Maria and Harrison for an affair you thought they had, but Isabel is the child of Harrison's actual lover, Anita. Now you lure Isabel here to kill her and kill yourself. You feel guilty after all these years, but you want to preserve the Caldwell bloodline. You shoot Isabel, then poison yourself with your martini."

"What?" Evelyn is still trying to grasp what he's saying.

"I'm sorry, Mom. I'm sorry it has to end like this."

Evelyn looks at the drink. "I won't do it."

Grant bites the side of his cheek. "This was never meant to happen." He shakes his head. "Even when I knew you'd betrayed me, I thought I'd still give you the benefit of the doubt and let you go out with some dignity." He hands the martini to her.

"Goodbye, Mother."

Rose

James bursts through the door, but it's empty. Relief floods Rose.

James looks around. "Where did that sound come from, then?"

"I don't know, but we're getting out of here."

James scrunches his eyebrows. "We can't just leave her."

Rose grabs his arm. "We don't know what that noise was." She tries to remain calm and rational.

"Mom, yes we do." He looks at her sternly.

"Let's go outside and we can call the cops."

Rose pats her legs, then grimaces, realizing she left her phone in the car.

"There's no time." James pulls away from her grip and runs from her again.

"James, no. Please!" Rose's whole body is shaking. She chases after him as he bursts through the stairwell.

"It's too dangerous, James, please stop." The thought of losing him is unbearable. She wouldn't be able to live with herself.

On the second floor there is another gray door.

"James!" Her lungs are burning to keep up with him. He bursts through the door. Her hand is on the handle when she hears the blood-curdling scream of her son.

Panic rises in Rose as she pushes through the burning in her legs and lurches through the door.

It takes her a moment to assess the scene. Isabel is bleeding out in the corner if she's not already dead. Evelyn is sitting hunched over on a cot with Grant standing next to her with a martini in his hand.

Rose thinks she is hallucinating. It's like being in a dream that feels real, but nothing makes sense.

Grant's face turns from shock to anger. He puts the drink down and picks up the gun on the desk next to him.

Anita's gun, Rose recognizes.

"Grant," she says shakily. "What's happened?"

"Rose, why are you here?" His voice is eerily calm.

"What are *you* doing here? What . . ." She turns again to Isabel. James is crouched on the floor next to her, trying to put pressure on the wound, his whole body shaking like a greyhound's.

"What happened to Isabel?"

Grant points the gun at Evelyn.

"She was hiding out here," he says. "She lured us here and tried to shoot us."

"What?" Rose is trying to catch up, but that doesn't make sense.

"Run, run while you can, please." Evelyn's voice is raw but urgent.

Rose looks at Evelyn in her weakened state. Her skin is ashen as she leans against the metal headboard of the cot.

Meanwhile, Grant stands tall and authoritative with the gun in his hand.

Rose realizes Evelyn doesn't have the ability to orchestrate this; she looks barely alive. Rose sees the desperation in her eyes and suddenly it all seems to make sense.

Evelyn has known all along.

The made-up illness was to get Grant away from Rose. This whole time, her apparent hatred towards Rose, the ultimatum to get her to make Grant leave her, hasn't been to protect Grant from Rose.

She's been trying to protect Rose from Grant.

"I'm handling the situation," Grant tells her calmly. "Take James and run, go get help."

"James," she calls, looking over her shoulder. She sees James's eyes are red. "Go to my car, call an ambulance now and stay outside."

James nods his head, unable to control his body's convulsions. He forces himself up and runs out the door.

Relieved that James is safely out of the room, she looks at Grant, then at Evelyn again.

Rose wants to run as well. She wants to believe Grant, but something isn't making sense. The light catches Grant's watch and suddenly something clicks inside her, like solving the final puzzle in an escape room.

"Grant, give me your watch," Rose says to him.

He looks down at it, then his eyes meet hers. "Why?" he says with caution.

"I want to see your watch," Rose says more firmly now.

Grant's gaze narrows on hers and with a deep, sickening feeling, she knows the truth about who he really is.

She can tell in his eyes; he knows it too.

"Rose," he starts.

She reflexively takes a step back.

"You of all people know what it's like to be in a position where it's you or them."

"What are you talking about?" Rose looks to Evelyn, but she shakes her head to say she didn't tell him.

"I've always known the truth about you. From the moment I met you I wanted to know everything about you, even what I knew you weren't willing to tell me." He puts his arms out. "I know who your father was, I know you killed him. I've just been waiting this whole time, hoping you would tell me." He steps towards her. "I wanted to tell you, Rose. I wanted you to know the truth about me and see that we're not that different, you and I."

Rose looks over at Isabel. "No"—Rose shakes her head—"we are not the same. I wouldn't kill someone innocent to save myself."

"Rose, I did this for us. If this all came out, we wouldn't be able to be together."

"No." Rose shakes her head violently. "You did this for yourself."

Grant stands there for a moment, staring at her. The tension in the room is so thick it's practically choking her.

Grant exhales slowly. "You continue to think what you did was justified, but really, you knew he had to die, and you took care of it, Rose. Just like I did. We did what we had to do. And what you couldn't do"—he looks at his watch—"I did for you. And you can't deny that you were relieved when he was dead."

Rose feels as if she's going to be sick. The room starts to spin, but she tries to proceed with caution, trying to avoid upsetting the situation further.

"You can still stop this." Rose points to Isabel. "We can get her help; we can fix this."

Grant shakes his head.

Rose puts her hands up towards him. "We can fix this. I wish someone had told me I didn't have to kill my father. There's still time to save Isabel's life."

"It's too late. I've already lost you." He gestures with his gun, "I've lost my mother"—he gestures back at Evelyn, causing her to flinch—"but I will not lose my inheritance."

Grant holds up the gun and fires a shot at Evelyn, her body jerking back onto the cot.

Rose lets out a terrified scream.

Grant turns, pointing the gun at her, his eyes now filled with tears. "I'm so sorry, Rose. I loved you, you know. I thought you loved me."

"I do love you," she hears herself saying. "And you're right. If I hadn't stopped my father, he would've likely killed me."

She takes a cautious step towards him. "I understand why you're doing this. And you're right, your life is over if it gets out what happened here." She takes another step. "But we can change that narrative, you and I."

Relief seems to wash over Grant's face.

As Grant lowers the gun, Rose takes her chance, charging as hard as she can towards him. Out of surprise, he fires the gun at her, but misses. She tackles him to the ground, the gun skittering underneath the cot.

He tries to reach for it, but she digs her thumbs into his eyes.

He lets out a cry of pain as he grabs her forearms and throws her off him.

She falls hard on her back, smacking the back of her skull. Spots blur her vision as she tries to regain consciousness.

Grant stands up, about to come at her again when she hears a gunshot.

Rose's body seizes from the sound.

When she opens her eyes, she sees Evelyn drop the gun back to the floor, her head slumping to the mattress.

Rose turns towards Grant, who drops to his knees, a pool of blood spreading from his heart before he falls to the ground.

She shudders. It's just like her painting. The abstract image with the bleeding heart. It *had* been a premonition.

She sees his watch, glistening in the ceiling light, and she reaches for it, unstrapping it from his wrist.

She flips it over and her throat constricts.

May all of our time on this earth be spent together. I love you, Rose.

Ian's watch. It's why they never found it on him. Grant had pushed him into traffic. He had killed him. Then he took his watch, wearing it in front of her this whole time.

Rose dry-heaves but swallows it down. She can't focus on this right now, she has to try to save Evelyn and Isabel.

She snaps her head back up. "Evelyn!" she cries. She stumbles to her, putting her ear to Evelyn's lips.

She's still breathing.

Rose then crawls over to Isabel to check her pulse; it's very weak, but still there. "Stay with us, Isabel," she says. "Help is coming."

A sharp pain in her head seizes her vision. Everything suddenly seems fuzzy, black spots taking over her vision as she slumps to the ground. She has no idea how long she's been lying there when the door bursts open. Rose hears a cluster of heavy footsteps scattering like wasps throughout the room. She calls out for James.

"I'm here, Mom." He appears beside her, reaching for her hand. She squeezes it tightly, before her eyes fall closed.

Evelyn

Evelyn looks out the window of her hospital room. It's open, allowing a cool breeze to come through. The Florida heat is finally breaking.

Rose is sleeping on a chair next to her bed, an itchy-looking hospital blanket draped across her.

"Evelyn." Missy comes into the room holding an oversized bouquet of lilies with a Get Well Soon balloon bouncing above it. She startles Evelyn and wakes Rose. "How are you, dear?"

"I'm fine, thank you."

"I had a feeling something terrible was going to happen to you." She turns to Rose. "Once I heard you were asking around about Anita, I knew trouble was brewing. Then, when you wouldn't answer your phone, Evelyn, I went as far as to call the house, and Martha had been told to say that you had simply gone back up to New York to handle the selling of your penthouse. I knew that was bull, because my daughter is your real estate agent." Missy looks at Evelyn and squeezes her hand. "Thank God you're okay."

Evelyn smiles, squeezing her best friend's hand, her eyes starting to glisten with tears.

"I have to get going," Missy says, wiping a stray tear from her own eye. "But you need to get better soon. You're running out of excuses for missing mahjong."

Evelyn blows a grateful kiss to Missy.

"Where's James?" Evelyn asks Rose.

Rose stretches. "I'm guessing I'll find him in Isabel's room."

"I hear she lost a lot of blood, but they were able to stabilize her. I'm glad she's going to make it," says Evelyn.

"Me too," Rose says.

Evelyn lets out a sigh. "I'm so sorry, Rose, for everything."

"You were trying to protect me, while still protecting yourself against him. I get it."

A tear falls down Evelyn's face. "I didn't know what to do. I couldn't let the murders get pinned on Anita when it was her gun he'd used. Once I found out she had died, I knew it was time to do something, but I was afraid."

"Afraid that if he managed to get out of it, he'd come after you."

"And you," Evelyn says. "I needed to get you away from him."

Rose feels her shoulders slump. "Oh, Evelyn, I can't imagine what it's been like for you."

"Can you do me a favor?" she asks Rose.

"Anything."

"Can you get the nurse in here? I need to ask her a question."

"We were able to fill your special request," says a woman in a nursing outfit an hour later. She tilts her head. "You're getting moved."

"Where are we going?" Rose asks.

"To Isabel," Evelyn says. "We all need to talk."

As she's being wheeled out in her bed, a wave of panic rushes over Evelyn. She's not sure how Isabel will react to everything she has to say. She may not be happy about it, but at least the truth will finally be out there.

"Here we are," says the nurse as they wheel her into the room. A curtain is closed around Isabel's bed, but James stands up out of his chair and opens it. The dark circles under his eyes show that he hasn't slept much either.

Evelyn sees Isabel awake and sitting up. She looks pale and somewhat weak, but she's alive.

"Isabel." Evelyn chokes on her words. "I'm so glad you're going to be okay."

"Me too." Isabel smiles weakly and puts her head back on her pillow.

"Is it okay if I join you?" Evelyn tries to make light of it, but she's also worried that she might've been presumptuous in assuming that Isabel would want to be in the same room with her.

Isabel nods.

Evelyn waits patiently as the nurses set up her bed and her various monitors. The room is thick with anticipation.

"All set," the nurse finally says, smiling. "I'll leave you all to it."

Evelyn smacks her lips together nervously.

"Water?" Rose asks.

"Yes, dear, thank you."

Rose stands up, pouring water from a pink plastic pitcher into a thin paper cup.

She picks her head up and smiles at Isabel. "How about you?"

"Yes please." Isabel's voice sounds scratchy.

She hands one cup off to James to give to Isabel and the other to Evelyn.

Evelyn takes a grateful sip and clears her throat.

"Okay." Evelyn exhales. "This has clearly been a long time coming. But now that there is no danger, it's time to tell the truth."

"I know that Anita is my mother," Isabel tells her. "And Harrison is my father. I figured it out."

Evelyn shakes her head. "No, dear, Anita is not your mother, nor is Harrison your father."

Isabel stares at her. "What?"

"I'm here to finally tell you the whole truth."

Isabel

Isabel's entire world tilts on its axis again. "Wait, what?" she says again, looking around the room as if she's in some sort of dream. Like she's not awake from her coma, she's still in it.

"Anita was my best friend. Yes, she was my maid, but she and I weren't that different. We had similar backgrounds, small-town people. My favorite part of the day was when Anita would finish up and we'd sit in the kitchen with tea. We'd laugh about, well, just about everything.

"But things started changing. Anita couldn't look me in the eye anymore. Eventually, I learned that she was pregnant."

"So, she did have an affair with Harrison?" Isabel can't help but feel a little sad. Mother, grandmother or not, she loved Anita and can't imagine her as the type that would have an affair.

"Not an affair," Evelyn corrects. "My husband was a scoundrel. There was one time that Anita was there when I was out at an event. Harrison came home early, and he forced himself on Anita. It wasn't her fault. She didn't want any of it to happen."

"And she got pregnant from it," Isabel concludes.

"I'll admit that when I first discovered Anita was pregnant, I said some horrible things to her." She shakes her head sadly. "But I quickly came to my senses and realized I needed to help her."

Isabel bites her lip.

"You see, she didn't want Harrison to know, in case he tried to make her get rid of it, which was against her beliefs. So, I told her to quit, and I'd find a way to take care of her in secret."

Isabel scrunches her nose. "But you just told me Anita wasn't my mother. Yet she raised me, and it was just her and me. There were no siblings."

Evelyn wipes a tear from her eye. "Anita lost the baby. After Maria died, she was so distraught from the stress and trauma of it all that it caused her to miscarry."

Isabel feels goosebumps run up her spine.

"Grant had always been in love with Maria, and he suspected that Maria and Harrison were having an affair." Evelyn suppresses a sob. "It wasn't even true.

"In the haste of leaving after what was discussed between us, Anita had left her purse behind. Later that night around nine, Maria showed up to retrieve her mother's purse. I was out with Harrison at a work function, leaving Grant home alone.

"Grant decided to confess his love for her, but she explained to him that she didn't feel the same way and that she was only nice to him because her mother worked for us."

Evelyn lets out a slow exhale, then swallows. "There had been an incident about three to four months earlier, when I was robbed at knifepoint in the park. Anita saw me in the aftermath of it. She showed me the gun she kept in her purse and urged me to get one as well, to protect myself. When she was showing me, Grant walked in on us. I thought I had been quick enough to hide it, but apparently I wasn't. So Grant knew that Anita had a gun in her purse.

"Before he returned the purse to Maria, he took the gun out. Then he followed her, and, I don't know, I guess he chose to confront her."

Evelyn's voice becomes shaky, and tears start to stream down her face.

Isabel exchanges a look with James and Rose, but their mouths are open, eyes wide. This is the first time they are hearing all of this as well.

"Less than a week later, I was cleaning Grant's room—since we no longer had a maid—and that's when I found the gun, hidden in the back of his closet, behind his hamper. It was then that I knew. I knew that Grant had killed her with Anita's gun.

"Harrison hadn't left for work yet and he heard me let out what must've sounded like an animal dying because I just couldn't believe it. It broke my heart into a thousand pieces.

"Harrison understood as well. He took the gun from me and told me he would sort it out with Grant. Two days later, he was dead."

"Oh my God," Isabel says, still taking it all in.

"So, he poisoned him?" James asks, looking between his mother and Isabel.

Evelyn nods sadly.

"Harrison had confronted Grant in the kitchen when they were making coffee. Grant must've sensed where the conversation was going and used residue from a peanut jar he had hidden in the back of our cupboard and rubbed it on the inside of Harrison's travel mug. Clearly, he always seemed to have a plan for Harrison and as the noose seemed to tighten around Grant's neck, he decided now was his time to use it. Grant methodically stormed out. In haste, Harrison chased after him and Grant led him onto a subway, away from any sort of help he might need."

"So that's why the details were kept from the papers?" Isabel asks.

"It looked suspicious, but nothing could be proven. The police agreed to keep it out of the press, for fear that because of who he was, it could create a scandal."

Isabel looks over at Rose, who has her head in her hands. James moves his chair next to his mother's.

Rose's back starts to jolt, in either dry-heaves or sobs. James puts a hand on her back. "You didn't know, Mom, you couldn't have."

Evelyn allows the information in the room to settle and Rose to compose herself.

Rose picks up her head and holds tightly to James's hand.

"It's over now," James reminds her.

Rose swallows down her tears and nods.

Isabel then turns to Evelyn. "So, where did I come from?"

Evelyn looks from Rose to Isabel now and smiles. "I was in a loveless marriage," she tells her. "I too had an affair."

Isabel raises her eyebrows in surprise.

"It turned out that I was not quite as far along as Anita was, but I had no idea. When I finally figured it out, it was after everything that had happened. When I told Anita what I suspected Grant had done, we were both devastated. I told her I was afraid of Grant and what he could do to me or the baby. We were both worried that we couldn't prove completely that it was Grant and the blame could fall to one of us. We both agreed that I hold the gun for safekeeping. Anita worried there was no way they would believe her, and we didn't see a scenario that would put Grant away. There simply wasn't enough evidence. We'd found the gun in his room, but we couldn't prove that. It could've turned back on either one of us." Evelyn wipes another tear that has fallen down her cheek.

"I told Anita that I was pregnant. And I was scared that Grant might try to hurt the baby." She looks at Isabel. "I didn't know you were a girl at the time." She smiles. "But I was glad when I found that out."

Isabel doesn't know what to make of it all yet. It's like she's watching herself be told this story from another angle in the room.

"Anita took my hand"—she clasps her own hands together—"and told me that if I could get away with having the baby without Grant's knowledge, then she would take you and raise you. She'd move out of the city, somewhere safe." Evelyn wipes her eyes again. "She said it would give her something to live for."

Isabel sees the story play out in her head, like reading a book. She can see them both confiding in each other.

"I wanted to protect you. I didn't want Grant to hurt you. I also knew that Anita was in a bad place. She needed you as much as you needed her. I don't think she would've kept on living as long as she did, if it hadn't been for you."

Now it's Isabel's turn to cry. She's happy to know that despite everything, they did love each other like family. And it's comforting to know that the love between them was pure. In the end, that's really, truly all that matters.

"I made sure both of you were always taken care of."

Now it all makes sense to Isabel. It was how they got to live comfortably. It was how her education at an Ivy League school wasn't an issue. When she looks back, she realizes despite everything, she did live a good life with Anita. She had a warm, safe, and loving childhood.

"I'm sorry that I couldn't do more for you." Evelyn looks towards her. "The moment I saw you in my house, I was so stunned I thought you were an apparition. Everything in me wanted to hug you, but you were standing next to Grant, and fear of what he would do to you just took over." The pain in Evelyn's eyes is so vivid Isabel can almost feel it herself.

"It makes sense," Isabel says. "I understand. But I still have questions."

Evelyn looks at her.

"Who is my father, then?"

"You actually already know him."

Isabel leans forward but then winces in pain. "I do?"

She nods. "Daniel Lopez."

"The head of Whitmore?" Rose asks.

"Yes." Evelyn nods. "We actually did love each other, but after everything that happened, I knew I was destined to be alone with my secrets."

"Does he know about me?" Isabel asks.

Evelyn shakes her head. "I couldn't tell anyone other than Anita about you. Well, her and Missy."

"Missy?" Rose questions.

"I was able to hide my pregnancy for a few months while Grant finished school. Then I sent him off to summer camp. Missy and I had never been close, but she knew Harrison for who he was, and I found myself trusting her. Missy sent me to her home in Geneva. She took care of me throughout the rest of my pregnancy. She helped with the documents so we could pass you along to Anita.

"Grant was at college then and we'd talk on the phone, but he was none the wiser."

Isabel rethinks her entire life, trying to rearrange all this information into one sequence in her head.

"My job at Whitmore," Isabel says. "They didn't really have a job for me. I was in administration, but I didn't have a real title."

"Anita told me what you wanted to do, and I called Dan for a favor. This was before I knew Grant was marrying Rose and James would attend the school. It was thankfully only for a year, and I hoped that you wouldn't make a connection.

"If I'm being honest, had I known what your plan was, I would've stopped you from coming to the Pelican Academy. I wanted to keep you safe."

Evelyn turns now to James. "James, can you please go get the nurse for me?"

"Now?" James says reluctantly, not wanting to miss anything.

"Now," Rose says firmly.

"Sorry," he apologizes to Evelyn. "Of course."

Once he leaves, Evelyn begins to speak again.

"I noticed how Grant was with you. He loved you, but it was very similar to how he was with Maria. I didn't want the same thing to happen to you. I thought I could keep him close and drive you away. I wanted him to see that you wouldn't fit in and hoped he would dismiss you. I did it to protect you."

Rose bites her lower lip, nodding like she understands.

"After everything with Maria, I wanted to feel safe, and I wanted there to be proof if something happened to me. So I installed hidden cameras around the penthouse. When you two started seeing each other, I understood you were a widow. Then, when I did a background check on you, I saw that your husband had been struck by a car, but I had a deep concern that Grant might've had something to do with it. That's why, after the wedding, I insisted you live in the penthouse, and I wouldn't let you redecorate. I was worried you or he might find the cameras, but I wanted to keep you safe, too."

Rose squeezes her eyes shut, trying to hold back the tears.

"Did he have something to do with your former husband's death?" Isabel asks gently.

Rose nods, her head in her hands, and starts to cry, but pulls herself together. She bites her lip. "My husband Ian. I had a watch inscribed that I'd given him on our wedding day." She steadies her breath. "Grant, he . . . he pushed him in front of a car. And took his watch. He wore it in front me, all this time." Rose lowers her head, humiliated and angry.

"I'm so sorry, Rose," Isabel says.

"I'm the one who's sorry," Evelyn says. "I'm sorry for all the lies, but I did it out of love. For all of you."

No one knows what to say. Everyone looks at each other instead in a stunned sort of silence.

"I want you all to know that whether you believe it or not, despite my past behavior, I consider you all my family. I hope that you will find it in your hearts to try to understand why I did what I did." Evelyn's voice catches. "I hope you can forgive me."

Isabel

Isabel pulls up to the Caldwells' house in her car. She looks up at the place in a new light. What previously had an old, haunted feeling to it now feels somehow softer and cheerier. Like the house itself has been released from its demons.

She gets out of her car, a bunch of roses in her hand, and knocks on the door.

A woman she remembers as Martha, the maid, opens the door with a cheery smile.

"Hi, I'm here to see Evelyn."

Martha nods. "She'll be very glad to see you."

Isabel goes to climb the stairs, feeling her stitches slightly pull, her side still healing.

Martha calls out to her: "She's downstairs in the guest bedroom. No stairs."

"Right," Isabel says, relieved. "Thank you."

She walks into a guest bedroom down the hall. It's less decorative than the others. The walls in this room are painted in a cheery yellow, with brown wooden beams across the ceiling. The floor is the same wood as the rest of the floor downstairs, but a yellow oriental rug covers the middle of it. Evelyn sits on a king-sized bed with a wooden head- and footboard. A white quilt rests over her frail body. She is sitting up; a plate of half-eaten toast and a cup of tea sit on a tray on the bedside table. The French doors are open, bringing in the soft breeze from the ocean.

Evelyn turns her head and sees Isabel. Her face lights up with a smile.

"Hi, Evelyn," Isabel says. She looks for a place to put the flowers, but to her surprise, Martha is still behind her. "I'll take those," she says.

Isabel hands them off to her, then takes a seat in a carved wooden chair between the open doors and Evelyn's bed.

The breeze feels cool on her back.

"I was hoping I'd get to see you again." Evelyn smiles.

"I just needed time to—"

Evelyn puts a hand up. "You don't have to say anything."

Isabel nods. "I'm sorry I came in and destroyed your big secret." She puts her hands up.

"Stop right there," Evelyn says. "You had nothing to do with this. Nothing was your fault. It was all Grant, and I'm glad he's gone. He was my son, and I loved him in some ways, but he was a bad person." Evelyn tightens her jaw, shaking her head. "I wish I could've done more to stop him. I wish I hadn't been such a coward. I had hoped that it was only Maria and Harrison, but it turns out it wasn't."

Evelyn starts to cry. Isabel takes a seat beside her on the bed, holding her shoulders as she falls into herself.

"You had your suspicions, but you had no proof. Police officers can spend their entire careers in situations like that. They know, but they can't prove it. It must've killed you, but there wasn't anything you could do. You had to protect yourself. And remember, you were trying to protect us as well."

Evelyn stretches out her arms and Isabel leans in, embracing her. Her real mother, finally after all this time.

"If it's okay"—Isabel pulls away—"I would like to take the opportunity to get to know you more. Understand who you are."

Evelyn smiles. "I would like that a lot. All my life, I've wanted to know more about you. When Anita told me you were going to Columbia, I was so proud of you. From the very beginning, I knew you were going to be someone special."

Martha comes back in, the bouquet of roses now cut and arranged into a blown-glass vase. "Where shall I put them, Mrs. Caldwell?"

"Please, Martha, call me Evelyn," she tells her.

Martha seems a bit confused but nods her head.

"We can put them on the dresser right there," Evelyn continues. "I like how the light catches the vase with the petals' colors."

"Sure thing . . ." Martha hesitates. "Evelyn," she finishes, as if testing it out.

"Thank you." Evelyn smiles and reaches for her glasses on the end table, along with a document that she pulls out of her drawer.

She hands it to Isabel.

"What is this?"

"It's my will and testament on the first page." She puts her glasses on. "Do you remember Anita ever mentioning A&E Financials?"

Isabel racks her brain. "It does sound familiar, but I'm not sure why."

"I always planned on leaving half of my fortune to you. Anita and I set up a trust for you called Anita and Evelyn Financials." She raises her eyebrows. "That's how Anita was paying for your upbringing."

Isabel is still trying to understand.

"This is your trust fund," Evelyn repeats. "Anita had access to it, but now with her gone, it's all yours to do with as you please. You will also inherit half my fortune when I die."

"Evelyn." Isabel scans the document. It's more than she could've ever imagined. "I can't accept this."

"You don't have a choice." Evelyn smirks. "You're my daughter and I will do as I see fit. The woman with the purse pulls the strings."

Rose

Rose is on a flight back from New York for the weekend. As Evelyn was incapacitated, she had sent Rose on her behalf to finalize the closing of the penthouse sale in New York – for real this time. Rose looks out the window as the plane is about to land in Palm Beach, the ocean view sliding into sand and lush palm trees.

These past few weeks have been an emotional roller coaster for her. Grant's betrayal sent her spiraling through a storm of emotions, from regret to anger but most of all heartbreak. Rose has been channeling that into her art, trying to make sense of everything, though after the Art Basel show next week, she's taking a long-deserved break. She needs time to heal with James, and to reconnect as a family again.

Evelyn has insisted they stay. She told Rose she wants to be her real self with her and for James to continue at the Pelican Academy with Isabel as his tutor and his friend.

Rose has agreed they will stay on until Evelyn is better, but she wants James and her to build a home for themselves.

Rose asked James if he wanted to stay at the Pelican Academy or transfer somewhere else. To her surprise, he said he wanted to stay, so Rose promised she'd be nearby should Evelyn need her.

Before Rose left for New York, Evelyn had handed her an envelope.

"Is this for the closing?"

Evelyn shook her head. "It's the details of Grant's trust money. It was forwarded to your bank account this morning. No strings attached. To do what you want. At the very least, you need it for your son's continued education."

Rose was shocked and had to force herself to speak. "Thank you, Evelyn. I don't know what to say."

"I'm not forcing you, but it would mean so much to me if you would keep your art studio here so I could visit you and watch you work. You really are a talented artist."

Rose smiled. Her heart had warmed towards Evelyn in a way that she hadn't felt since she was ten, with her own mother. "Thanks, Evelyn. It's a deal."

"Excuse me, miss?"

Rose turns her head from the window and realizes that the plane is already empty. A tall man with dark olive skin, strikingly handsome for a man in his mid-sixties, taps Rose on the shoulder.

"Are you alright?" He looks at her, concerned.

Rose blinks. She narrows her eyes on the man, whose face is now so familiar to her.

"Dan Lopez?"

"Yes," he confirms, then squints at her in turn, trying to figure out if he recognizes her.

"I'm Rose Caldwell. My son went to Whitmore last year." Then she puts her hand on her chest. "I'm Evelyn's daughter-in-law."

He smiles. "How is Evelyn?"

Rose is relieved he doesn't know about what happened with Grant. Evelyn pulled her strings again to keep things relatively quiet, though of course the gossip still ran wild at the Coconut Palm Country Club. But Evelyn was able to keep it contained. She told people that when Grant brought her to see the warehouse he had just acquired, they had been attacked by a squatter who had been living there. The squatter shot both of them, but sadly Grant didn't make it. An unfortunate tragedy. She kept Isabel out of it, and as far as the Pelican Academy was aware, Isabel had been shot in an attempted mugging.

Rose stands up, and Dan allows her to shuffle out into the aisle. "She's doing okay," Rose answers, regarding Evelyn. "You know she lives in Palm Beach full time now?"

"Yes, I believe she does." He smiles.

"What brings you to Palm Beach?" Rose asks while reaching for her bags in the overhead bin.

"My nephew just got a job as the head of the university here." He strains as he helps pull down her luggage.

"Thanks," she says. "Your wife's not with you?"

"I've never been married."

Rose considers this. "Well, if you have time, you should stop by the house. I think Evelyn could really use a friend, if I'm being honest."

Not wanting to make him feel awkward, she turns around and continues off the plane.

Dan catches up with her on the gangway. "I would love that."

"Mom!"

Rose waves to James from the sidelines as she climbs the bleachers.

"James, you're in," the coach calls.

"Go get 'em, James!" Rose searches the stands to find Isabel sitting on the last bleacher at the bottom, with Evelyn in a wheelchair next to her. Rose smiles, appreciating them for coming to support James.

"How's it going?" Rose settles next to Isabel.

"Last quarter, tied, about five minutes left in the game."

Rose grips Isabel's hand as James gets the ball, dribbling it up the field.

"Go James!" Isabel calls.

"Go, go, go!" Evelyn yells.

Another player goes to attack James, but he kicks the ball through his legs, continuing to push the ball forward up the field.

"Yes!" Rose stands up.

James gets it past two more people, then squares off with the goalie.

"You've got this, James!" Isabel calls.

A confident smile creeps across James's face, and in one clean motion he kicks the ball just above the goalie's head into the net.

The crowd erupts in cheers.

Rose puts her hands to her chest, watching as the team surrounds James, patting him on the back. For the first time in a long time, he looks happy.

"That was some game," Rose tells James as he settles into the car.

"I'm glad you made it; I heard your flight had been delayed."

"Me too." She grabs his hand. "Look, before we meet everyone for dinner, there's been something I've been meaning to talk to you about."

"Okay." He looks at her quizzically.

"I haven't been fair to you. I've been treating you like a child when I know you aren't anymore. You're a teenager now and I need to respect that you're getting older, and you have a right to know what's going on. I haven't always been honest with you because I've wanted to protect you, but that wasn't right. This is your life too and you should have a say in how you want to live it."

James gives a half-smile. "Thanks, Mom, I appreciate that."

"And I want us to be honest with one another. I've looked into a therapist down here to help both you and me not only deal with everything we've been through, but just help us communicate better with each other. I want to be a better mother to you. I hope that you're willing to do it with me."

James pulls his bottom lip in and nods.

"Thank you." She smiles with relief. She knows that she will have to eventually tell James the truth about Grant killing Ian, but thankfully with a therapist, it can be told to him at the right time, in the most delicate way possible. "You are the most important person in my life. And I'm sorry if I ever made you doubt that. From here on out, it's you and me as equals, okay?"

"Yeah." James smiles.

Rose leans across the console and hugs him. Her heart feels like it could burst with love for him. "I promise I'll always be here for you."

Epilogue

One year later

Rose and James sit next to one another on the back lawn of the Caldwell estate. The landscape has been trimmed to perfection. A band of white silk is draped down the middle of the grass, white folding chairs on either side. A wedding arbor covered in white roses overlooks the calm green and blue ocean.

A priest steps up, opening his book. Missy stands in a soft yellow dress holding a small white bouquet, and next to the priest stands Dan, in a black tux with a white rose on his lapel. His brother, who looks like he could almost be his twin, but is a few years younger, is standing at his side.

James taps Rose on the shoulder as the quartet in the back begins to play. Rose turns her head and watches as Evelyn appears. She's in a simple white dress, far more modest than anything Rose ever remembered seeing her in just a year ago, holding a bouquet of white roses. Her delicate arm is linked in Isabel's, who is wearing a soft yellow dress like Missy's and a white rose tucked behind her ear, her long hair cascading over her shoulders.

Rose feels her eyes prick with tears. Over the past year, Evelyn has really started to open up to both her and Isabel. She's told them everything from her abusive childhood and her toxic marriage to her fear of her son all these years. She really did live a tortured life. Now, as she sees Evelyn smiling brightly for the first time in a long time, she can't help but feel happy for her.

It's time for everyone to start over.

"Isabel!" Dan's voice echoes over the crowd. Isabel turns her head, a mouth full of shrimp, to see Dan and Evelyn waving her over.

Isabel chews her food embarrassedly and swallows before making her way to them.

"What are your plans for spring break this year?" Evelyn asks her.

Isabel looks from Dan to Evelyn. "No plans so far, why?"

Evelyn smiles. "We'd like to do a family trip together, all of us."

Isabel smiles back. "That sounds great, where are you thinking of going?"

Dan grins. "We discussed it, and we want you to decide."

"Wow!" Isabel's eyes widen. "There are so many places I've always wanted to go; I don't know where to begin."

"Think about it and let us know," Dan says.

Last year Evelyn told Dan the truth about everything. To her surprise, he still loved her as much as she loved him, and he had been elated to find out he had a daughter.

While they seemed to pick up right where they'd left off after Dan retired and moved to Palm Beach, they took things slow with Isabel, taking the time to get to know her. But with her now full-time job as a teacher at the Pelican Academy, she has been able to have weekly dinners with them. And now, it all feels like they really are truly a family.

"Uncle Dan." A middle-aged man approaches them. He smiles at Isabel and Evelyn.

Isabel recognizes him from the picture in Dan's office.

"Dad and I are going to get tickets to the Mets spring training game while he's in town. Did you want to join us this Tuesday?"

Dan smiles and looks at Isabel. "What do you say, Isabel, want to go to a baseball game?"

She grins. "I'd love that."

"Isabel!"

Isabel turns to see James snaking his way through the crowd. His suit jacket is already off, and his tie loosened. "Come on, I want to show you something."

Isabel allows herself to be led through the guests and back up to the house. It took her a year, but Evelyn has completely redecorated. The rooms that were once dark have now been painted fresh, light colors, which along with new modern furniture and light fixtures, gives the place a much softer, homier feel.

Rose is standing in the front hallway in a soft pink gown, standing next to a woman that Isabel doesn't recognize.

"Isabel, this is Lina Prose. She's my art curator."

"I just had to meet the woman that has inspired such beautiful work this past year from Rose."

Isabel looks confused. "Me?"

"Rose tells me that she hasn't shown you any of her recent work, but she's been painting the most extraordinary pieces. She told me that you, Evelyn, and of course James, have been her inspiration."

"I'm flattered." Isabel smiles.

"Now I'm about to cart all these back to New York for my gallery. They're selling like hot cakes, I tell you. But Rose insisted that before I do that"—she eyes Rose—"we allow you to choose a piece of art for you to have for yourself."

"You certainly don't have to," Rose says sheepishly. "But if you would like one, it's yours."

"Wow, thank you," Isabel says. "I'd be happy to look."

Isabel follows all of them up the stairs. She thinks the studio must be at the end of the hall, but then a door opens, and another set of stairs leads them up.

"Evelyn doesn't mind you still keeping a studio up here?" Lina asks.

"She loves it, actually. She comes up and watches me work while we chat," Rose answers.

Isabel takes in all the paintings lining the walls. There are so many that there are more stacked together on the floor.

"You've been busy," Isabel remarks. She wanders to the wall and starts to examine the paintings.

They're abstract, but the colors all compliment and flow into each other. There are images there, but they're what you want them to be. "This looks like James." Isabel smiles and points to a green painting. If she lets her eyes rest, almost like with a magic eye picture, she can see James kicking a soccer ball.

"You're right," Rose says.

Isabel continues to admire them. "Evelyn?" She notes the heavy gold in the picture.

"Yes," Rose laughs. "And Dan and Evelyn are keeping that one."

Then Isabel comes to a halt in front of a painting in soft yellow; in its center is a figure backdropped by white light.

"This is beautiful." Isabel feels herself becoming emotional, something she's never experienced with art before.

"It looks like you found yourself." Rose puts an arm around her. "That"—Rose points to the painting—"is the brightness that comes out of you. It represents your kindness, your positivity, your outlook on life despite everything you've been through."

Isabel starts to tear up. "Thank you."

"Thank you for being the light that brought this whole family out of darkness."

Isabel hugs her tightly. For the first time in her whole life, she feels whole.

Acknowledgements

This has been a long, but glorious journey and first and foremost I never would've made it here if it weren't for the encouragement of my family.

To my husband Paul and our two beautiful sons, who've kept me grounded and motivated even when it seemed impossible. Thank you for always continuing to push me.

Thanks to my parents, Ernie and Joan Muir, who have always supported me by reading my drafts and providing great notes. The same for my in-laws, Paul and Marylou Psak who also were always willing to read and edit early drafts.

To some of my good friends, Danielle McKenna for being another early beta-reader in exchange for wine. For all of my medical and hospital related questions, thank you Tanya Santoro, who is always there to answer even my weirdest inquiries. And for this particular novel, thank you Janis Chanin, for trusting me enough to tell me how I could possibly kill you with your nut allergy and get away with it.

Of course, none of this would be possible without Audrey Linton and the great team at Hodder and Stoughton who made this book the best it could be. And finally, to my agent, Nicky Lovick. The first person who took a chance on me from a slush pile and continues to help shape me into a better writer every day.

Most importantly, I'd like to thank all the readers out there. I know there are endless books to choose from and I'm so grateful that you chose mine. I hope you enjoyed reading it as much as I loved writing it.